LITTLE SISTER

DEV JARRETT

A PERMUTED PRESS BOOK

ISBN: 978-1-68261-126-5
ISBN (eBook): 978-1-68261-127-2

LITTLE SISTER

Cover art by Christian Bentulan

Permuted Press, LLC
275 Madison Avenue, 14th Floor
New York, NY 10016
permutedpress.com

This is for the little sister who named two of her teddy bears Leukemia and Polio simply because she thought the words sounded pretty.

Love you, Rabbit.

1

"Ma'am? Is everything all right?"

Sharon still couldn't respond. She was mesmerized by the box.

The UPS guy, wearing his uniform brown shorts and shirt, held the screen door open with one sunburned knee. Blond hair stuck out from beneath his brown ball cap, and his eyes were a light shade straddling the line between brown and green. His brow furrowed.

"Ma'am?"

Sharon shook herself out of her daze, finally tearing her eyes from the box. She didn't need to look at it. She didn't need to look at the address label, the invoice, or the receipt.

She knew who sent the box. Her father.

She didn't need to open the box to know what lay inside, either.

Behind her, the door to the trailer opened wider, and Lucinda ducked under her elbow. Questions sprang out of the little girl, ricocheting around like a double handful of Hi-Bounce rubber balls thrown into a spinning clothes dryer.

"Oh, Mommy! Is it a present? Is it for me? For my birthday? Mommy! Did someone send me a present? A birthday present? Who sent it? Ooo, it's so big! What is it? Can I open it?"

The questions went on and on, but Sharon tuned them out. For a moment, she considered scribbling "Return to Sender" all over the box, shoving it back into the UPS guy's arms, and slamming the door.

"Sorry," she said to the delivery guy. "It—you—startled me. I wasn't expecting any packages."

He smiled and held out his weird clipboard-shaped computer with its pen-shaped stylus attached.

"If you could sign here, please."

Sharon signed her name slowly in the pressure sensitive box, watching as the illegible scrawl of her signature bloomed in the display window at the top of the clipboard above her hand. The UPS guy turned and went down the wooden steps, then returned to the gravel road at the end of the trailer, where his brown delivery van was still idling.

She watched him climb into the driver's seat, check a block on his delivery schedule, plug the next destination into his GPS, and put his truck into gear. It rolled slowly to the entrance of the trailer court, disappearing in the thick foliage of the low oak trees. She heard the crunch of gravel beneath its tires fade as it turned onto the main road, and seconds later the sound of its engine faded as well, leaving Sharon holding a big cardboard box she suspected was for her lonely little girl who was about to celebrate a birthday.

Lucinda would turn seven in a few days.

Now her daughter's high, excited voice pierced Sharon's jumble of thought. She sounded frustrated at her mother's lack of response.

"Momm-*meee*! What is it? What's in the box?"

Sharon turned to her daughter and tried to smile. Her mind raced in an attempt to come up with different things to tell Lucinda, different excuses to make. She couldn't think of anything plausible, and she knew if she didn't take care of this before Deke got home, he'd wade in and start fucking things up. She couldn't allow that to happen. In the back of her mind, voices from her recent haunted past muttered warnings. She considered the parcel in her hand, and a voice of hopeful, unfounded optimism spoke up as well. *Maybe it'll be okay.*

She bent down with the box in her arms and set it on the floor. Lucinda's eyes grew wide, and Sharon saw the furious intensity in the girl's eyes as she studied the box. Her curiosity was as beautiful as she was. Sharon opened her arms to her daughter.

"Come here, baby girl."

Lucinda stepped into her mother's arms, pressing her warm cheek against Sharon's. Sharon inhaled, smelling the sweet scent, a mixture of fruit-scented shampoo and the salt of her daughter's perspiration. She held her little girl close, then leaned back to look in her eyes. She spoke slowly, choosing her words with care.

"I think you're right. This might be a birthday present for you," she said, tipping her head in the direction of the box. Lucinda began to squirm excitedly, trying to slip from her mother's embrace and get to the opening of the present.

"Hold on a second there, missy," Sharon said, gently restraining her daughter. "You remember what happened when your daddy sent me flowers last Mother's Day?"

Lucinda's face blanched, going from excited to sad and worried. "Deke got all mad."

Deke had indeed gotten "all mad." He had, in fact, visited the deep end of *going apeshit.*

* * *

In May, soon after Deke had begun volunteering to work extra hours at the auto parts store, Sharon received an unexpected gift. Ronnie, Lucinda's biological father, had sent Sharon a dozen roses, beautifully arranged in a brass vase. Such a lavish gift was strange coming from Ronnie, who, after returning from Iraq the third time, seemed to have retreated into a life of army regulations, field manuals, and guns. He'd lost touch with the people and things that had made him happy before. He simply wasn't the same man she'd known. The Ronnie she'd married had been replaced by a soldier who could never turn off the hoo-ah machine.

The very strangeness of the gift made it sweeter, and it touched Sharon deeply. The card simply said, "Thanks for all you do. Happy Mother's Day."

Deke had been drinking heavily and watching a baseball game when the flowers arrived. Lucinda and Sharon were baking M&M cookies, mashing the candies into sliced sugar cookie dough, and making silly faces at each other. Lucinda had given Sharon a card she'd decorated at school. It was made of pink construction paper and decorated with dancing stick figures limned in red glitter, and it made Sharon smile. With the cookies baking, she was trying to make the day special for them both. Deke, on the other hand, was an emotional interloper, a rock of barely-sheathed fury that the stream of their happiness had to flow around. He'd had nothing to do with Sharon becoming a mom in the first place, or with what she did as a mom now. The only thing he'd given her that day was a stale, morning-breath kiss that felt like someone wiped her mouth with a filthy bar rag, and he'd only done that much as a pretext for grabbing her tit. He'd started his beer-fueled channel surfing right after breakfast, and in the interest of peace, she and Lucinda simply steered clear of him.

Sharon had answered the door and received her flowers with a wide smile on her face. Lucinda, her face and hands covered with finely-sifted flour, had exclaimed at their beauty.

Deke had noticed, too.

As soon as the door closed, he stood in front of her.

"And who're these from?" he demanded.

"Ronnie. Lucinda's daddy." Even in those three words, she heard her voice cracking into stammered chunks of apology.

4

He snatched the card from the little plastic trident and singsonged its inscription. His eyes shone dangerously as he did so, turning flat and unreadable.

"'For all you do.' All you do. ALL you do. What's that really mean, anyway? You doing something I don't know about? These sure are some pretty flowers...he must really enjoy ALL you do. What ALL are you doing for your ex-husband? Maybe keeping a smile on his little soldier face while I'm at work every day? Is that it? Is that ALL?" His voice was already slurring from redneck illiteracy into full-blown drunken incomprehensibility.

Sharon sighed. She had known already that Deke was going to ruin the rest of the day. Once he started, it was nearly impossible to get him to stop. "Deke, you know it's nothing like that. He's thanking me for being Lucinda's mom. It's Mother's Day. Remember?"

His bloodshot eyes gleamed. "Remember, hell." He stuck a thick finger in her face. "You want to watch your tone with me, girl. I'll make it so you'll never *be* a mother again." His fingernails were dirty. They were *always* dirty.

"You're sick. Sick to even think of something so nasty! The hell's wrong with you, Deke?"

He snatched the vase from her and dashed it against the wall. When it hit, long-stemmed roses shot out in a clump, attached to a green cube of floral Styrofoam. The vase, the Styrofoam, and the roses all clattered to the floor, and water splashed onto the wall. The wall had a rounded dent in it, a bowl-shaped depression about the size of a child's head. Water dripped down and began to soak into the carpet.

"There's not a goddamned thing wrong with me," Deke growled. "Happy Mother's Day, you worthless bitch. And if I ever find out you are keeping company with soldier boy, I'll beat the dog shit out of both of you." He raised his hand and slapped her, rocking her head back on her neck. He turned, picked up his beer from the coffee table, and sat back down on the sofa. He pointedly did not look back at her, or say anything else.

How the hell did I get us into this mess? she asked herself.

That question rang out in her head every time Deke took out his anger on her or Lucinda. Thankfully, at this point Lucinda was still mostly beneath his radar. Sharon didn't have an answer for that question, but if she could figure it out, maybe she could figure out how to get *out* of the mess.

Her face stung. She looked back into the kitchen, embarrassed, angry, hurt, and scared. Lucinda, her lower lip trembling, met her mother's eyes. The delicate smudges of flour on her face looked like thin, downy feathers until a tear tracked through a splotch. As a six-year-old, Lucinda may not have understood everything Deke had said, but she certainly understood the ugliness of the feelings he'd shown.

* * *

Now Sharon looked into her daughter's eyes. Yes, Lucinda obviously remembered what had happened that day.

"Yeah," Sharon said. "Deke got all mad. We don't want him to get all mad at us again."

"When we get presents, it makes him mad," Lucinda said, sounding both awed and saddened by the conclusion she'd drawn. "What are we gonna do, Mommy?"

"Well, I think we'll have to keep this a secret, Punkin. We'll open your present, and you can keep it, but you've got to keep it hidden in your room. Can you do that?"

Lucinda nodded, adamant. "I promise."

"Okay. Make sure you don't mention it to Deke, though."

Sharon took her keys from the hook hanging by the door, and used the edge of one to cut the tape on the box seams. They opened the flaps of the box, revealing an interior stuffed with wadded newspaper pages. Nestled in the center was an object further wrapped with tissue paper and tape, and Sharon cut this tape as well. Lucinda tore through several thick layers of tissue with a child's eagerness and finally revealed what Sharon had known the box would hold: a doll.

Sharon held her breath and looked closely at the doll, remembering the horribly creepy-looking dolls her father had made for her when she'd been younger. To begin with, a few of them had been little more than sticks tacked or tied together and clothed in shapeless dresses, with ghastly heads made of apples. The apples were carved with facial features, and then, by design, as the days passed and the apples dried, the faces crumpled into the shriveled, wrinkly visages of old hags. While in theory these dolls might pass as a form of homespun artistry, they'd given Sharon nightmares.

Over the years, her father had advanced from apples, to wood and finally to plastic, but the dolls he'd made had always been unsettling to look at, and she'd never been able to bring herself to actually cuddle one in bed. Looking back on that time, Sharon wondered if the handmade dolls were as repellent as she remembered, or if her tastes were marred by the accident and her father's illness.

Despite Sharon's misgivings, the doll in front of Lucinda looked almost professionally made. Sharon sniffed the air wafting from the box and was again pleasantly surprised. The doll didn't smell like anything other than a doll, although there was a hint of pine-scented cleanser. The doll was even pretty, in a *don't play with it, put it on the shelf* way.

Lucinda owned a few Barbie dolls and some of the cheaper knockoffs as well, but she mostly played with her Dora the Explorer playset. The Barbies and their relatives were not much fun for Lucinda except to dress up, and Lucinda's Barbie wardrobe was severely limited. Sharon had hand-stitched most of the buxom little blonde's clothes from remnants of Lucinda's old castoffs.

The doll in the box before them looked to be based on a model from the early 1920s, with pale skin, curly brown hair, and a white dress with matching white shoes. She looked like something off of a nostalgic soft drink advertisement, almost like a china doll.

Lucinda lifted the doll out of the box, gently tearing away the rest of the padding.

"Oh, Mommy!" she said, drawing the words out in wonder. "She's so pretty!" Lucinda stroked the doll's hair as she examined the small, creamy, dimpled face.

"She sure is. And you know what else? I think your granddaddy made her especially for you. He used to make dollies for me when I was little, too, but none of them were as pretty as this one."

Lucinda pulled the doll into her arms in a fierce hug. "I love her, Mommy, and I'm going to take extra special care of her!"

"You do that, Punkin, and remember what I said. It'll be a secret from Deke, okay?"

"Yep, a secret. We don't want him to get all mad and tear up my new dolly. Can I have the box? She needs a bed, and she likes it in her box."

Sharon was glad to comply. This way Deke wouldn't see the box, either.

"That's fine, sweetie. Please don't forget and leave her out anywhere."

"I won't! I promise!" Lucinda gathered up the box and its padding and ran to her room. Sharon followed, basking in the beauty of her daughter's sudden happiness. She stood in the doorway of Lucinda's bedroom and watched as her little girl lifted the edge of her blanket and slid the box under the bed out of sight. She let the blanket fall back into place, the tugged at one side to straighten a wrinkle. She sat back on her heels, presumably accepting that the drape of the material looked natural, then reached down and peeked again under the blanket. She turned to Sharon.

"Mommy, what should I name her?"

"I don't know, baby. That's a hard question, sometimes. You can name her whatever you like. I know sometimes people name things because of a name they think is really pretty, and sometimes names are given in honor of other people. Sometimes, a name simply fits a person. Your middle name is the same as my little sister, your aunt Pearl. She died a long time ago, when we were little kids, but I loved her so much I wanted to remember her by sharing her name with you."

Lucinda seemed to consider this while Sharon's mind began to fill with the odd, sometimes ugly names she'd given the dollies her father had made for her. Granted, the names were fitting appellations to some of the creepy dolls, but she'd hardly ever used the names anyway. There was Spiderguts (the doll's skin was made of something greenish-brown and shiny), Footstop (the dolly's left foot had no toes and looked like they'd been chopped off), Wobble Head (her head didn't actually move, but it was oddly shaped, like a peanut lying on its side), Princess Burp (not sure about that one, but she thought the first thing out of her mouth after she'd opened it had been a belch), Monster kid (a little boy doll who for some reason had pointed teeth), and easily fifty others he'd sent before they'd finally stopped arriving in the mail. Her father had sent one for every occasion and sometimes for no occasion at all. She'd named them, she'd put them down, and then at night when it was bedtime she'd thrown them into the closet where they couldn't look at her. They disturbed her. They'd been creepy to start with, but at night they seemed to be worse. They stared intently at her, as if they were lurking, waiting for her to fall asleep, so they could attack her. She'd known that wasn't the case, though. She remembered seeing the baby food jars filled with the strange store-bought eyes her father had used, sitting on the counter in his weird little workroom in the scary hospital.

Lucinda's eyes lit up.

"How about Maryann?" Before Sharon could answer, Lucinda's face clouded with doubt. "Or maybe Angelica? Or Elizabeth?"

Sharon smiled. "It's all up to you, kiddo. Those are some good names, and I think she'd be pleased to have any of them."

From the end of the road, she heard the crunch of gravel and the growl of a large truck in desperate need of a new muffler.

Oh shit.

"Think about it all you want, sweetie, but put it away right now, okay?"

Lucinda shoved the doll's "bed" back under her own little bed, covered it, and then looked up with worry in her eyes.

"Deke's home," Sharon said.

2

As the afternoon sun sank into the treeline, Deke pulled the old pickup to the end of the trailer and turned it off. He reached down between his legs, did a little "scratch and adjust", and opened his door. He got out on one side while Raymond played fiddly-fuckaround with the window crank. It looked like he was trying to open the passenger door with it.

"Hey, dumbass," Deke called to him, then pointed about six inches forward of the window crank. "The door handle."

"Oh yeah, okay," Ray said, and he got out of the truck. He was a skinny son of a bitch with a late crop of angry-looking acne, an Adam's apple as big as a fist, and a lazy right eye that stared straight ahead, while his left looked off at some crazy angle. Dumb as a stump and uglier than homemade sin.

"Get the beer outta the back and come on in," Deke said, already unbuttoning his blue work shirt as he walked up the path to the porch steps. The pattern of sweat on the chest of his white undershirt looked almost like a long-tailed bat with its wings stretched all the way out.

"I'm home!" he yelled at the closed, aluminum-sheathed door of the trailer. *That silly bitch better not be on her ass on the couch. She better be in the kitchen, fixin' my goddamned dinner.* "We got comp'ny," he added. He pulled back on the screen door, making Raymond, his arms full of two cases of Bud, retreat a couple of steps.

His hairy fist swallowed the doorknob. He turned it and pushed then entered. Raymond followed silently. If Ray had any thoughts at all sparking in that hollow gourd of his, they were probably only about eating, drinking, and fucking, and they certainly didn't show in his dead eyes. Deke envied his simplicity a little.

The couch was empty, and ol' girl was standing over the stove. *Right where she goddamned ought to be*, he thought, almost regretfully. The little crumbsnatcher was nowhere in sight. A red pile of hamburger meat was beginning to sizzle in the skillet in front of Sharon, the scent filling the small trailer.

"What's for supper?"

"Hamburger Helper."

"Make some extra. Raymond here's gonna be eatin', too."

Sharon turned her head and looked like she was about to say something then stopped. She turned back to the skillet with a strained expression on her face, the wooden spoon stabbing into the ground beef. Deke grinned to himself. *'Bout time you learned to shut the fuck up, heifer.*

"You can put that beer down on the floor in there then get back out to the truck and get them bags of ice. I gotta get the cooler out."

Deke reached into the laundry room. Under the laundry basket was the big red chest cooler. He pulled it out and opened it up, ignoring the sharp scent of mildew that wafted out, and began to pull the cans of beer off their plastic ring templates. He covered the bottom of the cooler with a layer of red and silver cans before Raymond returned with the ice.

"Now we could'a put the beer in the fridge like any old jackass," Deke said, taking one of the bags of ice and tearing open the top of it. "Thing is, it takes about twenty minutes for a beer to get really cold that way." He dumped half the bag on the cans. "Doing this, we'll be drinking it ice cold inside of five minutes." Raymond made the appropriate appreciative sound at this little shred of beer wisdom, but Deke figured it was probably going in one ear and out the other. He turned back toward Sharon, who'd not moved since he last spoke to her.

"I thought I told you to make extra." The vulgar scent of threat was palpable in the air between them.

She looked up, but her eyes didn't rise all the way to his. "There's only so much that comes in the box, Deke. Y'all can eat this," she said, barely audible. "I'll fix sandwiches for Lucinda and me."

Deke shrugged. Just as well. He and Raymond had some serious business to discuss, and they didn't need any bullshit interruptions.

He dragged the cooler onto the carpet and sat on the couch. Only five feet of distance, but now he was out of the laundry room by the kitchen, and in middle of the living room. Raymond joined him, and he turned on the television, flipping channels and looking for something good. Commercial, commercial, news, game show, news. Finally, he found a baseball game. He opened up the cooler, got out a couple of beers, and gave one to Raymond.

"You see? What'd I tell you? Ice fuckin' cold." They opened them up, and before they'd polished them off completely, Sharon came into the living room with two paper plates. They were piled high with meat, sauce, and noodles. She brought them a couple of napkins and forks, then went back to the kitchen. A few minutes later she passed by one more time with two more paper plates. Each one of these had a peanut butter and jelly sandwich and half an apple on it.

She disappeared into the back hallway, and Deke grinned when he heard Lucinda's bedroom door close behind her. *Fuck yeah, good riddance.*

Raymond and Deke drank a few more beers and ate their supper, and before they got too drunk, the game ended. The Blue Jays got their asses handed to them again. No big surprise there. Deke sat back and took a deep breath then began his proposal.

"Ray, you remember what I mentioned to you at the store earlier today? I wasn't kiddin'. We could do it; you, me, and Earl, if he'd be willing to get off his fat ass."

"You think?" Ray asked. He looked like he wasn't entirely sure what Deke was talking about.

Deke drained off the last of his beer. "This is some serious shit, Ray. I'm gonna have to throw in a dip for this. You want one?"

Ray waved him off, and Deke pulled a round tin from his back pocket, tamped it out then opened it up. He pinched a generous wad of the cherry-scented tobacco in his blunt fingers and packed it into his lower lip. His most recently-emptied beer can automatically became his spittoon. He pulled a couple of fresh cans from the cooler, passed one to Ray, and opened another for himself.

"Hell yeah," he continued. "It'll be easy. Them stupidass cockholes at the bank will never know what hit 'em."

When Sharon brought the plates back to Lucinda's room, she opened the door and saw her daughter sitting on the floor by her bed, her hand under the hem of the blanket. Sharon thought Lucinda's fingers, still plump with baby fat, were probably touching her new doll as if to draw strength from it. She sat on the floor beside her daughter and held out a plate.

Sharon and Lucinda ate their meager meal in silence, scared of the potential violence that could erupt at the drop of a hat from the living room. Though the voices from the living room stayed fairly subdued, that did nothing to set them at ease.

They both earned their memberships in the Clean Plate Club then they played together in whispered tones. Halfway through a round of Candyland, Lucinda confided in her mother.

"Her name is Beatrice," she whispered. "She only likes to be called Betty, though. If I say Beatrice all out like that, it means she's in trouble, and no one likes to be in trouble." Lucinda's eyes were wide and solemn.

"That's for sure," Sharon said. "Well, tell Betty she sure is welcome in our home, and I hope she finds her new accommodations pleasing."

"Oh, Mommy, she's *very* happy to be here. She loves it here, even though she doesn't like Deke. She said he's a booger-head. She said she wants to be my best friend, too."

"Wow," Sharon said, hoping her tone wasn't too patronizing. "She must be pretty nice."

"Mommy, she's the best dolly ever."

They continued playing board games and sharing whispered conversation for a couple more hours, until Lucinda's speech began to be punctuated more by yawns than anything else. Sharon helped her change into pajamas then sent her to the bathroom to brush her teeth. As tight as they were on money, they certainly couldn't afford extra visits to the dentist.

Lucinda returned to her room and blew minty toothpaste breath into Sharon's face then climbed into bed.

"Can I sleep with Betty tonight?"

"Not tonight, sweetie. We'll figure out a way you can have Betty around all the time, and then you can cuddle her up in your bed every night."

Sharon already had the beginnings of a plan to make the doll an accepted part of the family in Deke's accounting, but talking about it now would only complicate things. Lucinda took her old standby Lumpy Bear to bed with her instead, and Sharon sat by her bedside and stroked her forehead while whispering the words to old songs from the sixties. The songs were the closest things to lullabies Sharon knew, and they worked as well as anything. One favorite was an old Elvis song called "Little Sister" that Lucinda loved. Even though she'd learned the actual lyrics now, in her head Sharon always heard it as "Little sister don't you cry." The actual words were about a boy telling a girl that she shouldn't run around with every guy like her big sister, but Sharon never remembered it that way.

Tonight, though, Lucinda asked for an old Temptations tune. "The Way You Do The Things You Do."

As Sharon whispered the words to the song, Lucinda's breathing slowly deepened, and the anxious care lines between her eyebrows smoothed. She slept.

"Sweet dreams, Punkin," Sharon whispered.

She sat in the dark in Lucinda's room and listened. The thin walls of the trailer offered little in the way of privacy, and she heard the steady mutter of Deke talking to Raymond. She couldn't quite make out what they said, but she could tell from their whispering and lack of humor that they were discussing matters of grave import.

After a time, she grew tired of trying to decipher their drunken speech based on the pattern of sibilant letters and vowel sounds, and she reached under her daughter's bed.

The box slid out easily. The wadded newspaper padding had been rearranged into a nest of sorts. In the nest, the doll lay on its back, its iridescent painted blue-green eyes gazing placidly up at nothing. Those eyes were strangely unsettling, and reminded Sharon of something she couldn't quite identify.

Sharon shuddered, thinking of all the dolls she'd been given over the years. The ones whose eyes had fallen out or fallen in, the ones that were jaggedly stitched like Frankenstein monsters, the ones whose stuffing included things normally found in a garbage can, or buried.

Don't think about that.

Lucinda's doll, on the other hand, looked like it had been made in a factory.

Mastering her remaining uneasiness, Sharon touched the doll's face. Made of a soft, thin rubber, it felt pliant. Its rosy color gave the impression of health. Beneath the rubber, some sort of fibrous stuffing kept the face in its pleasing shape. The eyes were painted on, bluish-green and coated with an acrylic that made them shiny. The hair had been inserted in tiny clusters and curled and styled lovingly. Sharon lifted the doll from the box and held it up for closer inspection.

The dress was handmade, but the stitching at each hem was careful and measured. Tiny blue flowers traced the dress's collar, and a matching flower was sewn onto each slipper.

Sharon was pleasantly surprised. This was probably the first one of her father's dolls that wasn't scary looking. Still, though, it creeped her out. She was about to replace the doll in its makeshift bed when she noticed the folded sheet of notebook paper at the bottom of the box.

It was a letter. The words had been written with a blunt pencil, pressed hard onto the paper. Sharon recognized the hand immediately. Her father had always written in perfect Palmer script except for his capital letters. Those were blocky, printed letters.

Dear Lucinda,

I hope you and your momma are doing well in Texas. I've been thinking about you and wondering what you're like. I made you this doll, and I hope she brings you happiness. You can tell her your deepest secrets and most frightening fears. Love her and keep her safe and keep yourself safe, too.

Happy Birthday,
Love Always,
Granddaddy

Sharon refolded the note and returned it to the box, then slid the box into its rightful spot under the bed. By the light of the bedside lamp, she watched her daughter sleep. Beneath her eyelids, Lucinda's eyes rolled from side to side. She was in the deep water of dreams. Sharon hooded the bedside lamp with a purple rayon scarf and crept out of the room.

As she passed the living room, Ray and Deke stopped talking and peered up at her. Suspicion and paranoia could be found in their expressions, and Sharon wondered what they could possibly be up to.

"What?" Deke grumbled at her.

"Nothing, nothing. Lucinda's asleep, and now I'm going to bed, too." She turned and walked into the bedroom. When she shut the door, she noticed that the conspiratorial whispers started scampering around again as soon as the door had hit the frame.

Lucinda, how the hell did I get us into this mess? she thought with a sigh. There had to have been something good between her and Deke at the beginning, but for the life of her she couldn't figure out what it had been. Maybe it had been the simple desire for security that had driven her to him.

Deke was an employee at an auto parts store, and in February, when she'd needed to replace the water pump in her old Nissan, she'd bought it from him and he'd helped her install it right there in the store parking lot. They went out on a few dates, and he'd stayed the night. A shirt got left at the trailer once, followed by a toothbrush, and then a pair of work boots, all of them simply overlooked the next morning. Objects began to pile up, and eventually Deke came to Sharon with the less than romantic *Well-shit-all-my-stuff-is-already-over-here* conversation, which amounted to a sort of passive-aggressive coercion to shack up more than any joint decision. So, Deke loaded up his pickup and moved the rest of his stuff in. He began to establish himself as the head of the household and convinced her to quit her job as an accounts receivable clerk at a rental car agency. Soon after, he sold her car. He gave logical-sounding reasons for both things, but in the end it only meant one thing: Sharon and Lucinda had no way to escape.

These days, Sharon's question of how she'd gotten herself and Lucinda into this mess flashed through her mind almost daily. No answer ever presented itself, and no possibility of escape ever became part of her hopes. They were practically living hand-to-mouth already. Lucinda would need at least a couple of new sets of clothes for school, but the money wasn't there.

Like always. Deke was more of a financial liability than anything. He gave her his paycheck and told her to take care of the bills then demanded an allowance like some overgrown kid. Without fail he'd drink away his beer money then ask for more. On a few occasions she'd even found him rooting through her purse. Between the money Ronnie sent for Lucinda and the aid money they received from Bell County, Sharon barely kept the roof over their heads and the electricity turned on. Deke got angry if she refused him more spending money, choosing to accuse her of mishandling things.

He'd not been physically violent with her since that horrible Mother's Day, but unstated threats ran through everything he said like a poisonous undercurrent. On the surface, she supposed Deke was a strong, solid man. Now that she really knew him, and was in too deep to get out, she saw that he had fundamental problems in his mind and in his heart. Sharon didn't know where those problems came from, and she certainly didn't feel the need to delve into the forensics of his soul, but she and Lucinda were between a rock and a hard place with him in the house.

She changed and slid into bed, hoping Deke would pass out on the couch. Sleep was quick to take her, and though she hoped to dream of taking Lucinda away and starting their lives over again, her rest was dark and dreamless.

4

Lucinda was dreaming.

The old man was in a little bed with plastic rails on it. The bed itself wasn't much bigger than Lucinda's. His head was mostly bald except around the edges. He wore round, gold-rimmed glasses like Santa Claus. He had no beard, but he hadn't shaved in a few days. His whiskery face looked at her and he gave her a slow, closed-mouth smile. It made Lucinda feel good, warming her from the inside. *Little sister, don't you cry. Ev'rything'll be all right* she thought the smile said, like Mommy told her when she was sad.

One time, when she was playing in the yard, she found an old rubber band. It was a big fat blue one, like the ones that go around broccoli bunches at the grocery store. She pulled it to see how far it would stretch, but it broke right away. When it popped her hand, it didn't even sting. She looked at it closely and saw all the cracks in it. When she went and asked Mommy about it, Mommy pointed to the cracks and splits in the rubber and called it dry rot.

That's what Lucinda thought of when she looked at the old man's seamed, yellowish face. Not that his face looked rotten, but it looked dried out and weathered in the same way.

She stood at the foot of his bed, where his feet were two indistinct lumps under the blanket. Beside the bed was a folding metal chair. A thin pillow on the seat offered a little padding.

"I'm Lucinda," she said into the silence of his smile. The old man bobbed his head in a nod then moved slightly. His wasted arm moved with what looked like a huge amount of effort, and he pointed to the chair beside him. Where his skin rubbed against itself, it made a soft, whispery sound.

"You want me to sit down?" she asked.

The man's eyes closed, and he lay his head back. He nodded again, and breath seemed to sigh out of him. Lucinda sat in the chair. She knew if she sat back properly the way Mommy told her, her feet wouldn't touch the floor so instead she sat forward. The old man's gaze followed her as she moved, and his hand spidered jerkily over the blanket toward her. On the side of the bed, thick leather straps dangled. They looked worn, but old, as if they'd been used a lot, but not recently.

A too-loud voice behind Lucinda spoke, and made her jump.

"John Tibbedeau, you done pushed yourself too hard!"

A stout brown-skinned woman swung into view like a speeding truck coming out of a fogbank. She startled Lucinda, and Lucinda cried out, but the woman spoke over her scream.

"I know you love your grandbaby, and you wanted to send her a present, but now look at yourself! Been a week, and you still can't even lift your head to look at me."

The old man looked steadily at Lucinda, the soft smile on his face suggesting that he and Lucinda shared a secret. Was this her granddaddy? The shape of his nose and the light in his eyes did resemble Mommy's a little.

"I sent it out the same day you finished it, like you asked. I guess she done got it by now," the woman continued. She had a large clipboard, and she checked a few blocks on it.

Lucinda nodded excitedly to the old man. "Yes, I got my dolly! Oh, Granddaddy, thank you so much! I love her!"

Again that barely perceptible nod, and this time one of his eyes gave her a slow wink. He sighed again. Lucinda impulsively reached out and held his hand. It was soft and cool, and it gently squeezed her hand in return.

The black woman continued to talk over her, to the old man. "In all my twenty years here, John, that's the prettiest doll you ever made. I thought I'd never collect enough dryer lint to suit you." She stopped and looked at the old man, seeming to consider something. "It's sure been a long time, sugar. You've made a lot of dolls."

She shook a tiny paper cup merrily. A couple of small tablets rattled back and forth inside it. "Time for your meds, John. Get you some good sleep, and maybe you'll feel like getting up tomorrow. I'll even give you a shave, too."

The woman moved forward, and when she reached up to the old man's face, her hand and the cup of pills passed straight through Lucinda's arm. The woman took another step, and her broad hip covered Lucinda's arm. Lucinda didn't feel it at all.

The woman touched Granddaddy and gasped. The paper cup fell to the floor, and the little yellow tablets rolled away.

"John? Mr. Tibbedeau?"

She shook his shoulder and got no response. His head tipped and fell limply onto one narrow shoulder.

"John?" her voice rose in alarm.

She reached down and checked his pulse at his wrist then she pushed a button on the wall. When she spoke, Lucinda heard tears in her voice.

"Oh, no. Oh, John."

She checked his pulse again, this time on the side of his neck. She stood there for a moment, and Lucinda thought she looked like she was praying.

At last the woman fetched up a big sigh, sounding resigned. "Yeah, John, it's been a long time. Sleep well, sugar. You sure deserve a rest, Lord knows."

The woman turned and left the room, her voice already rising in a cry for help. As she retreated, her voice faded. Lucinda continued to hold the old man's hand, and his eyes continued, even in death, to smile at her.

* * *

Little sister, don't you cry. Ev'rything'll be all right.

Lucinda opened her eyes and looked at her room in the hooded light of her bedside lamp. Lumpy Bear was all smooshed down under the pillow so she pulled him out, hugged him, and burrowed back down into her blankets. She thought about the old man, her granddaddy, and his soft, comforting smile.

On the tail of that, she heard Deke's dark, mean laugh from the living room, and it chilled her. It made her wonder whether things really *would* be all right.

Somehow, it didn't feel like it.

5

Sharon sprinkled another handful of potato chips on top of the tuna noodle casserole. Lucinda was in her room, presumably playing with her toys. A further presumption was that she was keeping an ear out for the ragged growl of Deke's truck coming up the gravel lane. Sharon herself automatically had her ear tuned to the sound. She slid the casserole into the oven a second time, to "crisp up" the stale potato chips.

In the last few days, they seemed to have fallen off Deke's increasingly dangerous radar, but it would be utter foolishness to forget that his hand was always ready to swing, and his words were always ready to hurt. Sharon again made a promise to herself: if he *ever* struck Lucinda, she and Lucinda would leave. No matter what. If they ended up homeless and hungry, so be it. Being free of his violence would be worth it. As long as Deke only put his hands on Sharon, she could persevere, dancing the jerky, arrhythmic dance of avoidance. She'd learned to read the signs and to adjust her actions on the fly.

As if her anxious thoughts of Deke summoned him, she sensed at the edge of her hearing the sound of his pickup. It idled at the entrance of the trailer park, and she could picture him checking the mail, opening their tiny box in the squat metal honeycomb. She heard the door to the truck close then the sound of the engine came closer.

Sharon tried to anticipate his mood. Given the time of the month, it was neither payday nor a day that bills usually arrived. Things should be relatively stable, especially considering that she had his dinner ready for him.

She took the casserole from the oven and put it on the table while she listened to the truck's engine come closer. A feeling rose in her. Not necessarily dread, but a kind of weariness. She always had to be so watchful, so guarded. The stress of it was exhausting her. She heard voices raised outside, and her already low spirits fell even further. Her preparations for a peaceful evening would not be enough. Were they ever?

The door slammed open and rebounded off the far wall.

"Keep your fuckin' lice to yourselves, you filthy fuckin' pigs!" Deke roared across the yard to the trailer next door. The voice of their neighbor, Darlene Whisnat, rose in response. Her shrill profanities sounded almost cartoonish, but Sharon knew all too well exactly how she felt.

"Fuck yeah! I'll be waitin' for him, you fat, stupid, knock-kneed slut! Send his scrawny ass over soon as he gets home, and I'll snap that roll uh dimes he calls a neck!"

Deke slammed the thin door, rattling the entire wall of the trailer. He growled, stomping into the living room. He glared at Sharon as if she were part of the problem.

"D'you see what that dizzy bitch is doin'?" he asked, incredulous.

Sharon looked out the kitchen window. Darlene was outside, on her tiny wooden porch. She had a kitchen stool set up in front of her, with her son sitting on the stool. He had a big flowered sheet draped over him. The boy's head was half shaved, and Darlene stood behind him with a cheap set of electric clippers in her hand.

"Shaving down her kids. Again," Sharon replied.

It was known throughout the trailer park that the Whisnats had a serious problem with keeping themselves clean. It seemed to go in cycles. The kids would get sent home from school with lice notes, the school nurse telling the parents to send them back to school after administering treatment. The Whisnat parents would wait, do nothing, and eventually take the children outside and shave their heads. No hair, no head lice. A workable solution, but their son and daughter had, on more than one occasion, been mistaken for leukemia patients. A few weeks or months later, and the children would be sent home again, with the same notes from the school nurse.

"Hell yeah, she's shaving down her nasty kids again! But it's windy, and all that shit's flying over here. All those fuckin' cooties cut loose in the breeze! Good Christ it makes me itch just thinking about it!"

"Don't worry about it," Sharon said in an attempt to soothe him. "It's never spread over here before."

He went on as though she'd not spoken. "And now that stupid trashy bitch says she's going to send over her little ringworm husband to tell me what's what! Fuck yeah, bitch! Bring it on, you nasty little shitbag!"

Sharon sighed. She couldn't defuse his anger now that he was already spinning so she watched, waited for the other boot to drop, and tried to ensure that she stayed clear of the storm and kept Lucinda clear of it as well when it broke. Without another word, she served their supper.

Lucinda peered from the dim hallway, not moving from the shadows until Deke was seated at the table and completely engaged in shoveling food from his plate to his mouth. She climbed into her chair, and Sharon served her a portion of the casserole and a spoonful of canned green beans. Lucinda was a smart girl, and she didn't need to be told what was going on. She ate in silence then excused herself to her room before Deke's baleful focus could fall on her. Sharon supposed in a normal household the family dinner table was a place where they would talk about events of the day, and possibly even bring up the impending birthday of the child. In their house, though, the family dinner table was a place of fear, to be escaped as quickly as possible.

For her part, Sharon kept Deke's plate full of food until the rate of his eating began to slow. She also kept a beer beside his plate. As he finished one can, she discarded it and replaced it with the next one. She knew that with a full belly and a couple of six packs, he'd start to get drowsy. Sharon hoped she could wear him down before Marty Whisnat worked up the gumption to come over.

Lucinda looked questioningly to Sharon from the hallway. Sharon flashed her a quick smile and nod. Lucinda vanished into the shadows of the hall, and Sharon saw a tiny flash of light on the hallway wall as her daughter opened the door to her room and escaped into it.

Keeping an eye on Deke, Sharon ate in silence. Quiet was the best tactic, because it avoided giving his rage any fuel. Let his anger either burn itself out, or burn itself down enough that it was manageable.

She began to think they were in the clear when the strident rapping began on the front door. Five quick, impatient knocks.

Oh shit.

The sudden smile that spread on Deke's face was positively evil. He pushed away from the table. Sharon saw that this was exactly what he'd been waiting for. He stood, picked up his beer, finished it off, and let the empty can clank to the surface of the table. He turned, in no apparent rush, and walked to the front door. Those five furious knocks came again, rattling the panes of glass in the small window by the door.

The tension rose palpably in the room as Deke reached for the porch light. He flicked it on and his hand dropped to the doorknob. Violence was coming. Sharon could feel it in the air and could taste it in her mouth. She saw the expression on Deke's face, the concentrated anticipation of his hateful smile so like the expression of a cat preparing to pounce on a wounded bird.

He turned the knob and pulled the door open. Marty Whisnat stood on the porch. Marty was breathing so fast it looked like he was hyperventilating. In one hand he held a green beer bottle.

Sharon stole a glance across the yard and saw Marty's family standing on their own front porch. Darlene was smoking a cigarette, her hand trembling so that the smoke drifting up was a stutter of Morse code. The two children—now shaved bald—stood close by. Their features were mostly masked because the light on their front porch threw them into silhouette, but Sharon detected their worry in the way they stood close together. They looked like ghosts.

Marty launched into a tirade he'd surely rehearsed in his head on the way over. His voice rose in pitch and volume as he spoke, his long, thin hair hanging over one eye.

"Deke, you got no call to talk to Darlene the way you did today! That was pure ugly! Here we are livin' right next door so we for damn sure gotta get along with one 'nother! You owe her an apology, and I'm gon' stand right here till you give it!" He panted, his chest heaving as he looked into the doorway of the trailer.

Deke's answer came with hateful good humor. "Would you look at this," he said in a tone of quiet wonder, speaking to no one. "Some sawed-off, narrow-assed little kid is trespassin' on our lovely deck. Looks threat'nin'. I may hafta scare him off."

Deke stepped over the threshold of the door, onto the sagging boards of the front porch. It was, by no stretch of the imagination, a "lovely deck," but no sane person would dare contradict Deke when he was half drunk and sounded so icily calm. Deke's chin was about even with the top of Marty's head, and for a moment, Sharon admired the smaller man for standing up to Deke. The admiration, however, quickly turned to pity. Marty would certainly get his ass kicked tonight.

"Now, Deke," he said, his voice cracking slightly, "you know you don't need to talk to folks that way. Darlene ain't done nothin' to you."

"Marty, go on back home. Git on back over there and slop that fuckin' sow you call a wife, and keep them fuckin' cootie-bug kids uh yours in your house. You don't want to have to go huntin' for your teeth in the dark, do you?"

"Goddammit, Deke, you watch your mouth!" Marty broke the green beer bottle against the porch railing and waved the jagged neck of it warningly in front of him.

Marty, you idiot, Sharon had time to think before Deke swung. Barely even visible as a blur in the porchlight, Deke's fist pistoned out between Marty's waves of the beer bottle. The thump of fist hitting face sounded meat locker ugly and was punctuated by the sound of Marty's makeshift weapon shattering into a million green jewels on the porch. After the one punch, Deke simply dropped his hands to his sides. Marty staggered a couple of steps backwards, his nose already spouting thick jets of blood and snot. It was surely broken. Sharon watched him as his eyes rolled back in his head. He took one more step backwards and flipped over the porch railing into the darkness.

From the next trailer, Darlene shrieked. A long, keening screech that wound down into a gobbling sob. She threatened to call the police as she rushed across the yard, dodging between the scrub oaks.

"Fuck yeah." Deke laughed. "Call 'em. Tell 'em how your numbfuck husband came over here trespassin', threatenin' me with a broken bottle, and still got his ass stomped! *Please* call the po-lice! I'd dearly love to tell them the whole goddamned sorry-ass story!"

She screeched a few more incomprehensible names at Deke as she lifted an unconscious Marty under his arms and began dragging him home. Sharon watched through the kitchen window, seeing Marty and Darlene's bald, alien-looking children on their porch. They clumsily held the door open for their mother as she dragged their father into

30

their trailer. Behind them, they closed the door, and a moment later they turned off their porch light.

Deke reentered the trailer with a satisfied smile on his face. The middle knuckle of his right hand was split, and Sharon watched as he finally took notice of it, drunken incredulity painting his face. He flicked off the porch light and brought his split knuckle to his mouth. When he noticed Sharon looking at him, his smile widened into a leer.

She could read his expression, and the chill hand of fear gripped her.

"Now that I've defended the sacred honor of this house, what should I have as my reward?" He stalked toward her, the violence in his eyes paired now with an animal lust.

Sharon knew she hadn't gotten enough beer into him for the alcohol to subdue him. He was in the spot barely before that, where he was a crazy, mean, horny drunk. He backed Sharon into the bedroom, and he took her. Forcefully and painfully.

* * *

When he finally passed out, Sharon went to the bathroom and scrubbed herself until her skin was red and raw. It didn't make her feel any cleaner.

She toweled off and got dressed then tiptoed into Lucinda's room. She found her daughter asleep on the floor. All her toys were neatly put into the big plastic toy box with the picture of the disturbingly big-eyed kitten on the side. One of Lucinda's hands was under her head, while the other was extended around the thin toddler bed mattress and under the bed. Sharon lifted the edge of the blanket and saw that Lucinda had fallen asleep holding her creepy doll's tiny rubber hand.

Sharon gently reached down and separated Lucinda's hand from the doll.

6

The Saturday morning of Lucinda's birthday party dawned quiet and beautiful, like a whispered declaration of love. Lucinda lay in her bed and listened to Deke's noises, knowing that after he was gone to work, she could get up and watch cartoons in peace. She heard Deke growl something at Mommy, rattle some stuff around in the kitchen, and leave. As soon as he was gone, Mommy burst into the room.

"Somebody's got a birthday today!" she smiled. The big bite-bruises on Mommy's neck from the other night had already turned from purple to yellow. In a couple of days, they wouldn't show at all, but Lucinda thought they still hurt. She smiled up at Mommy.

"Me! Me! Me!"

Mommy picked her up in a big hug and spun around the small room. "My big seven year old. I'm fixing you a birthday cake, and I've got a present or two to wrap, and you can play all day long, until it's time for your party."

"Can I help with the cake?"

"I don't know," Mommy said, sounding doubtful. "If you help, it won't be a surprise."

"That's okay, Mommy. Please please please can I help?"

"Well, all right, big girl." Mommy set her down on the floor. "We can get started right now if you really want to."

They went into the kitchen. Mommy poured a cup of coffee into her mug then got down another mug. She poured half a cup of milk into it, and a couple of spoonfuls of sugar, then topped it off with a splash of coffee. She stirred it then passed it to Lucinda.

"Coffee? For me?"

"Why not? You're getting so big I thought you might like to try it."

Lucinda took a tentative sip, swallowing while she decided whether she like it. She had trouble placing the taste at first then she smiled.

"It's good Mommy. It tastes like cereal-milk after you've eaten all the chocolate cereal out of the bowl." That wasn't the flavor exactly, but it was the closest approximation she could find.

Mommy got out two aprons and tied one over Lucinda's nightshirt. The tails were so long she had to wrap them around twice and tie them in front. Then she tied one on herself, and Lucinda was again impressed how Mommy could tie a bow behind her back without even looking. Mommy got down a box of cake mix and they set to work. They took turns stirring and mixing, but it became too difficult for Lucinda as it thickened. Mommy took over then poured the batter into two round pans, put the pans in the oven, and set the timer on the little microwave.

"You go get cleaned up while I wrap the presents," Mommy said, and Lucinda agreed. She looked down and was surprised to see how goobered up and messy her apron was. She untied it from her waist and put it in the laundry basket then shucked off her nightgown as well. Mommy's apron, she noticed, didn't have a speck of anything on it, and Lucinda smiled with the knowledge that someday she would be able to do that, too. She scampered off to the bathroom and began running a bath, and by the time she was ready to get into the tub, Mommy came into the bathroom.

"Wait a minute, here. This is no birthday bath," she said. She reached up to the top shelf, got down the big teardrop-shaped bottle, and drizzled a generous amount into the tub where the water was still flowing in. Thick bubbles boiled up in a fragrant froth, soon covering the surface of the water in wobbly white drifts. When Mommy turned the water off, Lucinda heard the low, crackly Pop Rocks whisper of the tiny bubbles as they burst. She stepped into the foamy cumulus with a giggle.

"*Now* it's a birthday bath," Mommy said. "I'll go get you a pair of clean undies, mermaid girl. You've got a few minutes playtime, but don't go under water."

"Okay," Lucinda said, scooping up a handful of suds as Mommy disappeared. She piled them on top of her head so that she wore a poufy white turban. Next she gave herself a Santa Claus beard and a pair of fat white mittens. Lucinda heard the distant beep of the microwave timer, and then heard Mommy open and close the oven.

A few moments later, Mommy returned to the bathroom with a towel in one hand and a pair of underpants in the other. She put them down on the lid of the toilet then sat by the tub.

Lucinda washed slowly, and Mommy talked with her. They talked about all kinds of things. School coming up soon, other kids in the trailer park, clothes, and what Lucinda wanted to be when she grew up. By the time they ran out of things to say, Lucinda's fingers were all pruney and the water was starting to get cold.

She got out and got dressed, while Mommy drained the tub, then rinsed and refilled it. Lucinda brushed her hair as it dried, and she watched Mommy as she undressed. Like the bruises on her neck, she had bruises on her upper arms and on her bottom. Lucinda wasn't certain how those bruises came about, but she knew that Deke was to blame. Looking at Mommy's injuries opened a puzzled blackness in her, and it made her angry and sad. Why did Deke always have to hurt Mommy?

Mommy washed quickly then dried off.

After they were dressed, Mommy sent her to check with the two baldheaded kids next door. Their daddy answered the door, and he looked scary. He had a dirty stripe of medical tape straddling his nose. Both his eyes had bruises beneath them. He seemed surprised that she was here inviting his kids to come over and have a slice of birthday cake, and he looked suspiciously over Lucinda's shoulder.

"Your daddy ain't home?"

Lucinda made a face. "Deke? He's not my daddy. He's at work, anyway."

"O-okay, then. They'll be over. They can't stay long, though, y'hear?"

"Yes, sir."

Lucinda came back home, and wondered if she or Mommy could think of anyone else to invite to the party. There was that one kid, Dustin, down at the end of the park by the playground, but they had a big mean dog at that trailer, and Lucinda was scared of it. If they were inviting Dustin, Mommy would have to go to his trailer and ask.

In the end, though, it was only the Whisnat kids and Mommy at Lucinda's party. That was okay, though. They had chocolate cake with chocolate frosting, and as a surprise Mommy served it with a scoop of vanilla ice cream on the side.

The Whisnat kids, Jeffrey and Sybil, were nervous, like their daddy had been, but after a while they began to smile and loosen up some. Their shaved heads, beginning to show a little bit of fuzz, looked strange. Even though they were born a year apart and one was a boy and one was a girl, with their heads shaved, they could have passed for sad twins.

They were about to watch Lucinda open her presents when Mommy looked up at the clock. Deke was probably on his way back to the house so that meant it was time for the Whisnat kids to leave. Mommy gave them each another slice of cake to take with them, then sent them back across the yard to their trailer. Lucinda watched as their pale, naked heads bobbed away between the trees, and they disappeared.

Lucinda and Mommy closed the front door and went back to the table. The second they sat down, they heard the rattling, laborious sounds of Deke's pickup turning off the main road onto the gravel drive of the trailer park.

In moments, he had come into the house.

"Supper's going to be a few minutes," Mommy said to him. "I got behind because I threw a little birthday party for Lucinda."

Deke came all the way into the kitchen and his eyes fell on Lucinda. Despite herself, she cowered under his appraising glance.

"Hmph. Well, happy birthday, young'un. You had a party?"

"Mmm-hmm. We had cake. I helped make it."

"Did y'all save me some?" No trace of a smile touched his face.

"There's some left," Mommy said. Lucinda noticed that her statement didn't offer any cake to him.

Deke's eyes finally left Lucinda's and turned to the two gifts at the other end of the table. They were both wrapped in comics pages from the newspaper. The smaller gift showed a frame of Dennis the Menace, and the larger gift showed several frames of Peanuts.

"Presents, too. Hmm, looks like it's a good day to be Lucinda." Deke's eyes turned toward her again, and Lucinda again felt uncomfortable. *If he keeps staring at me like that, I'm going to run to my room and hide.* He turned away and went to the fridge then returned to the table snapping open a can of beer. He seemed to have things other than Lucinda on his mind, and for that, she was glad.

"Go on and open them, honey," Mommy said. They're from Deke and me, and I think you'll like them."

Lucinda quickly tore into the small one, which was a strawberry-scented soap and lotion gift pack. She thanked them for it, and Deke rolled his eyes.

The big one was Lucinda's Betty dolly. Mommy had taken it from
under the bed and rewrapped it. Of course! Now Deke would think
Mommy got it for her! Now she could keep it out, and he wouldn't get
all mad. She took Betty out of the box and gave her dolly a big hug,
thanking Mommy and Deke again.

"Baby girl, we figured Lumpy Bear's about had it. He's ready to
retire, but you needed something new to cuddle at night. Do you
think you could take this dolly to bed at night?" Mommy's smile was
bright and clever, and Lucinda realized Mommy'd played a smart
trick on Deke. Lucinda played along, hoping her excitement and joy
masked her knowledge of Mommy's trick.

"Oh yes, Mommy, yes, oh thank you so much!"

Lucinda grabbed her strawberry-scented soap and Betty and ran
to her room.

That night, Betty slept in the bed right by Lucinda, nestled in the
child's small, warm embrace.

7

Deke had a bad fuckin' headache. He thought at first that it was a hangover headache, but the damned thing wasn't going away. Usually, coffee and a doughnut would knock a hangover back at least a little bit. Today it only made him feel like he was about to puke.

He had too much shit going on, and it was like a bunch of bowling balls crashing around inside his head. It wasn't that he was nervous about the plan. He'd thought it through over and over again, looking for holes in it. There weren't any. It was a good plan. It would work out fine, and then it'd be nothing but smooth sailing for them all.

At least it would until they needed to do it again.

Best not to worry about that until he had to. They probably wouldn't need to think anything about that for months.

Deke considered his immediate future as he drove into town, the radio droning a low, mournful song of loss. The three pistols he had picked up on the cheap from the pawn shop were snug in the glove box, along with a small box of nine-millimeter bullets. Hell, the bullets made Deke more nervous than the guns did. The pistols were nothing but chrome-plated pieces of shit. They probably wouldn't even shoot straight. They were *guns*, though, which is exactly what they needed. If everything went according to plan, they wouldn't even need to use them. They were mostly for show, anyway, but he'd bought the bullets just in case shit went bad.

He pulled into the nearly empty lot of Busby's Auto Parts and parked by the old brown Suburban Earl called his "Beast." To Deke, it looked like a rusty pile of crap. It was five after eight so Earl had only opened the store a couple of minutes ago. No real traffic would start for another hour or so, when mechanics would start either coming in or calling in with their lists of needed repair parts.

The mechanics in the area, both the certified and the shade-tree variety, all worked the same way. They'd diagnose the car's problem then find two or three more problems that might be "contributing factors." After bullying the car owner into getting all the problems fixed, the mechanic would place his order. He'd get the parts from Napa or Busby's or wherever, mark the price up about fifty dollars or so, and then charge an additional outrageous labor price. Changing out a five dollar fan belt, an easy fifteen minute job, wound up costing some poor ignorant shitass about seventy-five dollars. The other guys, the actual do-it-yourselfers, were a much smaller minority.

It was a racket, a complete hose job, but the car owners didn't give a fuck. Most of them figured they were probably paying for the convenience of someone *else* getting their hands dirty fixing the car. Prissy horseshit, Deke thought. Dirt and grease washes off, after all.

Deke got out of the truck while it rattled and jerked with the seizures of post-ignition. The sign over the door matched the big marquee by the road, a big cartoon bumblebee with a wrench in one hand and a spark plug in the other. A speech bubble over the bee's smiling head said, "NEED PARTS? JUST SAY BUZZ-BEE!" Stupid fuckin' bee. Deke would *not* miss this place.

The electronic chime that sounded like an actual doorbell announced his entrance to the store. Earl looked up from a clipboard in front of him, his eyebrows knitted together over his eyeglasses.

"Hey, Deke," he said, the tone of his voice betraying his uncertainty. "I thought you didn't come in until later on."

Deke strolled forward, saying nothing. Aisles stretched away to either side of him. The cosmetic crap was closest to the door; air fresheners, floor mats, steering wheel covers, and license plate frames. Many of the items sported the same black or chrome silhouette of a pinup girl. As the aisles reached toward the back of the store, the items became uglier and more integral to the actual function of vehicles. Wiring kits, dusty hoses, a wall of batteries, and easily two hundred serpentine belts lined up and hanging like dead ducks in a Chinese market window. As the products became more basic, the packaging became plainer as well, and the way they were displayed became more a question of function than of form. At the back of the store by the service counter, shelves were lined with small boxes whose tops had been cut off with razor blades. The boxes all had greasy fingerprints on their sides where they'd been pulled out, rummaged through, and pushed back onto the shelf. Inside these boxes were bolts, bushings, fuses, and brackets jumbled loose. The people who went through these boxes were generally the do-it-yourself types, not the stupidass yo-bros that thought they needed a stylized barbed wire license plate frame, or a Zombie Apocalypse Response Team window decal.

Behind the counter was a massive floor to ceiling display of tires in various sizes. The only break in the display was a doorway hole that led to the office, the restroom, and the storage area in the back.

"Yeah, I'm closing this evenin," Deke conceded, "but for now, I'm really only here to talk to you."

Earl put his clipboard down onto the glass-topped counter. Beneath the glass were the expensive chromed heads and manifolds for those fucktard hotrod kids that get such a hard on for car stealing games and car racing movies.

Earl tipped his head down, his neck fat mashing into double and triple chins.

Lard-ass bastard.

Deke had the whole deal figured out, all the way down to the point nine nine. The only problem was this fat fuck, Earl. He was a whatchacallit, a liability, to the whole plan.

"What is it you want, Deke?"

"You know goddamned well what I want." Deke struggled to keep his voice even and calm, but his patience was wearing thin. "Ray and I are ready to do the deal, and we're tired of waiting for your fat ass to get off the fence. You gotta decide. You gonna fish, fatass, or sit on the bank and cut bait? What's it gonna be?"

"Deke, come on, now. This is some serious shit you're talking about. We do this, and we're done in this town. Where the hell are we gonna go?"

"That's the beauty of it. It don't even fuckin' matter where we go. We can go anywhere we want. Hell, as far as that goes, we could all go to different places. Do the job, part ways, and never see each other again."

"But we can't ever come back here again, either!"

"You won't need to come back here again, Porky."

"Dammit, Deke, stop calling me names. Now you know there ain't nothin' wrong with what we got right now. Sure, it's work, and we won't never get rich, but that's okay. You might hit the Powerball someday or Mega Millions, and be rich."

Deke's head was throbbing, hurting worse than ever. He was fed up, out of patience with this big dumb jackass. It was past time to let him decide if he was going to shit or get off the pot. Deke slammed his fist down on the clipboard. Beneath it, he heard the glass crack. He leaned forward into Earl's face.

"It's not okay, you goddamned weak-ass cock-sucking pig. I'm not going to try to convince you anymore. You're in it already. You know what the plan is, and because of that, you're part of it. Fuckin' get used to it. You try to run out on us, I'll find you and I'll fuckin' kill you. You call the cops, they won't find anything, and then I'll hunt your sorry ass down and kill you. I'll fucking skin you and wear your face for a mask. You turn on me in any way, and you won't live to regret it. You fuckin' gettin' this?"

Deke sighed, and leaned back. "On the other hand, the three of us can do the job, split the money, and you live. You could even use your share to get one of those fat-suckin' operations. That sound better?"

Oily beads of sweat had popped out on Earl's forehead. They were slowly trickling into his red sideburns. *Scared? Good, motherfucker. I hope you pissed yourself.*

Earl's head bobbed spastically up and down, more a shudder than a nod.

"Good," Deke said. "Don't you fuckin' forget, neither."

Earl shook his head.

"I'm glad we had this talk, Earl. I'm feelin' worlds better. You?"

Again, that spasm of a nod.

"Well, all right. I'll see you in a few hours, partner."

Deke turned on the heels of his grease-covered work boots and strode to the door. Goddamned right. He did feel good, but despite Earl's panicky, bobble-headed assurances, worry still nagged at the back of Deke's mind.

Could that chicken shit bastard be trusted?

8

Sharon woke with a gasp, wondering if she'd screamed out loud. If Deke's sour smelling snores were any indication, she hadn't. She lay still while she caught her breath, waiting for her heart to stop racing.

Deke had left for the store early in the day, was gone for an hour or two then he'd come home, and then later he'd gone back into the store for his regular shift. When he'd finally returned for the night, he'd been as irritable as usual, but thankfully he'd also been too distracted to take notice of either her or Lucinda. He farted in his sleep then groaned through a smile. She avoided wondering what sort of repugnant dreams he might be enjoying.

Sharon had been dreaming of her father and of what had happened. She thought she'd gotten past it, but the memories had lain in wait, after all these years, to ambush her while she slept. She suspected that Lucinda's new dolly triggered the dream. For a fleeting moment, she wanted to go into Lucinda's room, rip the doll from her daughter's arms then take the thing outside. Douse the plastic and thin cloth in lighter fluid and throw it in the barbecue grill. Burn the damned thing up. Despite the thick scar tissue of time and distance, it only took one dream to make all the old horrors shiny and new again. No matter what people had told her at the time, how they'd explained that sometimes adult problems were unfixable, she'd never been able to understand her father and her mother and the tragedy that had broken them.

These days, when Sharon happened to think of it, she was only able to think about the way her sister Pearl had smiled. So like her Lucinda. Only rarely did her mind turn to the day Pearl got run over by the mail truck.

Sharon never thought about those horrifying times that came after. Not consciously, anyway. Not anymore. Her father and mother going to pieces separately, each exacerbating the other's self-destruction, was a memory best left alone.

Especially the last part, in the workroom. Her father had gotten sent away to the special hospital after that.

Sharon sat up in bed trying to clear her head. The red numbers of the clock said it was only four in the morning, but with the devils of her memory running amok though her head, she didn't figure she'd get back to sleep anytime soon. She got out of bed slowly. She didn't think Deke would wake up, but there was no sense in taking unnecessary chances.

Sharon went to the kitchen and started a pot of coffee then went down the narrow hall at the other end of the trailer. Lucinda's door was open a crack, and a thread of light from the muted glow of her bedside lamp shone into the hallway. Sharon eased the door open to avoid making it squeak.

Lucinda had kicked free of the blankets as she did every night. They were mounded like a pile of laundry at the foot of the bed. Her princess pajamas were twisted and bunched from her nocturnal wiggling, and her Betty doll was being held in a tight hug. The doll appeared to sleep as well, its eyes closed and its arms stretched up to Lucinda as if returning her embrace.

Something was odd about that. Sharon couldn't put her finger on it, but something was weird about the doll. She considered it for a moment, but still couldn't figure out what was out of place. She shook her head and dismissed the feeling of uneasiness.

She thought the feeling was an echo of her own grisly memories, brought forward by her terrible nightmare. The dream was so terrible it made her wish she'd never let Lucinda have that doll. Who knew what materials had been used for its stuffing? Old bread? Hair? Roadkill? She sighed as she looked down at her daughter. Despite Sharon's misgivings, the doll seemed okay. Whatever horrific associations she'd made hopefully existed only in her mind and in the past.

Lucinda's breathing was slow, deep, and even, and her expression was calm. Whatever dreams visited her tonight, they must be soothing. They seemed to wrap her small form in safety and warmth.

Sharon stepped into the bedroom and pulled the sheet and blanket up to Lucinda's shoulders. Lucinda shifted, snuggling down into the blankets with a contented hum. The gesture made Sharon feel better, but without a doubt the blanket would be down around Lucinda's ankles again within ten minutes.

She tiptoed out of the bedroom and returned to the kitchen. With a cup of coffee in front of her, she looked at her reflection in the kitchen window. Her hair was in need of washing, and the crow's feet growing around her eyes showed, in harsh relief, the accumulated strains of her life.

"Oh, Lucinda," she whispered into the darkness, "how the fuck did I get us into this mess?" She smiled ruefully and sipped her coffee in the morning silence. Although she took it with sugar, the taste of it was bitter in her mouth.

She sat, eyes unfocused, trying to center herself in her world. Lucinda depended on her. Deke, in his own hurtful, selfish, abusive way, depended on her, too. But who did *she* have to turn to? Who'd help her when push came to shove? Who could she depend on?

Sharon caught sight of her reflection again and raised her coffee mug in salute. "Guess I can always depend on you, ol' girl."

She tipped back the last of the coffee in her cup then refilled it. As she set it to cool on the table, she watched the steam rising from the mug and tumbling lazily over itself like the goo in one of those lava lamps.

Then it hit her. The doll.

She shook her head. She must've made a mistake, her eyes playing tricks. She returned to Lucinda's room.

As expected, the top sheet and blanket were down around Lucinda's ankles, and the doll was pressed firmly against her chest. Sharon stepped forward and looked closely at the doll. It lay inert in Lucinda's arms, its shiny blue-green eyes gazing in placid emptiness at the ceiling.

Just as she'd reassured herself.

For some reason, though, Sharon couldn't dislodge the remembered image. The first time she'd come into Lucinda's room, the doll's eyes had been closed.

Impossible, though. They were painted on.

Could it have been a trick of the dim light? Shadows cast across the doll's face?

But Sharon distinctly recalled the thin black crescent lines and remembered thinking the doll had looked like it was asleep, too.

9

"You be extra careful out there, girlie-girl," Mommy said to her as she stood at the door. "If you see or hear a car coming while you're on your way, get all the way out of the road."

"I will."

"I'll finish the vacuuming then when I come get you, we'll come back here and have some lunch."

"Okay."

"And don't run off and leave Betty lying somewhere. Some other little girl might find her and try to take her home."

Lucinda hugged her doll extra tight. "Don't worry about that, Mommy. I'll keep her safe."

Mommy smiled and held the screen door open for her then went back to cleaning the house. Lucinda heard the tube-thingy on the door hiss as it pulled the screen closed, but she didn't turn around. She held Betty under one arm and held the splintery wooden railing with her other hand until she reached the bottom of the four steps. Once on the ground, she shifted Betty around so the dolly was riding on her shoulders. The dolly's legs were astride her neck, and Lucinda held her dolly's hands the way Mommy sometimes did with her.

She was excited. This was the first time she'd taken Betty outside to play, and as she walked, she gave a running commentary to Betty about all the trailer-houses they passed and the people who lived in them. Some of the trailers had inhabitants she'd never seen so at those points the commentary shifted from reality to characters from television or movies. Betty didn't seem to mind.

The trailer park wasn't much, defined by a straight gravel road that ended in a muddy, rutted turnaround. The trailers lined the road at an angle, making the park the shape of fish bones or a feather. The turnaround had three things around it: the big doublewide trailer where the park manager lived, the playground, and a pair of big, brown dumpsters. The first trailer this side of the dumpsters was where Dustin and his daddy lived.

The playground was a small, fenced area equipped with a few castoff playground pieces from remodeled public parks. At the front, a small gap stood in the fence where a gate would fit, but Lucinda didn't remember ever seeing a gate there. The playground had a short slide, a long slide, a big metal jungle gym, and a couple of cracked fiberglass seesaws. The playground equipment sat in full sun for most of the day so in the summer Lucinda only ever went there in the morning. By midday the slides and the jungle gym got hot; too hot to sit on in shorts. Lucinda and Betty had left the house early today, though, and would have plenty of time to play. The silvery sparkle of dew could still be seen on the grass that was in the shade.

As Lucinda approached Dustin's house, the dog came charging from beneath the skirting, dragging a fat, rusty tow chain in the orange dust of the yard. It was a huge monster of a dog, gray with white splotches. It had a broad, square skull and its ears were cut off so they were nothing but little stubs of gristle poking out of the sides of its head. Scars puckered the flesh between its ears, making odd ridges on the top of its head. Mommy always warned her to stay well clear of this dog, but Mommy didn't really need to say anything. In Lucinda's eyes, the beast was ugly and mean. There was nothing nice about it.

"Rrrr-OW-ugh! OW-ugh! OW-ugh!" The dog lunged against the end of its chain, the growls in its throat finally erupting into vicious barks. Its black lips were pulled back above its yellowed teeth and purple gums. For a moment it stood on its hind legs, straining to escape the limits of its chain as it barked and snarled. The area of the yard the dog could reach was trampled down to raw dirt and rock; no grass could grow under the constantly gouging, galloping feet of the dog.

Lucinda hurried to the relative safety of the playground, Betty bouncing on her shoulders. She climbed to the top of the slide and looked back at Dustin's mean dog, all monstery and loud. After looking around to make sure no one was watching, she stuck her tongue out at the dog. It glared at her, growled again, then snorted and returned to its hollowed-out spot under the skirting of the trailer. It lay in the dirt, keeping a baleful eye on her and occasionally huffing canine threats.

Lucinda played with Betty, teaching the dolly her games. In one they were astronauts who had to escape the mean aliens on the space station by going through the secret passageway (sliding down the tall slide), then climbing into the pilot's seat of the escape pod (at the top of the jungle gym) to fly away. In another, they were pirates. They were the nice kind, who went from island to island exploring and finding buried treasure. They had to escape from a band of mean pirates on one island by following a hidden trail (running down the short slide), then climbing up into the rigging of their ship to the crow's nest (at the top of the jungle gym), to chart their course so they could sail away. The seesaws rarely came into the pretending, because she'd hurt herself one time trying to get on one of them while no one was on the other side. She'd gone down hard on her backside, and since then Lucinda only pushed them up or down without actually mounting them. She promised Betty that she'd let her ride on them sometime.

All the mean guys in her pretending looked like Deke and his friends, but she'd never said so to Mommy. It would make Mommy sad, she thought.

Lucinda slid down the tall slide again, with Betty in her lap. She sat at the bottom and told Betty about going to school at Cimmaron Hills Elementary. It would be starting again in a few weeks, and Lucinda would be attending second grade.

The slope of the tall slide flattened out several feet before the end of it, so Lucinda always had to either scoot forward by pulling with her hands on the side rails, or stand up and walk to the end of the slide and jump off. This time she stood, with Betty dangling from one hand.

Then it happened.

Maybe it was because Lucinda stood quickly, moving into the dog's line of sight so suddenly she startled it. Maybe it was because the dog had been asleep, dreaming its violent and bloody dog nightmares. Maybe a bee stung the dog. It could have been caused by any of those things, but the cause didn't change the effect.

The dog attacked.

When Lucinda stood at the end of the slide, the dog sprang up. It shot from its hollowed-out spot under the trailer and bounded out to the end of its chain, growling and roaring.

Lucinda knew that when the dog hit the limit of its chain, several feet shy of the fence, it would stand up on its hind legs again, pushing its neck forward as hard as it could. Its front paws would paddle at the air, and its lips would pull up on the sides of its short muzzle. It would make a lot of scary noises at her until it either got tired of doing so, or when it'd established itself as the dominant animal. Then it'd go back under the trailer and sleep in the shade some more.

That's what always happened before.

This time, when the dog reached the end of its chain, the surge was only checked for the barest second. Lucinda heard the sharp squeak of a large nail being pulled loose. Gravity and momentum pulled the dog forward, well outside the limit of its chain. It bounded ferociously into the fence surrounding the playground, closing its jaws savagely on the steel diamonds of the chainlink.

Lucinda screamed and stepped back by reflex. In doing so, she tumbled over the side of the slide and landed in the sparse grass. A chunk of sharp rock scraped her elbow, which began to bleed. Beneath the roaring growls of the dog, she could hear the machinelike click each time its jaws slammed shut.

The truth of the dog's freedom finally seemed to dawn on the animal, and it ran around the corner of the fence toward the opening. The heavy links of the tow chain dragged behind it, skipping over the rocks as lightly as a crepe paper streamer.

Ignoring the stinging in her arm, Lucinda picked up Betty and sprinted to the other corner of the playground where the jungle gym stood. Behind her she heard the deep, percolating growl of the dog coming closer and the jangly hiss of the chain trailing behind it in the dirt.

With Betty in one hand, she mounted the first couple of bars, expecting at any moment to lose a leg to the monster dog that was about to catch her. She lifted her trailing foot off the second level of rungs in the nick of time and actually felt the dog's nose bump the back of her ankle a hair above the lip of her sneaker.

"Mommy!" she screamed, weeping as she pulled herself higher. The dog would get her and gobble her up like a big bad wolf. It would grab her in its teeth, drag her down onto the ground, and eat her all up. It would even eat Betty.

She sat at the top of the jungle gym, hugging Betty against her face as she cried. Below, the dog stalked around the foot of the metal frame, its red-rimmed eyes looking up at Lucinda. The dog's lips were drawn back in a snarl, and the chain it dragged in its wake rattled noisily against the legs of the jungle gym.

With an effort, Lucinda lifted her eyes from the dog and looked up the road. Through the glare she could see the front end of their trailer, but Mommy was nowhere outside. Lucinda's tears started again as she glanced back down at the dog. Its feral eyes seemed amused at having treed Lucinda. It briefly reared back on its hind legs, hanging its front paws over the lower crossbar.

"Go home!" she yelled down at the dog. Tears blurred her eyes for a moment then rolled down her cheeks. The dog's panting mouth hung open almost like a smile, and it studied her with a predator's eyes.

Lucinda heard the thin crack of a screen door closing, and hope swelled in her chest. She saw Mommy appear around the front of their trailer.

"Mommy!" Lucinda screamed, waving one hand frantically.

At first Mommy didn't hear the terror in Lucinda's voice, and she smiled and waved.

"Help! Help me, Mommyyyy!"

Mommy's hand dropped to her side and her face fell. She began to run toward the playground.

Lucinda turned to the dog beneath her. It paced back and forth like a caged tiger, its eyes never wavering. It growled deep in its throat.

She held Betty close, determined not to lose her grip on her dolly.

Mommy approached the playground and saw the huge, ugly dog beneath Lucinda's perch. She stopped and changed her course, and Lucinda saw that she was headed toward Dustin's dad's trailer.

Mommy crossed the weed-filled yard and mounted the stacked cinderblocks that served as the unsteady front steps of the trailer and beat on the door.

"Hey! Get out here and get your dog!"

Lucinda heard a mumbled reply from inside the trailer.

"Hurry up! The damn thing got loose! If your dog hurts my daughter, I swear I'll kill it!"

Relief flooded Lucinda's mind. She drew a deep breath, and it hitched and hiccupped in her chest. She looked down at the dog.

It was gone.

She saw it. Skulking low along the fenceline, its rusty chain dragging behind it with a hiss. Its furious eyes were on Mommy.

"Mommy, look out! The dog!"

As she called out, the dog charged. Unlike its loud warning behavior when it was chained up, it made no sound as it ran at Mommy. Standing on the top cinderblock, she turned, the anger on her face crumbling into fear. She raised her arms as the dog leapt.

Lucinda watched as the dog flew through the air and hit Mommy, knocking her backwards off the steps. On the ground with the gigantic dog straddling her, Mommy screamed, and the dog's growl was a roar. She held it by its thick neck, her arms locked at the elbows. While Mommy did keep it from biting her, all four of its claws dug and scratched at her, shredding the front of her shirt. The tow chain slithered heavily in the dust, a big metal snake.

Lucinda shrieked and began to climb down, unmindful that she was once again putting herself in reach of the beast. She held Betty tightly under one arm and sprinted around the fence.

The trailer door swung open and Dustin's daddy appeared. He looked like he was half asleep. His greasy hair stuck out in all directions, and over his bare chest he wore an ancient pair of overalls with a pouch of Beech Nut sticking out of the unzipped breast pocket. In one hand he held a steel dumbbell with a big "10" engraved on each octagonal end.

In no particular hurry, he climbed down the steps and approached Mommy and the dog. He grabbed the dog by the back of its worn leather collar and swung the dumbbell over handed.

The dumbbell hit the top of the dog's head with a loud <u>thock!</u> It sounded more like it had been thrown onto a cement floor. The dog didn't collapse, but the blow stunned it enough that it stopped lunging. The dog's jaws clicked together, and Dustin's daddy yanked back on the animal.

Lucinda ran to Mommy, who was struggling into a sitting position. Tracks of her tears cut through the orange dust on her face, and her shirt was in shreds. The dog's claws had left huge, bleeding welts down her chest and stomach. Lucinda hugged Mommy, crying. The sharp intake of breath told Lucinda the hug hurt Mommy so she loosened her grip. She didn't let go entirely, but Mommy pulled back to look at her through red, puffy eyes.

"Are you okay, baby?"

"Yeah, I...I was..." Lucinda said, and was overwhelmed by tears. "I was so scared, Mommy!" she sobbed. "And then I got all scared for you!"

"Okay, girlie-girl. It's okay. I'm all right." Mommy hugged her again. "I was scared, too."

They got up from the ground slowly. Dustin's daddy stood there, with the dog's collar in one meaty fist. The dog sat attentively, as if it were the best-behaved dog in the world. The dog had a fresh gash on its head in the crisscrossed nest of scars between its ears. A trickle of blood that had mostly stopped flowing traced a thin line down between the dog's wide-set eyes and around its muzzle, but other than that, it seemed completely unaffected. Its wide tongue licked out, smearing the blood by its lips.

Dustin's daddy watched silently as Mommy stood. His eyes never left the torn front of her shirt. She looked at him then angrily crossed her arms over her chest. He blinked twice then spoke slowly as if unused to it.

"You all right?"

Mommy got right in his face and screamed at him.

"That goddamned dog is dangerous! I'm calling Animal Control as soon as I get back to the house! That dog needs to be put down!"

"Hold on, now. He didn't hurt your young'un, and you're mostly all right."

"Bullshit! And you'd better be goddamned glad he didn't touch Lucinda, or I'd kill you both!" Taking Lucinda's hand, she stormed out of the yard.

"I'm sorry he scared you," the man called after them.

"Fuck your sorry! I'm calling Animal Control!"

The man got angry then. "Fine, you bitch! You do whatever you think you need to do! You're wastin' your fuckin' time! Ain't nobody takin' my dog, nor putting him down, neither! You got that, bitch?"

Lucinda looked back as they crossed the gravel drive and saw the dog watching them with a vacant, inert expression. Dustin's daddy flipped them the bird as they went away. Lucinda hurried along with Mommy, with Betty held firmly under one arm.

That was the last time Lucinda ever went to the trailer park playground.

10

"Are you out of your goddamned mind?" Sharon yelled into the phone receiver. "It's by pure luck my daughter and I aren't in the hospital, or worse!"

"Well, ma'am, like you said, the dog didn't bite you, and it only reacted when you trespassed on private property." The man's friendly condescension only served to fuel her anger.

"The dog came into a playground to attack my seven-year-old daughter!"

"Ma'am, I'm sure that's what she *told* you, but how can we know if that's the truth?"

"Because I know she's not an idiot that would tease a dog. Especially a pit bull!"

"First of all, ma'am, that's exactly what Mr. Whistler said your daughter did, and second, the dog in question has been reported as a mixed breed of Weimaraner and Mastiff."

"*Mr. Whistler?* Mr. Whistler's full of shit! And so are *you!*"

Sharon slammed down the phone with a scream of frustration. Again a sharp twinge of pain stung her right side, at the bottom of her ribcage. She didn't know if anything was broken, but if not, it was the worst bruise she'd ever had. The force of the dog's claws was compounded by its weight. The damn thing outweighed Sharon by at least thirty pounds. The welts from the dog's claws were like burns etched into her skin. They were red, raised, and angry, and even though some of the claw marks hadn't broken skin, they still stung. Her old shirt was trashed beyond saving and was now the newest item in the rag bag. Every movement she made caused the t-shirt she now wore to shift and brush against the welts, rekindling the pain.

Sharon heard Deke, sitting on the living room sofa, snickering at her frustration. When he'd gotten home, his first reaction had been the same as Aaron Whistler's. He'd ogled her bare chest. After she'd changed shirts and told him the whole story, he'd only shaken his head and grumbled, "Well, damn, what the hell were you thinking with? That dog coulda killed both of you without even breakin' a sweat." as he'd turned away.

She stood in the kitchen, seething at his continued insensitivity. At the table, Lucinda watched with solemn eyes. Her lips were blue from the Otter Pop she'd finished a few minutes earlier. Her scraped elbow had been cleaned, disinfected, and bandaged, and other than that she'd only been incredibly scared. Betty was still clutched under one arm, held more like a football than a baby.

"Sure, sit there laughing, Deke. You're no goddamned help at all!"

As soon as the words left her lips, she knew it'd been the wrong thing to say. Deke's mean smile twitched, and in the fraction of a second the twitch lasted, she was confident that her angered remark had been deposited, catalogued, and set in a safe place inside the hate machine that was Deke's mind. He would bide his time and exact his retribution later, when her guard was lowered. He continued grinning now, as he turned back to the television. The smile didn't touch his eyes but was frozen to his mouth. His eyes reflected the blue and white tones of the news broadcast, and his smile seemed demented, joyful over the report of the rising death toll in the Middle East over the last few weeks.

Sharon went to the refrigerator and pulled a beer from a six pack. She wanted to make sure Deke was passed out drunk before she fell asleep. He took it without a word and cut his eyes over at her as he brought it to his lips. Sharon figured he probably knew what she was doing in serving him a beer. Then again, he probably didn't give a shit. By the time she turned away from him, he'd already guzzled more than half the can.

Sharon sank into a chair beside Lucinda. Her little girl's eyes were wide and still puffy from her crying earlier. Sharon reached out and took Lucinda's hand, and the child returned her squeeze with soft, damp fingers.

"How you doin', sweetie?"

"Mommy, I'm still scared. That dog tried to hurt us. What if it gets loose again?" Her breath started hitching in her chest as she contemplated further dog attacks.

"What if it comes to get us again, Mommy?" she wailed, her tears beginning again. Sharon needed to stem the flow of what ifs before it grew into a flood.

She took Lucinda in her arms, whispering empty reassurances that everything would turn out all right. She hugged her daughter and made the promises every parent makes, all the while praying her child would be protected from the bad, hurtful possibilities of life.

"Mommy?" she said after the worst had passed again. Lucinda shifted her grip on Betty, holding the dolly by one arm.

"Yeah, baby?"

The weary, terrorized look on Lucinda's face grew into an expression of fierce determination, and for a split second, Sharon glimpsed the knife that would sculpt Lucinda's soft, sweet face into grim adulthood.

"If I was bigger," she spoke slowly to Sharon, "I'd kill that dog."

"Kill it, Lucinda?"

"That way it couldn't ever hurt anybody again."

58

That promise of violence sounded so foreign coming from Lucinda's angelic little mouth. In Sharon's mind Lucinda's mouth was better suited for eating ice cream and blowing kisses. She still had most of her baby teeth, and the harshest curse she'd ever heard Lucinda utter was to call someone stupid. Threats of death had no place in this tiny mouth with its blue-popsicle-colored lips.

Sharon saw the sincerity in her daughter's eyes, and a sudden chill coursed down her back.

11

The gibbous moon rides across the summer sky on a chariot of cumulus, the cold white glare of its shine dimming the brighter stars and eclipsing the fainter ones altogether. A warm August wind hisses through the possum pines and the leaves of the scrub oaks, spreading ghost whispers and phantom laughter.

Out beyond the entrance to the trailer park, a rusted out Camaro roars down Chaparral Road leaking laughter and music. Its occupants are on their way home from Rooster's Roadhouse and are thoroughly shitfaced. Above the tubercular growl of the muffler, the stereo blares a Hank Williams Jr. song, his voice mashing and stretching in a cartoonish Doppler as the Camaro speeds away across the rural landscape of Texas hill country.

The trailer park itself is quiet. Even the trailer near the park entrance, whose tenants rented it for use solely as a meth lab, is quiet. Darkness and quiet rule together over the blue world of Texas night.

The quiet, like the darkness, is far from absolute. In many trailers, sleepers snore in blissful oblivion. Barely heard is the occasional strange shriek of insomniac peacocks from an exotic bird farm a mile distant. From beneath the trees comes the panicky skittering and scurrying of rodents as they forage through layers of mulch for crumbs and bugs and other bits of sustenance. With a quick snap, a coiled copperhead reduces the rodent population by one gray mouse, and for a moment, after the snake adjusts its grip so that it can swallow the mouse, quiet truly reigns. It is as if the entire world is holding its breath.

As that moment of silence ends, a stealthy metallic click sounds from a trailer door. A hinge squeaks, and a ghostly white swish of cloth hops and flows down the wooden steps. The white thing moves jerkily, unfamiliar with the differential equations and physics of predictive locomotion that spatially translate to manual dexterity. Even so, as it moves, it becomes more practiced, like a newborn fawn learning to move on its stiltlike, wobbly legs.

It moves from the sheltering shadow of the trailer and into the uneven gravel of the drive. Its slow, tentative movements attract the attention of a barn owl soaring high above, and the bird tips its wing. It dives, accelerating in gravity's grasp. The owl extends its thorny talons.

A fraction of a second before the owl would take its pale, fluttering prey, moonlight reflects in a silver flash from a shiny blade. The small, ghostlike figure raises the razor-sharp fillet knife. It moves to one side as it thrusts the knife upward, piercing a thick layer of feathers and grating against the owl's breastbone. With an injured *squawk!* the owl blunders its wounded, unsteady way back into the sky, forced to search for easier prey elsewhere.

The soft plastic hand adjusts its grip on the fillet knife, and the dolly called Betty moves to the other side of the gravel lane.

Once in the tall weeds on the opposite side of the drive, the doll turns left. She slowly picks her careful way across several lots, the victory grass on every side bowing and nodding with her passage. A raccoon atop a rusted garbage can glares at her with reflective eyes before turning back to its secret scavenging, licking crumbs out of the foil seasoning envelope from a packet of ramen noodles.

The dolly moves silently, her brown curls bouncing with each movement. She holds the fillet knife at her side awkwardly; it is overly large for her body, more like a long-handled sword than a knife. Her cloth slippers whisper softly as she moves.

At the edge of the last lot before the playground, she stops and looks for movement, her painted-on blue-green eyes scanning the nightscape. Stillness and silence radiate from the trailer with the wobbly cinderblock steps. She studies a GI Joe action figure discarded in the grass, its head turned around backwards. It is ridiculously muscled and missing an arm. The dolly dismisses it. A rusting pickup with no tailgate sits in the yard. A huge steel cage takes up half of the bed of the truck.

The dolly moves forward into an area of the yard where the grass is sparse from constant trampling. Beneath the fiberglass skirting of the trailer, the dog exhales a phlegmy snort. The dolly creeps closer, the knife blade catching a last flash of moonlight before she advances under the trailer. A tiny dot of owl blood is at the point of the knife. It looks black and alien in the darkness.

Beneath the trailer, the dog snores again. It lies in a trough hollowed out by many years of shifting, wallowing naps. It dreams, kicking in its sleep. Perhaps it is dreaming of fighting and killing, of catching and biting and tasting blood.

The mark of the blow the dog received earlier is a swollen goose egg on its head, and the blood is a smeared black line in its fur. The tacky blood is now crusted with dust. The dolly steps closer and raises the knife.

The dog's flank inflates as it takes a breath.

She slices the knife down onto the dog's closed muzzle. The knife blade shears the front half of the dog's nose cleanly off, the wide-set nostrils and the soft, moist flesh of the nose fall unceremoniously into the dirt as the dog screams and jumps up, throwing Betty aside and into a steel strap of trailer underpinning. The dog charges out through the gap in the skirt in an excruciating panic, snuffling and snorting blood, bellowing its agony at the night, and snapping at the empty air. In less than a second it reaches the limit of its newly reattached chain and jerks itself to the ground. It reaches up with one foreleg to its bleeding face, rubs it once, and the pain sends it roaring back to its domain under the trailer. Its horrible pain makes it stagger into the skirting twice, splashing wide swaths of blood on the vinyl before it finds the opening into its den. It steps on the black blob of its own severed nose and huddles in its trough among the spiderwebs, underpinning straps, and thin elbows of PVC pipe. It howls through blood.

Betty stands on a buckle of underpinning, the knife held firmly in her tiny grasp. The yowling dog is bleeding, pawing at its face as it screams. Movement begins above the dog and the dolly, in the trailer. The man shifts his weight off the bed and steps heavily across the floor over Betty's head, each footfall a loud thud. He opens the door and yells down at the opening in the trailer's skirting.

"Shut up, you goddamned idiot dog! Leave them fuckin' coons alone and they won't fuckin' scratch you! Goddamned stupid ass! Fuckin' shut up!"

The dog's conditioned response, born more from fear than from a desire for praise, silences its yowling. Despite the fiery pain in its head, the pit bull is terrified of the man. It stops its screaming but continues to whine and whimper, licking and pawing at its ruined face, bleeding and dribbling snot into its own mouth.

Hidden beneath the sounds of its suffering, Betty is able to move closer to the dog without being noticed. The dog smells the blood on the knife blade, but recognizes it as its own. Betty approaches the dog on its blind side, staying clear of its legs and paws. The dolly raises the knife again then stabs downward.

The thin blade bites solidly into the dog's back, driving through thick hide, muscle, and gristle before severing the fibrous stalk of its spinal cord. The knife sticks fast between the dog's vertebrae, the bones locked together by spasming muscles. The tip of the blade punctures the dog's windpipe. Betty releases her grip on the knife. It has done its job and is no longer needed. Blood wells around the handle of the knife, spreading through the dog's fur and pouring onto the ground.

Though the dog shrieks again, it does not move. It cannot. From above, the man stomps his foot and curses again as the dog's scream descends into a wet gurgle. It stretches its neck, trying to reach the knife in its back, but it is unable to escape the pain. It whimpers, its strength ebbing. Betty steps before it, and the dog snaps feebly at the dolly. Its fear is evident in its rolling eyes and bubbling respiration.

Its bowels run loose, spilling out of the dog in a foul rush as its nerveless muscles relax. Betty backs away as the sounds from the dog degenerate into wet snufflings. It swings its head back and forth, straining its neck against its body's unresponsive muscles as it begins to feel the effects of blood loss.

The dolly called Betty returns the way it came, in stillness and darkness, leaving behind the weakening moans of the dog's fleeing mortality. She moves more fluidly now than when she first started. Far off, a peacock screeches, sounding like a distant, crying child.

The girl Lucinda would be safe now. The dog would die. It would never hurt the little girl, or anyone else, again.

The dolly enters the trailer, pads silently to the girl's room, and climbs back into bed. The dolly's dress is now heavily soiled with red dirt, cobwebs, and errant splashes of spilled canine blood.

Betty crawls across the sheets and gently burrows under the arm of the girl as she sleeps. Lucinda wakes, and looks blearily at her dolly.

"Hi, Betty," she whispers, her eyelids at half-mast. They roll close again.

Betty's soft plastic hand reaches up and gently touches the tip of the girl's nose, feeling the child's warm exhale as she sighs back to sleep.

"Night-night, Betty." The girl hugs the dolly close, and the dolly smiles in the dark. An errant crease of worry in the girl's brow smooths itself. The girl sleeps peacefully, and the dolly is secure in her embrace.

12

Despite the goddamned pile driver of a hangover, Deke woke up before the alarm clock went off. He swung his legs off the side of the bed as he sat up, his pulse throbbing in his head like silent thunder. With hooded eyes, he looked at the other side of the bed where Sharon lay sleeping. He turned off the alarm and sighed, scratching his ball sack as he considered the coming day.

It all came down to today. He deserved this, a chance at fame, fortune, and a little more than the thankless bullshit he always put up with. He was leaving Sharon today. Her and her goddamned loud-mouthed kid. About fuckin' time he got away from her. He'd have the money to go wherever he wanted, and he'd never need to worry about getting a piece of ass. Stupid Mexican sluts were always looking for someone with a handful of money to throw a fuck in them. In Deke's eyes, deep down, every woman was a whore, givin' up that ass for pay. Some took your money, while others took your time.

All Earl and Ray had to do was stay calm and do what the fuck they were told then the three of them could light out and never look back. Ray was all right, nothing to worry about there. He was dumber than dirt, and his goddamned face could make a train take a dirt road, but he was solid. He'd follow instructions. Earl, on the other hand, was different. He was a chicken shit, for one thing, but for another, he thought too goddamned much. It made him slow. Deke hoped he would either grow a pair of balls, or shut off his brain for the day. The plan was so cock-sucking simple he didn't need his brain anyway.

The gates of Fort Hood were, for many years, wide open, letting any cars through at any time. Then there was Al Qaeda, and now there was ISIS. Now that the goddamned Arabs were all over the place trying to crash shit into buildings and blowing hard-workin' American folks to bits, the open gate policy had been changed. Now the gate guards had to stop each car, check the ID cards of all the occupants, and then either wave them through or make them pull over for a more thorough inspection.

The necessity of the ID check combined with the fact that Fort Hood was one of the biggest military posts in the world made the front gate busy. Add in the fact that the post had only two other entry gates and the fact that everyone started work at the same time, and the busy gate turned into a morning clusterfuck, every day. The traffic was ridiculous. Every morning from about 8:45 to 9:15, the traffic got backed up for miles in both directions.

A quarter mile from the gate was a turnoff into a strip mall, and the only way into or out of the strip mall was onto the highway. The only tenant of the strip mall was the Lone Star Federal Bank, Fort Hood Branch. Many soldiers kept their money there, and today was payday. The bank would surely be stocked up on cash for the soldier boys to go slipping their dollar bills into some pole dancing hooker's G-string. Give enough, and they might get a *pole* dance of their own, right?

With traffic keeping the cops from getting to them, Deke, Ray, and Earl could get the money from the bank and hightail it out of there before the police arrived.

They'd be walking in high cotton then. Wouldn't need to lift a finger for months. Hell, they could even turn it into a career. Rolling from town to town, living like kings until the money dried up. When it did, they could move again, making sure they robbed another bank on the way out of town. Deke couldn't let himself think about that now, though. He'd do best to keep his mind on this job first then they could see where it led after that.

He shuffled into the bathroom and shaved. The dull razor nicked the hell out of his upper lip. He growled and cussed under his breath, pissed off but not wanting to wake up Sharon. If there was one thing he absolutely couldn't deal with this morning, it was that whining bitch.

Those other two motherfuckers better not forget to shave, he thought as he looked at his red eyes and cut lip. It bled for a moment more then he licked the blood from his lips. He got dressed in jeans, a Lynyrd Skynyrd t-shirt, and a camouflage ball cap. Not the usual work uniform. He'd never wear that stupid-ass Busby Auto Parts shirt again, and thank fuckin' God for that.

He moved through the house in silence. The sun was barely clear of the treeline in the east, and watery daylight had begun to turn everything in the trailer an unpleasant yellow-gray. Unpleasant or not, though, dim light beat the fuck out of no light at all; Deke had cracked his shins on the goddamned coffee table more than enough times to know that.

He left the house, closing the door as quietly as he could and getting into the truck. He started it up, and then the last pretense of a peaceful morning lay broken in the obstreperous echoes of the struggling engine. The truck was on its last legs, but that, too, was something he wouldn't have to worry about after today.

He pulled out of the trailer park and turned on the radio. Toby Keith and Willie Nelson started ordering whiskey for their men and beer for their horses, and that, to Deke, sounded like a pretty good sign. It was like they were destined to succeed. The three of them would be celebrating tonight, he was sure. He cranked up the music loud enough that it drowned out the sound of the engine, and he tapped out the rhythm of the song on the steering wheel.

Instead of driving north into town, he drove south and parked in the lot by the boat ramp at Cedar Gap Park, on Stillhouse Hollow Lake, where Ray was supposed to pick him up.

There were already several trucks in the lot. They were parked with empty boat trailers behind them, their owners already out casting for bass. Most of the trucks were as beat to shit as Deke's was, but he was damn sure the boats they towed were waxed and polished and tricked out with every goddamned piece of electronic fish-finding crap possible.

Deke sat, irritably watching the minutes tick past on his wristwatch. He wished he'd made a pot of coffee this morning, but that probably would've made too much noise in the trailer. He always made it too strong, anyway. He reached into his back pocket, settling instead for a dip of Cope'.

Today was the day. Today Deke would finally make good on the advice he'd been given so many years ago. That advice had not come from his father, but from the other man who'd been fucking his mother.

Deke's father was a machinist in Houston who lost his job in the seventies and had to come up to Waco to find work. None of the leads he'd been given ever panned out, and he ended up being a school bus driver in Killeen.

Deke was sitting in the yard, his bicycle upside down in front of him, its handlebars and seat in the dirt. He'd been sent outside, as he often was when Mr. Pratt from up the street came to visit Momma. Deke's bike's chain had slipped off so he was spending the time trying to rethread the chain to the sprocket. Deke was trying to pop it back on by hooking a couple of links into the sprocket then pedaling the rest of it into line. It wasn't working and he was getting frustrated with it when his father showed up, coming home from work early. He told Deke that the easiest way was to loosen the wheel, put the chain on, and then retighten the wheel to keep the chain in place. He went up the sidewalk, smiling and telling Deke that the easiest way was always the best way. Deke followed him up to the house.

Inside, Deke's father found Mr. Pratt in bed with Deke's mother. They were both naked. Deke's father didn't get violent. He didn't do anything. He stood there trembling, with tears squeezing out of his eyes and flowing down into his thick beard.

"Deke, go on back out yonder 'n' fix your bike." Deke turned to the door and heard his father finally speak to Mr. Pratt and Deke's mother. "Get out of my house," he said. Deke went out to his bike, and a few moments later Deke's mother and Mr. Pratt came outside as well.

As they passed Deke in the yard, Mr. Pratt smiled. It wasn't an expression of happiness. It was only a declaration of victory. He stopped and spoke.

"Let this be a lesson to you, boy. If you decide you want something, all you got to do is go get it. No matter what it is, no matter what the cost."

"Don't you speak to my boy!" Deke's father cried, his voice cracking from the front porch. Mr. Pratt rolled his eyes and continued.

"If you want something bad enough, fucking go get it. Half the time," he looked up at the porch, where Deke's father stood, silent and red-faced, "you don't even have to ask. They'll fucking give it to you, anyway."

Mr. Pratt and Deke's mother walked up the road and out of Deke's life. Deke never saw either of them again.

Even though he'd been young at the time, Deke wasn't stupid. Since that day, he'd never been able to look his father in the eye. His father had stood there and let the two of them shit on him. He'd taken the easy way, as he'd only moments ago advised Deke, and they'd disgraced him.

But Deke had always remembered Mr. Pratt's advice. He'd come to understand that the man was right, that his father was weak. And today was the day that Deke would put that advice into action.

The growl of an engine brought Deke out of his fetid swamp of memories. Ray, grinning like a damned jack o lantern, drove into the lot in a stolen car, with Earl in the passenger seat. Naturally neither one had taken a razor to his face in days, despite Deke reminding them over and over again. Ray looked the way he always did, ugly and stupid, and Earl looked, as usual, pale and scared shitless. Deke shook his head, disgusted, but he wondered how Ray had managed to get that Nancyboy Earl into the car. When they got out of the car, Deke lit into them.

"Can't either one of you follow simple fuckin' instructions? Shit! I'd do better to team up with a couple of fuckin' houseplants."

"Uhh, what?" Ray blinked at him.

"Forget it. Why didn't you dumbasses shave?"

Ray's eyes lit up as though he'd finally gotten some obscure joke. "I knew we forgot somethin'!"

"Ya think, you fuckin' retard? I'm amazed you even remembered to get the goddamned car." Deke leaned left and spat a brown stream to the pavement, then wiped his mouth with the back of his hairy wrist.

Ray declared that things had worked perfectly with the car. A neighbor of his worked at the Oak Hill Nursing Home, and on occasion this neighbor borrowed the car keys of patients. Apparently, this neighbor's reasoning was that if no one drove the car, the engine would get all gummed up so he was actually doing them a favor by taking their cars out. Ray had gone to the guy with some dumbass hard luck story about his car going into the shop, and the neighbor had been more than willing to help him out with a set of wheels for a day or two. Ray had taken the offered car and had swapped out the license plates with a different neighbor's truck to further throw off any police pursuit. The car was a 1969 Chevy Nova with a current Fort Hood decal stuck into the bottom corner of the window. It was an old car, but it was in pretty decent shape. It certainly ran better than Deke's truck.

"Yeah, yeah, great. We can talk about how everything went perfectly tonight, when we're sippin' cold bottles of Shiner in San Antonio. Till then, keep your fuckin' cock holster shut. Get in the car. We got shit to do."

They got into the Nova, and Deke passed them each a pistol. Ray took his silently, but Earl hissed, looking around in terror.

"Don't start cutting up, neither. They're loaded," Deke said, and Earl looked down at the gun as if it had turned into a rattlesnake. He daintily put the weapon onto the floor, and sat back in the seat.

Ray drove, with Deke in the passenger seat. Earl sat in the back, withdrawn and pale. He looked like he'd shit himself at the slightest noise.

Deke made them pull in at the first convenience store they saw and sent Ray in for disposable razors. Again Raymond looked at him with a question on his face then the gears in his brain caught, and he nodded and smiled. He got out of the car and walked into the store.

A few moments later, he strolled back out. He had a pack of Bic single-blades stuffed into his jeans. After getting into the car, he fished them out and opened the pack.

Deke was dumbfounded. He couldn't find his voice until Ray had already started dry-shaving, dragging the razor across his stubbly cheek.

"Ho. Lee. Shit. You *lifted* them? You fuckin' idiot! Right when I think you've hit bedrock stupid, you go deeper. If you'd'a got caught, the whole plan would be down the drain! The hell's wrong with you?"

Ray tried to apologize but only succeeded in cutting a gash in his jaw. Deke ignored him, looking back into the convenience store. The clerk, some greasy little college dropout, had apparently not noticed the theft. He sat behind the counter exploring the depths of a nostril with a finger while idly flipping through a magazine.

Moments later, they were back on the road. Ray's jaw had stopped bleeding, but both he and Earl had razor burned faces that were an angry pink. They went through Killeen and got onto the highway but turned off right before the entrance to Fort Hood. It was 8:00 AM, and a gradually thickening trickle of soldiers' cars moved off the highway and onto post.

The Southgate strip mall was quiet, and other than the Nova, the only other vehicles in the lot were bank employee cars. The bank itself was still closed, but lights were on inside and Deke saw signs of movement through the tinted windows. He imagined the tellers trading jokes and lies about what they'd done last night, sipping coffee and eating doughnuts as they counted up their drawers. It was a military payday, after all, and he was sure they expected a busy day.

Busier than you think, he thought and smiled to himself then turned to Ray. An anxiety began to crawl up the bone trellis of his spine, threatening to blossom into fleshy black orchids of paranoia.

"Shit. I know I should have asked this before we got into the car. Tell me you remembered the goddamn ski masks."

"'Course I 'membered 'em," Ray said proudly, pulling a plastic grocery bag from under the seat. He passed the masks out to Earl and Deke and took one himself. Thankfully, Deke saw that Ray had at least made sure they were all black.

Time seemed to slow as they waited, torturing them with its elasticity. As the minute hand inched around to 8:15, Deke saw the first of the gate congestion begin as the soldiers started arriving for work. Cars and trucks joined the line faster than the gate guards could clear them. The guards had to look at the military ID of all the passengers in each vehicle. A few of them got randomly pulled aside for further inspection, but the vast majority was waved through with barely a glance. Deke was counting on that being the case later.

At 8:55, Deke looked at the highway and smiled. Gridlock in both directions, until the highway curved out of sight. A solid logjam of cars stretched from the Copperas Cove horizon in the west to the Killeen horizon in the east. Perfect. Several cars had by now pulled into the parking lot of the strip mall. A few of them held soldiers, but most of the customers seemed to be older folks and some merchants getting their daily supply of change for their cash registers.

A couple of minutes before 9:00, the security guard came doddering to the door. He was older than dirt, with a set of glasses so thick they could probably see into the future and a pistol that had probably never been drawn on duty. The maroon leather holster was lovingly polished, as were his wide belt and his black shoes. He stepped slowly to the entrance with a smile and a wave to the small crowd of customers gathered outside the door. From his pocket he pulled a thin ring of keys that was attached to a belt loop with a spring-wound cable. He flipped to the correct key and spun it in the lock, then stepped back as he opened the door, nodding and grinning at each person as they crossed the threshold. The bank was open.

"Almost time, boys. Remember the plan." He looked at Ray and said, "Don't fuckin' get stupid." He looked at Earl and said, "And don't fuckin' get scared."

Another customer entered the bank, and for the moment, no people were in the parking lot, only cars. Deke pulled the ski mask onto his head.

"All right. Remember, in and out of there as quick as we can, and we'll get away like we planned. No fuckin' up, and no addin' in any dumb shit you saw on TV last night. Ray, go pop the trunk, and leave it so it's barely open."

Ray did so and got back into the car.

"Now put the keys back into the ignition. Leave the fuckin' doors unlocked, too, brain child."

Deke pulled his mask down, straightening the eye holes and the mouth hole. The damn thing already itched like hell. Ray and Earl followed suit. The three of them got out of the car, pulled their pistols out, and rushed into the bank.

13

Aaron Whistler scratched his ass with one hand while he used the other to dig the crumbs of crap from the corners of his eyes. Morning had come too early, like always. He watched dust motes slide through the shaft of sunlight shining in the window. He heard cartoons playing from the other end of the trailer. Dustin must already be up. Good. Aaron had a lot of shit to do before this evening, and Dusty was a good helper. The kid was silly most of the time, but he seemed to be growing up way too fast. In some ways, he was already becoming the distant, angry kid Aaron had not expected to meet until the boy was a teenager.

Dusty had no reason to be difficult. Aaron didn't keep after him about anything. If the boy didn't do his homework, that was fine with Aaron. Dusty would have to deal with the consequences. The price of bad grades was an ass whuppin', as the boy was well aware.

In fact, most transgressions in the Whistler house were paid for with an ass whuppin'. Spare the rod and spoil the child, right? Hell, everybody knew that. It came straight from the Bible so it was the Word of God. If God told Aaron to whup his kid, Aaron was going to obey. Couldn't nobody argue with that.

Aaron didn't really have to beat the boy much. Didn't have to. Dusty was pretty good most of the time. He'd get into trouble, take his licks, and usually he'd learn from it. Aaron had often told Dusty if he ever got into a fight at school, he'd better make damn sure he won it, because he'd be getting an ass whuppin' for fightin' when he got home, and it would pure suck to get your ass beaten twice in one day. As a result, Dusty had not gotten into any fights. As far as Aaron knew, anyway. Aaron almost hoped the kid got into a scrap or two this year, though. That kind of shit builds character. Hell, just look what it had done for Diablo.

He looked at the clock. 9:15 AM. He sighed, scratching the several days' growth of whiskers on his oily jaw. He lit a cigarette from the pack of American Spirits on the nightstand, and sat on the edge of the bed. He exhaled through his nose, thinking how Dustin had once said he looked like the angry bull in the cartoons when he did that.

His eye fell to the set of dumbbells on the floor. One of them had a dark maroon splotch on it, right by the zero. Must have been from yesterday, when he had to call Diablo off that slut from down the road. It was kinda nice seein' her with her shirt all tore up, them big pale hooters bouncin' out all over the place. Picturing them, Aaron absently tugged at his cock a few times. The memory didn't do enough for him to make it worth his while, and he didn't really feel like beating off, anyway. He finished his smoke then stood, got dressed, and shambled out to the kitchen like a zombie.

The kitchen was a complete goddamned mess, as usual. He was never able to clean it up as good as Stacy had, and Stacy was long gone.

She'd gotten sick a few years back and had simply never gotten better. She didn't complain about it or anything. But one day she took to her bed. A few months later she died in that very same bed. When Aaron had called the ambulance about it, they came right out. After a brief look around, they called in the Bell County Sheriff's department. They said Stacy had died of some kind of infection. They were pissy about it at first, saying Stacy had not received proper care while she'd

77

been sick. Aaron told them he'd done the best he could. Desperate to provide an explanation, Aaron told them that in Stacy's religion, she didn't believe in doctors. If the Lord wanted her healed, he'd'a healed her. As much as it pained him to do so, he had to honor her request that no doctors be called. It was a goddamned lie, of course, but the word "religion" had power. It was like saying a magic word. *Oh, doctors were something against her religion? Well, fuckin' okay, bud, why didn't you say so to start with? We're real sorry for your loss. Yeah, pure tore up about it. Fill out this form and you'll start receiving a portion of her Social Security benefits.*

So now he and Dusty lived without the influence of a woman. It was all right most of the time, but the nights got lonely and the mealtimes were spare, and there was a lot less laughter in the house. For the nights a little sipping whiskey usually did the trick, but for mealtimes he was plumb out of his depth. The stovetop gathered dust, because Aaron's cooking skills were confined to foods that went from the freezer to the microwave or the regular oven, and then to the table. Aaron still salivated when he remembered the venison chili Stacy'd fixed every time he'd gotten a chance to get out and go hunting, and he still got horny when he remembered the loving they'd shared for the few years they'd had together. He missed her every day, and Dusty sometimes still cried about it, but mostly the two of them got on with their lives as best they could.

He looked at the coffeemaker, which still had a couple of inches in it from the last time he'd made coffee. He couldn't recollect whether it had been two days ago or three, but he didn't see any blue-green mold growing on the surface of the liquid. He poured a cup, put it into the microwave, and heated it up.

"Dusty!" he called. "C'mere, boy!"

The television clicked off, and Dusty trotted out of the back of the trailer. The waistband of a dingy white pair of briefs protruded from his shorts, and his bare chest was sun-browned and thin.

Aaron lifted the coffee mug to his lips and took a sip. He grimaced at its bitterness then answered Dusty's questioning expression.

"Diablo's got a fight tonight, boy. We got to get him fed and crated up then get him over to Jose's."

"Daddy? You think Diablo's gonna win tonight?"

"We'll see. I reckon he'll do all right."

Dusty ran out of the room. After a minute or two, Aaron heard the screen door slamming on its spring with a clap. Yeah, Diablo would do fine tonight. Aaron was certain his dog would win. Aaron had seen the competition, and it was pathetic. The dog Diablo was going up against tonight was nothing more than a bait dog, despite what his owner might think. The owner, some kid from the projects on the east side of Killeen, was a punk looking to make a name for himself without working for it and without having to fight his way to the top. The kid would have to learn the hard way, like everyone else. It'd be embarrassing for him, too. Jose usually held the fights in a condemned house on the outskirts of Harker Heights. Aaron could picture it already. The place would be packed tonight, and the big plywood walls of the fighting ring would be red with that bait dog's blood. After tonight, that kid wouldn't be able to show his face at Jose's again till he earned it.

Diablo, Aaron's current pit bull, was a champ. A perfect goddamned killing machine. He'd killed or crippled more dogs in the past year than any other dog in town, and he hadn't sustained any real injuries in several months. Because of the winnings, Aaron hadn't had to spend a dime of his county assistance money.

Diablo was tough, quick, and had savage instincts. Aaron had no doubt that tonight's match would be a quick fight and that Diablo would come through without a scratch.

"Daddy!" Dusty called from outside.

Aaron went to the door and looked out. Dusty was still shirtless, but he'd put on an old pair of jeans. He was on his knees by the cinderblock steps, peering into the darkness under the trailer where Diablo usually slept.

"What is it?"

"Diablo ain't comin' out. I can see him under there, but he didn't come out when I put the food in his dish, and he don't come when I call him, neither."

The first tickle of worry tightened the skin at the back of Aaron's neck. He stepped outside and descended the steps to the ground.

"Diablo!" he yelled. "Git on out here! Now! Come on, Diablo!" He clapped his hand against the skirting of the trailer and noticed a smear of blood near the opening of the skirting.

There was no sign of the dog, and no sound of his movement. Aaron got down on his knees beside his son and leaned forward under the edge of the trailer. He smelled the familiar scent of dog, mixed with a sewage smell so strong it was almost medicinal.

"Diablo!" he yelled, getting angry now. "Git out here, goddammit!"

Still he saw no movement from the dog. He tried to focus on the lumped figure of the dog in his hollowed-out spot in the darkness, but he was unable to make out any details.

"Diablo! Come on!"

Still no answering canine groan or clink of shifting chain. Nothing. Aaron pushed as far forward as he could, his head and shoulders fully under the trailer. A storm of flies buzzed loudly. The dog smell was stronger, as was the other odor, which had settled into a harsh ammonia scent that Aaron immediately recognized.

It was the smell of blood. It was an odor that was thick and heavy, an odor that Aaron had smelled many times at the dog fights after Diablo had ripped out the throat of another animal. Aaron didn't want to think about what it might mean, but the thoughts forced themselves upon him. He remembered the fuss Diablo had kicked up in the middle of the night. He'd dismissed the racket as the usual assin' around Diablo sometimes did with the damn raccoons, but now, with the scent of blood in his nostrils, he didn't know what to think. The buzz of the flies under the trailer was constant, almost maddening. Diablo had gotten scratched up by coons before, but maybe one of them had really put a hurtin' on him this time.

Aaron got to his feet and turned to Dusty.

"I think Diablo musta got hurt, boy. I can't get in under there to get him, so I need you to get in there and pull him out."

"Pull 'im out, Daddy?" There was hesitation in Dusty's voice. The boy was no idiot. He'd taught Dusty that if you approach a hurt dog, especially a hurt fighting dog, you'd better have a heavy chunk of pipe ready to swing. Otherwise, you stick your hand in there you're liable to draw back a stump. Still, what other option was there? Sit around and wait? Hell no. They had to get Diablo up and out for tonight's match. If Aaron didn't show up with the dog at Jose's tonight, he'd be out a thousand dollars. That didn't even count the $600 dollar side bet he'd already laid down on the fight.

"Yeah, goddammit, get in there and bring Diablo out. Quit messin' around. We got shit to do."

"But, Daddy..."

Aaron slapped Dusty across the head, and the boy went sprawling in the dirt. Dusty put a hand to his mouth and looked up at his father with wet eyes but said nothing more.

"If you're through sassing me, get to it, boy. We ain't got time for this."

Dusty picked himself up out of the dirt, sniffed, then crawled under the trailer. Aaron watched his son's bare feet disappear under the side. A few moments later, he scrambled back out, scraping his arms, legs, and back in his haste to get free of the underpinning. He staggered away and threw up into the weeds.

Aaron stood over his son and waited for the worst to pass. Old cobwebs were woven into the boy's hair, and his forearms, knees, and elbows were scored with abrasions. When Dusty spoke, a string of errant saliva still hung from his mouth.

"Daddy. Diablo's dead."

"Dead? The fuck do you mean *dead?*"

"He's all bloody and he's not breathing. He's lying there like a piece of meat. He's too heavy for me to move, Daddy."

No, no, this can't be. Those goddamned raccoons couldn't have killed Diablo! And on the heels of that, a whisper of guilt came unbidden.

Did I really hit him that hard yesterday?

Aaron had an idea. He let go of the boy and went to the edge of the trailer. He grabbed hold of the chain in both hands and hauled backwards on it.

He pulled the dead weight of the dog out from under the trailer, and when he saw Diablo's corpse, he roared in anger.

Dusty was right, Diablo was dead.

The dog was coated with tacky, muddy blood. His head showed the huge knot where Aaron had pounded him with the dumbbell, and below that the dog's nose was a gory, ruined hole. The dog's eyes were glazed and cloudy in death, and a few grains of red sand were gummed onto the edge of the eyelids. Diablo's mouth hung open, his tongue furred with dirt and blood.

"Oh no...Oh God, no."

The dog's flanks were covered with dark blood, thick and sticky like syrup. Aaron turned the dog over, following the path of gore, and found a straight stick poking out of the dog's back.

aw shit

A stick? But it looked like

It must have been

a knife! A goddamned knife handle! He couldn't be sure with all the blood, but it looked black with yellow stripes.

That bitch

The handle was sticking up from the dog's backbone, squarely between its shoulders.

That rottencrotch bitch killed my dog

That stupid slut that Diablo almost bit. From down the street. Her and her kid. When she'd threatened to call Animal Control, Aaron had known she wouldn't get anywhere with Lars. Hell, Lars was practically Diablo's corporate sponsor. He'd been the one that got Diablo's training started, right there at the City Pound. He'd even sent a few strays Diablo's way, too, as bait dogs. And so the dumb bitch must've come back in the middle of the night and stabbed Diablo dead. Oh shit, she was gonna *pay* for this. Big time.

Aaron roared, dropping the dog's carcass in the dirt. Diablo was the best fighting dog ever, and that bitch had killed him! Aaron felt hot tears on his face. How dare she take away something he'd worked so hard to get?

"Daddy? Are you okay?" Dusty asked, a tremor of uncertainty in his voice. The boy'd never seen Aaron cry, not even when Stacy died, but now here he was, bawling and blubbering in front Dusty like some kind of baby.

"Get in the house, boy!"

"But, Daddy...?"

Aaron knelt down and grasped the handle of the knife. The blood was gummy, like half-dried glue. He worked it back and forth, and finally the blade came free. He pulled the knife from the dog's spine, and the dog's body slumped heavily to the ground.

"Get in the house, boy. Right now."

Aaron held the knife before his face, looking at the maroon-streaked blade. A fillet knife. Thin blade, sharp. Nice. A fly buzzed around his hand, then landed lightly in the smeared blood. He smiled at it, and it buzzed away.

White-hot anger flared in his chest. That bitch would pay.

Just fuckin' wait I'll show that bitch how to use a goddamn fee-lay knife

He turned his smile to the blue trailer up the lane. The girl and her mother had retreated to that one yesterday.

I'll carve them goddamn hooters right off her chest.

14

Going into the bank, Deke knew that a plan was only perfect as long as it was only a plan. Start acting the plan out and random shit was bound to happen.

The best bet was to stick as closely to the plan as he could, keep control of the situation, and pray to God that neither of the retards with him opened their goddamned mouths. If they did that, they'd fuck everything all to hell.

The three of them went through the door silently, and the first thing he did was pistol-whip the guard across the back of the head. The old boy fell down like a sack of spuds, and the sound of his falling was what made everybody turn toward them, and toward the door. In response to the surprised gasps he heard, Deke smiled. He figured the smile would probably be visible in the ski mask, but he didn't care.

The people in the bank were mostly older folks, taking their pension money out to pay their rent or buy some groceries. A few people were wearing fast food service uniforms, most likely either dropping off the receipts from last night or getting a supply of change to fill their cash registers for today. Several soldiers were in the bank, probably drawing out enough money to party through the weekend. Get drunk, go out to the titty bars up in Harker Heights, maybe get a tattoo or something before they shipped out to some shithole in that Arab sandbox over there. In their eyes, he could already see their minds ticking, trying to figure out the best way to stop this from happening. Deke almost wanted one of them to attack so he could make an example of the asshole to any other would-be heroes.

"Don't fuckin' say anything, don't fuckin' do anything. Just fuckin' stand still," Deke said, loudly enough for everyone to hear. He made sure his voice wasn't threatening or menacing in any way, but he wanted it to sound like its owner had very little patience left and a low bullshit tolerance. He figured they looked plenty threatening and menacing as it was. Three masked figures popping out of nowhere, stalking around the room with guns. "All except you tellers," he added. "Y'all step back from your counters, and if any of you touch your little panic buttons, I'll touch a panic button of my own." He waved the pistol in front of him for effect.

"I don't need to tell you what we're doing here. I don't need any questions from you. I need quiet and cooperation and for all of you to keep in mind that any money lost by this bank is insured. As long as we all get along all right, you might be delayed a few minutes. You might have to talk to the police. If you fuck up and get me pissed, then the deal's off. The next person you'll be talking to *that* way is Saint Pete. You don't want that, I know. I mean, I don't give a shit one way or the other, but I'm sure you do."

Deke tapped Earl on the shoulder and could feel the nervous trembling of his partner's muscles. Earl was barely holding his shit together. *Don't screw this up, you limp dick jackass,* he tried to mentally project at Earl. At the same time he said, "Go 'round and gather up their cell phones, fat boy."

Earl jumped like someone rammed a knitting needle up his ass then moved forward with a plastic grocery bag. He went behind the counter first, and all the bank employees obediently dropped their phones into the bag. He didn't say anything to them and for that, Deke was thankful. He glanced over at Raymond for a second and saw that his other partner was as cool as a cucumber, not panicky or nervous at all. He also saw that anyone who was acquainted with Raymond would certainly see his identity through the ski mask. His one eye looked straight ahead, while the other seemed to be checking out the ceiling in the far corner of the room, and the bottom edge of the ski mask didn't quite cover Ray's ridiculous Adam's apple. Looked like Ray'd swallowed a damned baseball.

"After you give up your phone, I want you to lie face down on the floor. Don't worry, it won't be but a minute or two. Then we'll leave, and you can get back to whatever you were doing."

From one corner, an elderly woman's quivery voice spoke up. "You can't *do* this!"

Deke rushed to her and pressed the barrel of the pistol up against one of her veiny, pale nostrils. She shrieked, but he held her close with his other arm. A tear leaked from the corner of her eye onto the business end of the gun.

"Oh, yes, ma'am, I can. And if you want to live to tell your grandchildren about it, I suggest you shut your fuckin' pie-hole." As punctuation for both sentences, he pressed the pistol harder into her nose. "You got that?"

Her eyes rolled back, showing only yellowed corneas and thin red threads of vein, and the old lady crumpled to the floor in a faint.

Or a coronary.

Either way.

Inciting that kind of fear made Deke feel good.

It made him feel *powerful*.

After that, everyone lay down on the floor without further objection. Deke took the bag of cell phones from Earl and gave him two new, empty grocery bags. Earl went back around the counter and opened all the tellers' drawers, unceremoniously dumping in all the bills from their denomination-segregated slots.

It looked like a good haul, based on how the bags filled up. Earl still moved jerkily, barely keeping a grip on himself. The rolls of fat on his upper arms were visible below the short sleeves of his t-shirt. They quivered like pale dishes of stretchmark-etched jell-o.

A few minutes more, dumbass, just a few minutes more.

He picked out three soldiers approximately the right height. "You, you, and you. Get up. Strip. Leave your wallets in your pants."

The soldiers obediently got up and began taking off their uniforms. They cast the clothes aside then lay back on the floor. One of the soldiers had been unfortunate enough to choose today to "go commando." Maybe it was laundry day or something, but after only a second's hesitation, he took off his trousers. Red-faced, he joined his friends face down on the floor. One of them snickered nervously as his buddy's pale, naked ass pointed toward the ceiling, and Deke figured the cold linoleum beneath him must be mighty uncomfortable.

One by one, Deke, Earl, and Raymond put on the discarded uniforms. The fit wasn't perfect, but it'd do for a few minutes. Long enough for them to get away, as long as no one looked too closely at Earl. The Army would never let someone as lard bucket as him stay in.

After they put on the boots, they backed toward the bank's door.

A shot rang out behind Deke, loud and echoing in the enclosed bank lobby, and a keening screech rose from Earl. Deke turned to see what had happened.

Earl was unhurt, but blood had splattered all over him and he was noisily losing his mind. Raymond had been shot, the skin around his eyes and mouth gone suddenly pale as dark red roses bloomed in his midsection, turning the digitized gray dots of his stolen uniform into a wet maroon puddle. The geriatric guard held his smoking service revolver in both hands, turning it toward Deke and blinking. His eyes were magnified into big green blobs by his glasses. He hadn't gotten up. He was lying on his belly, supporting his pistol aim with his elbows on the floor.

Goddammit! You dumb old fuck!

Deke pulled the trigger of his pistol twice before the old man could draw a bead on him. Two small dark holes appeared in the guard's high forehead, and the velocity of the rounds kicked him up and backward for a second. Then gravity took hold and the old man rolled forward. The slack skin of his face hit the linoleum with a smack, and his glasses skittered away. A little blood poured from his mouth and nose while his surprised, dead eyes stared at Deke's boots. Deke stepped over to Earl and slapped him hard, shutting him up. Earl's eyes still rolled like a horse ready to bolt, but at least he stopped screaming like a goddamned girl.

"To the car, Nancyboy," Deke said, shoving him out the door. To the rest of the bank he roared, "Stay down, motherfuckers!" Deke turned and helped Ray stand, then walked him to the door. Ray was crying and weaving and only half conscious.

By the time they'd reached the far side of the parking lot, Deke was nearly carrying Ray. No way they could get him through the gate like that. He lifted the lid of the trunk, and put Ray in on top of the spare tire. He put the bags of money in as well then shut the trunk and got into the car. Right before Deke turned the key in the ignition, he thought he heard distant sirens. They took off the ski masks and stuffed them under the seat then they both took off their uniform overshirts and lay them on the seat, careful to fold them so the spatters of blood were hidden. They pulled out of the lot into the mostly stopped traffic, and eased over a few lanes to distance themselves from the strip mall and the bank. Now, for all appearances, they were a couple of soldiers on their way to work.

The traffic moved at a steady pace, about twenty feet at a time. In the rearview mirror, Deke saw two police cruisers pull into the parking lot of the strip mall and police officers hustled out. They'd take a minute to find out what happened then they'd call it in. Deke could imagine what was being said.

"Yes, three masked men robbed the bank and shot old Gus the guard. One was wounded. One was a chicken shit. And the mean one scared an old lady so bad she passed out. Now they've got on soldier uniforms, and they're headed toward Fort Hood."

Deke pulled up to the gate, and he and Earl pulled the soldiers' wallets from their pockets and handing the MP guarding the gate their stolen IDs. Their resemblance to the soldiers was slight at best, but hopefully the gate guard would give them no more than a passing glance.

No such luck. The guard took the cards, turned them over, examined all the fine-printed data on the back, and then glanced in the back window. He gave the Fort Hood sticker on the car a long, studious look.

Despite the benign smile on Deke's face, his heart was thudding so hard he could feel it in his fingertips. He was more nervous now than he'd been at the bank. To give his hands something to do, he turned on the old car's radio. It was the factory original, so it was straight AM. He spun the tuning dial until he came to the first station. A commercial for Gold Bond powder was playing so it was impossible to tell what sort of station he'd found. It was AM, so it was a good bet that it was either news talk shit or religious shit. The really good music only came on FM these days.

The fucking guard was taking forever.

Deke was growing nervous. These guys had guns, and unlike the dead bank guard, they probably used them all the damned time. Would he be able to shoot them and get away in time? Somehow, Deke thought those odds weren't very good.

"Aw-right, Sar'n, have a good one," the guard finally mumbled, and Deke breathed a sigh of relief. He took his foot off the brake and pulled slowly forward.

Then the guard started yelling for them to stop.

15

Sharon and Lucinda finished their breakfast quietly. Sharon brought the coffee mug to her lips and watched Lucinda take a sip of milk from her Hello Kitty cup. She saw the puffiness under her daughter's eyes that said even though yesterday was over, it might not be over in Lucinda's head for a long time.

Sharon herself had also slept badly. The dreams that haunted her night were of the dog attacking her and Lucinda again. It was too easy to imagine the dog whipping its head back and forth with Lucinda's frail body clenched in those muscled jaws.

As Sharon cleared the table, Lucinda picked up her dolly and went to sit in front of the television. When she sat before the TV, with its bluish light washing over her blonde hair, Sharon got the strangest sense of déjà vu. For a moment, Lucinda had looked like the little girl in that old movie *Poltergeist*. Not the dumbass remake of a couple years back but the old one, the original. Creepy.

She shook off the chilly feeling and started on the daily chores that kept Deke fed, in clean clothes, and in a clean house. She took a pack of thin pork chops from the freezer, setting them on the counter by the sink to thaw for dinner.

This was one of the better days, so far. It always was, Sharon decided, when Deke left the house before she and Lucinda woke up. Go figure. She woke briefly when he'd gotten out of bed, but she knew that if she acted like she was awake, he'd start bitching at her to make him some breakfast or pack a lunch for him. She'd stayed still, pretended sleep, and eventually he left and her pretending became reality. She drifted back into thin sleep and survived, by default, another morning with Deke. She jerked awake when she heard the tired old engine of the truck start. After it faded away down the road, she got out of bed and woke Lucinda.

Now all she had to do was win the lottery, and she could escape him for good. *Sure, whatever*, she told herself as her throat tightened. Frustrated tears rose to her eyes, but she willed them back down. The fears and the frustrations were all too much to face. She had Lucinda to worry about. She gathered up Deke's dirty clothes from the bedroom floor, and added them to the small pile she'd begun accumulating at the doorway between the kitchen and the laundry room.

Lucinda sat on the living room floor, wearing a thin pink sundress over a white t-shirt, with her Betty dolly clutched tightly under her arm. She'd been watching TV for a while, and Sharon could tell that boredom was beginning to set in.

In the laundry room, Sharon found something oddly out of place.

Deke's green tackle box was open on the floor in front of the washing machine, with plastic bobbers and lures scattered across the floor in front of the washer. What had he been doing with this? He certainly hadn't gone fishing this morning. The very idea was crazy. In the time that Deke had lived with them, she'd never known him to go fishing. The rusted barbs on the hooks in their tiny compartments were mute testimony to the idea that any interest he'd had in fishing was far in Deke's past. Sharon turned, her foot kicking something thin and plastic across the tiny room, where it lodged under the hot water heater. She bent and picked it up from the tile floor and saw that it was a sheath of a knife. The black plastic had bright yellow stripes but no brand name. She suspected the knife probably fell into a lake or river somewhere when Deke was too drunk to care. The image was easy to conjure. In fact, it was difficult to picture him fishing sober.

What did I ever see in him? she wondered as she put the fishing junk back into the tackle box. Her usual thought chased that one through her heart. *Oh, Lucinda, what the hell did I get us into?* She pushed the clasps shut and slid the tackle box back onto the shelf.

She returned to the kitchen and topped up her mug of coffee, and when she turned again, Lucinda was in front of her.

"Mommy, my Betty dolly needs a bath." She held Betty up for Sharon's inspection, and Sharon saw that Lucinda was right. The dolly looked like a baseball team had been using it for home plate. It was filthy. The doll's skin was a mass of gray smudges, the hair was knotted with bits of dead grass, pine straw, and what appeared to be spiderwebs. The dolly's dress was covered with dusty orange smears of dirt and dark red-brown splotches that almost looked like blood. Betty dolly—for damn sure and no doubt about it—needed a bath.

"Okay, girlie-girl. Let's see what we can do." Sharon took the dolly from her daughter. Betty was warm, radiating the stored heat of Lucinda's embrace. Sharon gently worked the dress loose from the dolly, being especially careful around the shoulders. Beneath the dress, the dolly's underwear was modest and sewn to the body. The dress was hand stitched, and the seams, even in the few days of wear and play that it had seen, were already strained.

She put the dolly on the kitchen counter and took the dress to the laundry room, where she dabbed the maroon spots with hydrogen peroxide. Lucinda followed, watching in silence. The peroxide foamed as it reacted with the spots, so Sharon concluded that it must be actual blood, probably from her own wounds inflicted by the dog. The dark spots turned lighter and lighter until they were nearly gone.

Sharon pulled a pillowcase from the shelf and put the doll's dress into it, then knotted the mouth of the pillowcase shut and put it into the washer with a small load of clothes.

"All right, sweetie. Let's let it run on the gentle cycle for a few minutes then we'll see what else needs to be done."

They went back to the kitchen and picked up Betty dolly. Sharon showed Lucinda how to use a dishtowel and warm water with a little soap to remove the smudges from Betty's face, and Lucinda took the dishcloth and the dolly from her. The little girl talked to the dolly as she rubbed at the dirt, reminding Betty to be good for her bath so that it wouldn't take as long. She was gentle but fastidious, and eventually all the smudges on the dolly's face and hands had been removed.

Lucinda didn't need Sharon to show her what to do with the brush. The girl's small hands were careful with the dolly's hair, and soon it, too, was free of debris. The chime of the washing machine sounded, and mother and daughter went to see how successful the wash had been.

Although some of the blood spots still showed as slight pink stains, the dress was much cleaner. Almost as good as new. Sharon was relieved the stitching had survived the washer. They put the dress back in the pillowcase then transferred the load of freshly washed clothing to the dryer.

Sharon spied her daughter's beautiful look of intense concentration as she set the timer on the dryer and turned it on. Tiny buttons tumbled in the dryer, sounding like stray pebbles in a drum, and Lucinda peered over the edge of the dryer, staring at the knob with all its settings. It gave Sharon a small smile, thinking about all the little instances of Lucinda helping her and how many of these instances were actually teaching Lucinda the skills she would need later in life. On impulse, she knelt and hugged Lucinda.

"We'll take care of Betty, sweetheart. I know you love your dolly."

"Mommy, after you, she's my best friend."

The sentiment saddened Sharon. Not only that the doll still unnerved her, but also that Lucinda's statement was completely factual. That Lucinda considered the doll her best friend did nothing to soothe the pain that Lucinda had no real friends, no real family. When she walked away from Lucinda's smile, the enthusiasm in her little girl's voice echoed in Sharon's head. Lucinda returned to the living room and sat before the television, while Sharon went to her daughter's room.

Instead of making Lucinda's bed, she stripped the sheets from the mattress. The sheets, like the dolly, were grimy, and covered with dirt, blades of grass, and a couple of unmistakable blood smears. Sharon didn't realize she'd bled so much onto Lucinda after yesterday's encounter with the pit bull.

She fed the bedclothes into the washing machine then sat down for a moment. Something was amiss, and nagging at her. She mentally retraced her morning, following her path from one task to the next, but found nothing wrong.

Something *was* wrong, though, she knew it. She simply couldn't identify the problem, or shake the feeling. She tried to relax and listen to the clothes dryer, hoping the identity of the problem would dawn on her before she got distracted by something else. After a few near-hypnotic white noise moments, she still came up dry.

She sighed. *If it's important, I'm sure I'll remember it soon.*

The clothes dryer beeped, and the concern fled her mind. Sharon opened the dryer and fished out Betty dolly's dress. It was clean, dry, and warm, and when she handed it to Lucinda, she said, "Give this to Betty and she'll probably cuddle up in it and go right to sleep. I love putting on clothes straight out of the dryer. They're all fluffy and cozy."

Lucinda took the dress but looked intimidated.

"I don't want to tear the seams of it, Mommy."

"Don't you worry, sweetheart. Be careful, but give it a try, and if you need a hand, I'm right here. All you have to do is call me."

Lucinda took Betty to the sofa, all the while whispering reassurances to the dolly. Sharon watched for a moment while her daughter carefully bent the dolly's arms into unnatural positions in order to get the dress around the odd bends and corners of the tiny physique. After a bit of stretch and tug, the dress made it over the dolly's head then one arm was worked through a sleeve. Lucinda gamely tried to get the other arm properly situated, but after a moment, gave up in frustration. She sighed then looked to Sharon.

"Mommy, I'm stuck. Her arm won't go into the hole."

Sharon sat beside her on the sofa, smiling.

"Hang on, Cinda-girl. There's a trick to it. Let me show you."

She held out her hand for the doll, and Lucinda gave Betty to her. Again Sharon was amazed at how warm the doll's plastic skin had become. It was almost as if the doll itself had come out of the dryer only moments ago.

She backed the doll's arm out of its sleeve then aligned both of the arms to their sleeves. After that, she simply rotated the dress half a centimeter at a time, until each hand protruded from its proper sleeve.

"You see what I'm doing, Punkin?"

"Wow."

"Remember, little girl, once upon a time I was a girl with dollies like you." The similarities started and ended right there, because unlike Betty, Sharon's dollies were disturbing in a way that made them hard to care about.

"Let me get it, Mommy," Lucinda said, and took the dolly back from Sharon. She worked the dress around slowly and carefully, and soon it began to line up properly.

The door of the trailer suddenly bent inward on its frame with a sound like a shotgun. Sharon jumped to her feet, and Lucinda shrieked and clutched at Betty. The door now had a crease running up the center of it. If the deadbolt hadn't been fastened, the door would surely have burst open like the lid of a jack in the box.

At the center of the crease in the thin door, a narrow knife blade erupted from the enamel-sheathed aluminum. On the other side, an inhuman scream rose—bloodcurdling, loud, and full of rage.

"You killed my dog, you fucking bitch!"

16

"Oh shit, oh shit, we're toast; we're fucking toast. Oh man, they got us," Earl started gibbering. His breathing sped up again.

"Shut the fuck up, lard ass," Deke whispered. Earl's eyes rolled like a panicked horse. "Shut the fuck up or I'll fucking beat your face inside out." He braked, and the MP trotted up from the rear of the car. Deke lifted the pistol beside the seat, holding it below the level of the window. He drew the hammer back as he sucked in a deep breath and held it then he turned to the gate guard approaching the door.

"Hey, Sar'n', you forgot your IDs." The guard held out the laminated cards.

Deke snickered, exhaling harshly. His mind was overstressed, like a spring wound too tight; it was about to break and send his brains squirting out his ears. He nearly raised the gun and shot the guard anyway.

Thousands of dollars in stolen money in the trunk, along with a gut-shot dumbass in a ski mask, another dumbass about to piss himself on the seat beside me, an old dead dumbass back at the bank with two of my bullets in his head, and you've got your dick in a knot about some fuckin' ID cards! Even those are stolen, you dipshit!

He let go of the pistol and reached out the open window with a smile he hoped looked relieved and embarrassed. A bead of sweat

98

rolled down into his eye, stinging. He blinked it away and took a quick look into the rearview mirror. No cops were on the way. Yet.

"Aw shit, don't want to do that. First Sergeant would have my ass then. Thanks, man." Deke took the IDs and put them on the seat between him and Earl.

"No problem, Sar'n'. Oh, and there's one other thing. This is a real nice car, a classic an' all, but it looks like you got a Class three leak in your oil pan. You might want to get that checked out, 'cause you're dripping oil all over the road." The gate guard's pronunciation of oil was "ohhl."

"Hey, thanks, man. Here's some advice from someone who knows: never get an old car and try to restore it. It'll friggin' nickel an' dime you to death."

The guard chuckled and turned around, walking back to his checkpoint as Deke drove away. Earl was practically hyperventilating, wheezing and gasping in the passenger seat like a carburetor sucking an empty tank of gas. It was really a surprise that the guard hadn't looked over at him stroking out like he was having a damned seizure. If they'd been caught, it would have been that fat fucktard's fault.

Deke knew what the guard had been talking about. It probably did look like oil, all thick and dark and reddish. But it wasn't the oil pan leaking onto the road.

Raymond was doing the leaking, bleeding out from inside the trunk. For a second, Deke wondered what condition all that money was in, whether it was getting bloody. He supposed it'd still spend as well as pretty money, but he didn't want to deal with the obvious questions that would be asked about blood-spattered cash.

The old Nova entered Fort Hood, made a right onto Battalion Avenue, drove about two miles then exited through the east gate, directly into Killeen. As they pulled onto the main road, Deke turned and watched the guards pull the gates shut. Lockdown, right on cue. He slowly accelerated, keeping the car well under the speed limit as he passed the seedy liquor stores, pawn shops, and payday loan stores that had sprouted right outside Fort Hood's east gate.

They'd made it. The cops had trailed him onto Fort Hood, and the MPs, as they were trained, promptly locked it down. It'd probably stay that way for the better part of the day. While the MPs were dicking around with searching post for them, the city cops outside the fence wouldn't start the search for him anywhere else. They were so predictable. And now they were screwing up while he drove sedately away. He looked over at Earl, who was still white-faced and terrified, his brown eyes bulging and his breath coming in harsh pants, and Deke laughed. Earl looked like he was practically having a coronary sitting there.

Deke punched him in the shoulder.

"Hot damn! We made it! WeeeeHawwww!"

Earl looked at him, rubbing his shoulder. He didn't seem able to comprehend what Deke was saying. His expression was pure misery, and Deke laughed again.

Home free. He'd pulled it off. He could finally escape this shithole of a town. This shithole of a life. Starting today, he'd be famous. A real-live bank robber. Every time he pulled another job, his legend would grow. Like Billy the Kid or John Dillinger.

Deke reckoned he ought to feel some sort of guilt about killing the old guard, but he found no shred of remorse in his heart or his head. The only thing he felt was a wild elation, a spike of adrenaline from actually getting away with not only a bank robbery in broad daylight, but murder as well. The untamed sense of such a nefarious accomplishment made him feel powerful like some terrible, unstoppable machine.

But it still left him with a question.

What was he going to do about Ray?

As they pulled onto the highway, the radio station identified itself as "The Home of Today's Praise" and said that today's Message in Praise was centered on the parable of the Good Samaritan.

So, the radio station wasn't talk-radio shit. Instead, it was religious shit. Same difference. Deke let it continue to bray its whiny prayers as he drove.

He stopped at a convenience store to fill the gas tank on the old Nova and to stock up on some essentials. A log of Copenhagen, a case of beer, and a handful of beef jerky packets would probably take care of things until they had time for more leisurely shopping. He got back into the car, and the questions of *what next?* assailed him again.

He couldn't take Ray to the hospital or to any doctor. That would lead to too many questions that didn't have reasonable answers. He couldn't leave him in a ditch somewhere. Well he *could*, but he'd rather not. If he had to pick, he'd rather shoot Earl and throw his fat dumb ass in a ditch.

The only solution that came to mind was to take Raymond back to the house. Yeah, he wanted to be free of goddamned Sharon and her goddamned kid, but she was the only person Deke knew with any medical skills. She said she'd nearly gotten her nursing degree before she'd gotten together with her ex. She still talked about going back to school to finish up someday.

Deke knew the truth, though. She'd never be anything except that goofy kid's mom. She'd whelped a brat, and that was the highlight of her life. It was the end of the road for her. The best she'd ever be.

Even though they'd only been living together for about five months, it was *way* past time to cut her loose. Hell, she wouldn't even let him fuck her for the last couple of months. Ever since that horseshit with her old flame sending her the damned Mother's Day flowers, she'd acted all high and mighty. You'd think her cunt was gold-plated. Once or twice, though, he'd had to let her know who was in charge and had taken what he'd wanted. And regardless of what she said afterward, he could tell that she'd liked it. They were all sluts deep down, after all, weren't they?

If you want something, boy, take it. Half the time, they'll fucking give it to you anyway.

Despite the fact that Sharon was now old news, she had what he needed right now. She could at least take a look at Raymond, and maybe she could even fix him up. He turned off the highway and pointed the old Nova toward the trailer park.

Best to take Ray there. Deke could figure out what to do next while Sharon was checking out Raymond's injuries and hopefully patching him up.

17

"Go into my room and close the door, baby," Sharon whispered to Lucinda. "Don't come out till I tell you to." Lucinda did as she was told, hugging Betty tightly to her chest. Fear showed in her eyes as she ran through the kitchen to the big bedroom, and the door clicked closed behind her. Over the screaming outside, Sharon couldn't say for sure that she heard the lock engage, but she was confident Lucinda would turn it.

Sharon turned toward the front door in time to see the knife blade working itself up and down. Finally it moved freely enough to slide out of the stab hole. It withdrew, and the voice screamed again.

"You killed my dog, and now I'm gonna kill you!"

"What are you talking about?" she yelled out the door.

"You know goddamn well what I'm talking about, bitch! I found my dog dead this morning! You killed Diablo like you goddamn said you would!"

BAM! Something hard hit the door, either a fist or a work boot.

"And now I'm gonna fuck you up!"

BAM! It hit the door again.

"Fuck you up eight ways from Sunday, slut!"

BAM! Sharon reached for the phone and dialed 911.

"Carve them hooters off your chest—"

BAM! The operator picked up in the middle of the first ring. "Killeen Emergency Services, how may I direct your call?" The voice sounded very officious, bland, and vaguely female.

"—get me a new dog—"

BAM! Sharon gasped into the phone. "A man's breaking into my house...he's crazy...he's got a knife, and he's trying to kick the damned door in."

"—and then I'll feed him your tits! How 'bout that, you fuckin' bitch!"

BAM! The voice on the other end of the phone transformed dramatically, changing from zombie switchboard operator to high-octane emergency dispatcher. "Yes ma'am, police are on the way. Please stay on the line as long as you can..."

Sharon had already dropped the receiver onto the kitchen counter, and had backed into the laundry room.

Someone killed Aaron Whistler's dog? He thought *she* was the killer? It didn't make any sense, and it was far too much to try to figure out with him practically inside the house with a knife. The front door wouldn't hold up much longer under his onslaught.

She cast her eyes about her, looking everywhere for something she could use as a weapon. In the laundry room, there were only cleaning supplies, the old tackle box, a cooler, and a few dusty board games up on a shelf. Nothing with any significant heft. She thought about getting a knife from the kitchen, but that would be stupid. He had a knife, rage, and at least a hundred pounds on her. She wouldn't have a chance.

Ruling out fight left only flight as an option. It would surely only buy her a few moments, but hopefully that would be enough. The laundry room was also where the trailer's back door was located. They never used it, because there were no back steps. It'd be a four foot drop, but what other choice did she have? They'd have to make a run for it.

"Lucinda! Come on, let's go!" she called into the back room. Whistler was still trying to beat down the front door. Sharon saw that a couple more solid blows would finish the job.

"Lucinda!" she hissed. "Come here!"

Lucinda poked her head out the bedroom door. Her eyes were round with fear, and her face was pale.

BAM!

"Best fuckin' dog in the world, you stupid bitch! That was the last mistake you're ever gonna make!"

BAM!

Lucinda scurried over to Sharon, her white-knuckled fist tight around Betty's arm.

"We've got to get out of here, sweetie! Come on!"

Sharon shoved the cooler out of the way, into the kitchen, and unlocked the back door. The door stuck at first, its rubberized seals like glue with age and disuse. Sharon gave a final push, and the door finally popped open with a sound like duct tape being ripped off a roll.

"Go go go," she whispered to Lucinda as she lowered her daughter and the little girl's bare feet touched the ground. Behind her, Sharon heard the front door explode inward on its hinges, and Whistler's voice howling in triumph. She grabbed a pair of flip-flops from the floor, and tossed them on the ground ahead of her.

Sharon took a breath and leapt to the ground. When she landed, her left heel was half on a rock, and her ankle rolled when her full weight came down. Sharon gasped but kept moving, grabbing the flip-flops and staggering away from the trailer. She and Lucinda went out to the gravel lane, and all the while Sharon racked her brains trying to figure out if any of the neighbors she knew were home.

She looked back at the wide open back door, and saw Whistler's head sticking out. He grinned at her like a sweaty great white shark then lightly jumped down from the laundry room doorway. He seemed to have no problem with his landing, but every step Sharon took brought fresh pain to her foot.

She limped forward, hand in hand with Lucinda, and saw their salvation approaching in a cloud of gravel dust.

Coming up the drive was an old white car. She didn't recognize it, but that didn't matter. She hobbled toward it, afraid to look behind to see how fast Whistler and his knife were catching up with them. She waved and yelled as she moved up the drive toward the car.

When she saw that Deke was behind the wheel of the car, the realization of what she'd missed hit her. Deke had left early for work, but today was his day off.

She looked closer. What was he wearing? It looked almost like a soldier's uniform. Whose car was this? Why were he and Earl in it? The questions sprang up at her like evil funhouse clowns, but she ignored them and scrambled into the backseat, hustling Lucinda in before her.

In the distance, she heard the wail of an approaching police siren.

18

Lucinda was so scared. Even though she had Betty with her, all she wanted to do was cry until all the bad people went away.

She sat on the floor of the backseat of this strange car that smelled like old people and rust, while Mommy cried and screamed about the crazy man who'd come into the house with a knife. The crazy man was Dustin's daddy, and he was now standing in front of the car. Lucinda hugged Betty tightly to her chest. She bent down and whispered to the dolly to not be scared. Mommy would save them like she did yesterday.

Betty whispered the same words back to her, and it made her feel a little safer. Lucinda didn't think that anyone else could hear Betty's voice, and it didn't actually sound like a dolly voice, but it comforted her anyway.

From the front seat, Deke barked at Mommy.

"Whistler did what? Why the fuck would he do that?" He paused for a moment, and when Mommy told him about the man's dog being dead, he asked, "So *did* you kill his dog?" Lucinda could tell he was smiling his mean smile even though she couldn't see his face.

"Of course not, Deke! Goddammit, stop playing around and get us out of here! He's standing right there!"

Lucinda put her hands on the cracked vinyl upholstery and sat up on her knees, peeking over the seat and out the windshield of the car.

Dustin's daddy was standing in front of the car, still holding that knife. His arms were down by his side, and he had an ugly look on his face as he peered into the car.

"Deke? That you?"

Deke rolled down the window on the driver's side, despite Mommy whispering swearwords at him and telling him to stop. He spoke conversationally to Dustin's daddy, like everything was normal. "Aaron. How you doin'?"

"Now Deke, you know I ain't got no argument with you. It's that stupid bit… that *woman* you're shackin' up with. She went and killed my dog with this knife, and you know Diablo was the best fightin' dog in the whole county. Let me talk with her." He waved the knife around, showing it to Deke.

"Deke," Mommy whispered, "don't you even think about it. Close the damned window and drive away."

The seat shook. Deke seemed to be chuckling. "You *did* kill his dog. How the hell else would he get my knife?"

"Your knife?" Mommy asked, sounding puzzled.

"Aaron," Deke called out the window, "you get on home. I ain't got time to deal with your stupid shit right now, and I ain't lettin' you get near her with that damned pig sticker."

He rolled up the window most of the way and turned around to look at Mommy. "Raymond got hurt, and I need you to help me with him. If I didn't, I'd shove your ass out of the car right now. Don't think for a minute that it's anything more than that saving you from the pointy end of that knife. And it had to have been you that killed his dog. That's my old fishing knife. Don't fucking lie to me, bitch."

His eyes rose from hers and he looked out the back window, and Lucinda became aware of the police siren as the squad car came around the corner and pulled into the trailer park. Lucinda stretched up and turned, and saw the white cruiser pull up close behind the car they were in. The blue light flashed, and the headlights blinked on and off.

"Fuck!" he yelled at Mommy. "You stupid whore! You called the cops?"

From behind the car, the police siren shut off and there were several loud clicks. The policeman's voice came over a loudspeaker, sounding like they did on TV. Lucinda gripped Betty, and the dolly told her in tiny secret whispers that everything was going to be all right. Lucinda wasn't so sure that was the case.

"Sir! You, in front of the car! Drop your weapon and back away slowly!"

Deke growled and beat on the steering wheel.

"If that goddamned cop comes up here, he's going to do all his investigating shit, and he'll see me and Earl, and he'll look in the goddamned trunk, and then the shit will hit the fan."

"What are you talking about?" Mommy asked. "What's in the trunk?"

Deke didn't answer her question, and Lucinda saw his head move slightly. It was as if he was looking at the policeman in the rearview mirror, then glanced out the front of the car at Dustin's daddy again. Beside Deke on the front seat was that fat man that he worked with at Busby's, who always looked worried and sweaty. His name was something that started with an E, but Lucinda couldn't remember what it was. Right now he looked extra sweaty and worried. He shook whenever he moved, as if he was as scared as Lucinda was.

In front of the car, Dustin's daddy stood there, his arms slack at his sides. He was still holding the knife, but he wasn't waving it around.

From behind the car, the policeman called to him again. "Sir, please put down the knife and step away from it."

Lucinda turned again, and she saw the policeman. He had his door open, and was standing with one foot on the ground and one foot inside his car. When he spoke into his handheld radio, his voice crackled from the speaker on the top of his car. His sunglasses hid his eyes behind two shiny mirrors, and his flat brimmed hat kept his face in shadow.

"Deke! What have you got in the trunk?" Mommy's voice was no longer a whisper. It sounded like she was ready to start shouting some more.

"Sir!" the policeman said again. "This is your last opportunity to put down your weapon. Do as I say, sir, and no one has to get hurt!"

Dustin's daddy seemed to dimly consider that suggestion a moment longer. Comprehension finally dawned in his eyes, and he dropped the knife. It hit the gravel and Dustin's daddy raised his hands as he backed up a few steps.

Lucinda turned to see what would happen next. The policeman got fully out of his car and moved from behind his door, then strode forward in the direction of Dustin's daddy. He walked past the back seat, looking in at Mommy and Lucinda, then past the front seat, looking in at Deke and his sweaty friend. As he passed the front fender of the car, he again turned his attention to Dustin's daddy. Lucinda followed him with her eyes.

In one fluid movement, Deke popped open the door and stepped out of the car. The policeman turned in response to the sound, a question on his face. With no hesitation, Deke raised a gun from his side and shot the police officer. The sound wasn't very loud, but it was a sharp crack! that could easily be heard over the running car engine. The policeman fell, lifeless, to the gravel. He didn't move after that, and Mommy screamed.

Lucinda couldn't breathe. She was shocked. She'd always known Deke was mean to her and Mommy, but he'd shot a policeman! Policemen, soldiers, and firemen were the good guys—Mommy taught her that. They kept everyone safe. Deke had killed one.

Lucinda knew what that meant.

Deke wasn't simply mean.

Deke was one of the *bad* guys.

Lucinda watched as Deke stepped closer to the fallen policeman, and she still couldn't inhale. She didn't know if she was more scared of that, or of the fact that she and Mommy and Betty were in a bad guy car. Her mind struggled with the complete obscenity of what Deke had done. She looked up at Mommy for some sort of reassurance, her eyes wide in terror and panic. Mommy's hands were in her hair, her mouth hung open, and her eyebrows were raised and mashing her forehead into furrows.

Finally Lucinda's mounting fear overflowed her paralysis. She sucked in a great whoop of wind, and screamed. Not a word, but a solid barrage of hopeless, heartbroken sound. Tears rained from her cheeks as she scrambled onto Mommy's lap, hiding her eyes against Mommy's chest.

Deke walked back to the car. When he'd fired the pistol at the policeman, Dustin's daddy had run off. Lucinda wished she and Mommy could run off, too, but they were in a bad guy car. They couldn't get away. They couldn't. The bad guy would shoot them, too.

The sweaty fat guy must be a bad guy too, but he wasn't acting like he was. He sounded the way Lucinda imagined him in her head. Lucinda heard him muttering, "No, no, no, no..." over and over again.

She looked up at Mommy's face and saw confused emptiness, like she, too, was trying to figure out what had happened. One tear slid down Mommy's cheek.

Lucinda clutched at her mother again but was determined not to let Deke out of her sight. Through tear-blurred eyes she saw him get back into the car as if he'd gone to get a milkshake. He slapped the sweaty guy across the face and told him to shut up then he turned to the backseat and spoke to Mommy.

"Raymond's in the trunk. He got shot. We robbed a bank. Don't fucking say anything. I was coming to get you to fix him up at the house, but now we don't have time. We've got to get the hell out of here. There's gonna be cops all over the place soon, so now I've got to take you and your stupid brat with me, and I don't know how soon we can stop running so you can look at Ray's wound. Shit. You had to call the damn cops, didn't you? Why do you keep fucking up my life?"

Mommy looked at Deke uncomprehendingly. Her eyes were big, and her lower lip quivered.

"Raymond got shot? You robbed a bank? But—"

Deke held up a thick pointing finger. "Huh-uh. Not another goddamned word."

Lucinda squeezed Mommy's arm, willing her to stop talking. Couldn't she see that Deke was a bad guy? He'd shot a policeman, so he'd have no trouble shooting the two of them. Lucinda pulled herself as close as she could to Mommy, ducking awkwardly under her arm and holding Betty under her own arm. A small hole in the musty upholstery was a tiny black window into the trunk compartment, and when she sat back against the seat, a puff of foul air came out of the hole. She didn't want to think about what she smelled.

Deke changed gears then backed around the police car. It was still running, its driver's side door was open, and the blue light was still flashing. As they passed, Lucinda could hear the squawk of his radio through the window. Someone was trying to call him, but the policeman would never answer that call.

Deke turned the car around and got onto the main road, and then he pointed the car away from the morning sun. The shadows of Mommy, Betty, and Lucinda lay sharp and dark on the back of the front seat before them then flickered and fled when they drove under the overhanging branches of oak trees.

Although the sun warmed the crown of her head, and was bright all around, Lucinda had never known a colder, darker day. The only comfort she got was from Mommy's hugs and from Betty's secret whispers.

19

This was great. Oh, this was fuckin' rich! It took the cake and the goddamned plate it was sittin' on, too.

Well, what the shit, let's fuckin' shoot everybody. Stack 'em up like goddamned cordwood by the side of the road and lighten the motherfuckin' load a little bit!

Deke was starting to come unraveled. He could feel panic in his chest flapping hungrily around like a big roadkill-eating vulture, but he couldn't do anything about it. His grip on the steering wheel kept involuntarily tightening. He'd force his fingers to relax then he'd look away for a second, and the next thing he knew, his hands would cramp up from white-knuckling the wheel again. The radio was still playing religious crap, and the talking and preaching made it hard for Deke to think about what he needed to do next. He reached out and snapped it off and saw from the corner of his eye that Earl flinched at his sudden movement. *Goddamned idiot.*

"What's the matter, fatty?"

"Deke, please don't call me that." It sounded more like a whine that anything. Deke snorted.

And all the shit kept piling up. First Raymond, then the guard, then the goddamned cop, and now he was dragging Sharon and her whelp across the state. Couldn't very well leave them behind now.

Couldn't goddamned go to San Antonio now. Hell, it was bad enough that Whistler was still drawing breath. Deke knew he should have killed him, too, but the dumbass redneck had vanished when he'd opened up on the cop. Cop killing. Jesus. What the fuck, right? No use half-stepping when you're trying to get a job done. Fuck doing things the easy way, no matter what his father had said. He'd found what he wanted, and he took it, like Mr. Pratt advised him so long ago. And now there was no going back.

Earl looked like he was waiting for the goddamned car to slow down enough so he could jump out and escape, and Deke figured the only reason Sharon wouldn't do the same thing was because of her kid. She'd wait until she was sure they could both escape safely. Earl, on the other hand, didn't have anything holding him back. Nothing, of course, except the fear of flying bullets.

They're all against me.

The thought came out of nowhere and disappeared from his conscious mind as quickly as it had occurred to him, but for a split second he was utterly convinced that everyone was conspiring against him. Earl, Sharon, Aaron, and the cop were all in on it, purposely slowing him down so he'd get caught. His mind cleared and he drove on.

First things first, then. He had to get them far enough away from Killeen that he could consider them in the clear then he could stop somewhere and let Sharon take a look at Raymond. He was starting to get a little worried about Ray, bleeding back there in the dark. He idly wondered if Ray was dead already.

He pulled a packet of beef jerky from the bag and tore it open with his teeth. After deciding the jerky tasted like petrified shit, he threw the rest out the window, threw in a dip of Cope', and cracked open a beer. He drove southwest.

Originally, the plan had been to swap back to his truck and drive down to San Antonio, where there were big crowds of tourists, so they could blend in until the dust settled a little. That option was now out the window. With what had happened at the trailer park, the cops would be all over the place looking for them. Hell, they'd probably even call in the Texas Rangers. Then they'd eventually connect the shooting to the bank robbery, and they'd call in the Feds. The idea of Federal Officers looking all over the state for him made Deke feel damn near *notorious*, like some kind of infamous uncatchable badass. Imagining the "extensive manhunt" being talked about all over the TV and radio, Deke grinned.

That they would be out looking for him all over the state made him stick to the back roads instead of the Interstate, despite the fact that getting anywhere took much more time. They needed to avoid the places where any law dogs were likely to see them.

He meticulously followed the posted speed limits out of town. They drove through tiny truck stops with strange names that somehow still qualified as towns. When they drove through Joppa, Sharon told him that they needed to stop to let Lucinda go to the restroom. He laughed and kept driving, but he finally agreed that he didn't want the car to smell like piss. Once Joppa's one and only three-way blinking stoplight was a few miles behind them in the wobbling heat haze, he pulled over onto the shoulder and invited the kid to cop a squat in the bluebells on the side of the road.

When they got back on the road, Deke heard a shift and a thump from the trunk. They had to get somewhere safe to check on Ray. Maybe Sharon could bandage him up and he could sit up front in the car, but if he was all bloody and fucked up-looking, there would be no way. Too much of a risk. Ray would understand. He was a dipshit, sure, but even he could see the logic in that. Deke hoped he was okay. Between him and Earl, Deke would pick Ray any day of the week.

After a few more miles of empty two-lane road, Deke saw an old, rust-pitted mailbox peppered with buckshot holes on the right. The mailbox looked like it hadn't been used in years. Beside it, a dirt driveway that was nothing more than a pair of barely visible wheel ruts arced through a field of tall weeds. While the state of the mailbox didn't necessarily mean no one lived there, the condition of the driveway clinched it. If anyone used the driveway on a regular basis, the center swath of weeds wouldn't be nearly so tall. Rather than stopping around the first hilltop, he drove the driveway to its end to make sure, and he was rewarded with finding the burned ruins of an old farmhouse.

The only part of the house still standing was its chimney, crookedly erect and blackened. Deke grinned as he congratulated himself for being so observant and finding the perfect spot to stop, check on Raymond, and stretch. He briefly wondered if anyone had been in the house when it burned down. Probably not.

"Here's the deal," he said. We're stopping here for a few minutes. Earl, Sharon, you're both getting out with me. Don't get any fuckin' bright ideas about *anything*. Earl, if you try to run off, I'll put a hole in your head. Sharon, if you do anything stupid, I'll put a hole in Lucinda's head. You two understand what I'm saying?"

"Yeah," Earl croaked, sounding like he was trying to keep from swallowing his tongue. Sharon nodded with a scowl. Sullen bitch. Better be glad I do need you alive, whore, or you wouldn't be. Don't fuckin' push me.

At first Lucinda clung to Sharon when she tried to get out of the car, but relented when Deke glared at her. The three of them got out together. Deke kept the gun handy and visible, using it to gesture toward the trunk. They moved to the back of the car, and Deke opened it up.

Earl said, "Ommahhgahh," and puked all over himself. He staggered back, turning and hanging onto a pine tree as he emptied his guts and noisily dry heaved.

Sharon clapped a hand over her mouth, her eyes rolling in horror. She swallowed several times as she blinked and involuntarily took a step backward.

Deke's jaw flexed, unclenched, then flexed again as he looked down at Raymond's body. Ray was sweating and pale with blood loss, but his chest was visibly rising and falling. Ray had one gore-covered hand on his midsection, and his other arm was wrapped around the spare tire. Sitting in the pool of Ray's blood, the white plastic grocery bags full of money looked like fat, well-fed maggots.

"Ray? How you doin', man?"

Ray opened his eyes, wincing. "Not too good, Deke." He tried to smile, but failed. "Did we get caught?" Deke couldn't help but hear the note of hope in the question. The poor bastard was hurting.

"No, Ray, we're practically home free. I got Sharon here to see about that gunshot wound of yours. That old bastard got off a lucky shot, but I got him for you. Twice in the head. He ain't braggin' to nobody."

Raymond's eyes shifted to Sharon. "Hey."

Sharon, having finally gotten a grip on herself, stepped forward. Deke backed up, both to give her room and to escape the smell.

"Hey, Raymond," she said. "Let's see what's up with you." She reached out to him and delicately lifted his hand away from the wound, then lifted the Army uniform and the t-shirt beneath. Blood flowed sluggishly from a round black hole about four inches to the left of his navel.

"Hang on, Ray," she said then felt around his back for an exit wound. He squeezed his eyes shut and shrieked as she shifted him, scaring a family of blue jays whose nest was in the remains of the chimney. They exploded into the sky, scolding and screeching. Sharon gently lay Ray back down. She checked his pulse, and checked to see if he could feel her touching his leg. Deke smiled. She was a regular goddamned Florence Nightingale in action.

"I'll be right back, Ray," she whispered, but he didn't respond. She took a few steps away from the car and spoke to Deke. She tried in vain to wipe the blood from her hands with an ancient flowered bath towel that had been left in the trunk.

"I can't do anything with that, Deke," she hissed. "I'm surprised he's still living after all the blood he's lost. He needs a hospital, a doctor, and a transfusion, at least. This half-assed roadside first aid isn't going to help at all. You're killing him, doing this."

"The fuck I am!" Deke countered. "I didn't shoot him. I dragged his ass out of the bank! I saved him. I didn't have to, but I brought him."

"It was a stupid idea, Deke. Not your bringing Ray out of the bank. You did that to keep him from telling the cops your plan. No, I'm talking about the whole ridiculous bank robbery business. How did such a stupid idea get into your thick head?"

Deke's free hand whipped up and out in a blur, backhanding her with a loud smack. She spun and landed hard on her hands and knees in the dust, his handprint already standing out in red on her cheek.

He looked up and saw Earl staring, slack-jawed, at the two of them. "Get your fat ass back in the car, you worthless, mouth-breathin' sack of shit. The next time you start cryin' or pukin' over something, I'm gonna knock a few of your teeth down your throat. It's about time for you to cowboy up and stop actin' like a fag." Earl moved back to the passenger side of the car and got in. He pulled the door shut behind him then sat perfectly still, with his eyes forward.

Deke turned and looked down at Sharon. "And you. Don't you *ever* call me stupid again. Saying that ever again would be a really stupid idea. The stupidest ever." He gestured with the pistol in his hand. "You understand me?"

She stood silently, her eyes less scared now. More than anything, she looked angry.

"Deke what I'm saying is that I can't help him. Seeing all that blood in the trunk, I don't know how his heart is still pumping at all. On top of that, the wound smells horrible. The bullet must've torn through his intestines. So he's bleeding blood out all over the place, and he's bleeding shit into his bloodstream. He's got two holes in him. The bullet went in the front and out the back, and I think it opened up his large intestine on the way. If you don't get him to a hospital right away, he's going to die."

"Oh no," Deke said. "No, you're going to make sure he stays alive all the way into Mexico, and I'll get him a doctor there."

"Deke, there's no way."

"You'd better fuckin' find a way." He leaned in, close to her face. She could smell his breath, and the Copenhagen-spit fumes from his mouth made her eyes burn. "See, that's the only reason you're here. If he dies before we get to Mexico, you won't have anything else to offer. I'll shoot you and little Miss Lucinda out on the side of the road and let the damn coyotes fight over you. So if you and Lucindarella want to live a little while longer, you've got to find a way to keep Ray alive."

"Goddamn you, Deke. There's nothing I can do!"

"Well, that's entirely up to you, bitch." He smiled and winked at her. "But I've got faith in you. After all, you know I'd shoot Lucinda first." He walked away, chuckling to himself.

Sharon cleaned Raymond's wounds as best she could and didn't say another word to Deke. They found a bottle of aspirin in the glove box so she gave Ray a couple of those, then put a bandage on both the front and back bullet holes.

"I reckon I'm gon' die," Raymond said as he looked up at her. Beads of sweat covered his face. Below that, his Adam's apple bobbed up and down jerkily, and his hands trembled.

"I sure hope not, Ray."

Deke stepped forward when she stood up. He passed three warm beers to Ray and a packet of the nasty beef jerky. From one of the grocery bags, he withdrew a wad of bills. He pulled the keys from the trunk keyhole and looked down at Ray.

"Raymond, I'm as sorry as I can be about this, but I gotta leave you in the trunk for a little while longer. If someone was to see you while we're on the road, they'd call down the law on us so fast our capture would make the six o'clock news. You understand, right?" Without waiting for a response, he closed the trunk. A muffled thump was the only noise that followed.

Sharon and he got back into the car, and he started it up.

"Well," he said, "there is one bit of good news."

"What?" Sharon asked, her voice flat and defeated, her brow furrowed.

"It's a good thing we put the money in those plastic grocery bags. Now it's not getting bled on at all!" He snickered to himself as he turned the car around and followed the wheel ruts through the weeds, steering the car out onto the main road.

Deke hadn't realized that he was heading for Mexico until he said it, but it seemed like the best bet, all things considered. San Antonio was definitely out. Cops and rangers would swarm all over that town, probably worse than in Dallas. On the other hand, they always said Mexico didn't extradite criminals back to the States so if he could get across the border he'd be home free.

He mopped his sweaty brow and pulled his damp t-shirt from the center of his chest. The day was shaping up to be a hell-hot one. He turned the radio back on and drove west into Texas hill country, seeing fewer stands of trees and more clumps of prickly pear cactus as they went. The boiling heat from the sun made the unspooling blacktop road ahead of them shimmer like water in the ever-unreachable distance. Far off on the left, he saw a few turkey buzzards circling high in the sky, drawn by the smell of something dead or dying.

20

Lucinda dozed, lulled to sleep by post-traumatic exhaustion and the steady drone of the car's engine. The radio evangelist's hectoring voice had long ago receded into disjointed, nonsensical syllables that even in incomprehensibility still sounded threatening.

She opened her eyes. With her head on Mommy's lap, she looked up and saw that Mommy was asleep. Mommy's chin rested on her chest, and her hair was shiny in the bright sunlight. Lucinda held Betty tight in her arms, cozy-warm and safe. She looked at the hole ripped in the seatback, and wondered about Deke's friend Raymond. She'd understood what she'd overheard between Deke and Mommy, and she knew Raymond was hurt really badly. She'd even peeked through the upholstery hole when they'd had the trunk open, but she'd only been able to see lots of dark blood in the trunk, and the struggling movement of a body lying across the recessed spare tire.

Lucinda's thoughts were confused. Yes, Deke was a bad guy. He took money from a bank, he killed a policeman and some other man, and he was mean to Mommy. Earl, up front beside Deke, was different. Was he a bad guy too? She didn't think he was a good guy, because he didn't do anything to try to stop the bad stuff from happening. He was involved with Deke's bank robbery, but he seemed very sad about it. It looked like all the killing and blood upset him, too. Maybe he

121

was going to be a bad guy, but then he realized that being one meant he had to do all kinds of ugly, nasty stuff like the bad guys on TV. Maybe Earl was never going to be a bad guy, but he wasn't strong enough to avoid getting dragged into Deke's snaky meanness. Deke *liked* to do bad guy stuff. Lucinda could tell from the hateful-looking happiness she saw in him when he shot that policeman, and when he hit Mommy. Deke was a bad guy through and through, but the more she considered it, the more she thought that Earl wasn't a good guy or a bad guy, but only a regular guy.

The question grew in her mind until it became a fundamental value that could be assigned to everybody. Her eye was drawn to the hole in the back seat. What about Raymond? He'd been in on the bank robbery too, but he'd gotten shot by one of the good guys. Did that automatically make him a bad guy? He hadn't, as far as Lucinda knew, killed anyone. Was he a regular guy like Earl?

She saw a brief, furtive movement at the edge of the hole. A finger, tattooed with dried blood, reached out though the hole and felt blindly around the frayed edges. After a moment's exploration, it retreated back into the darkness.

Without saying anything, Lucinda reached up and shook Mommy's thigh. It flopped loosely back and forth. Lucinda shook it harder, but Mommy wasn't waking up.

The finger returned to the hole, picking and obscene. It felt around quickly, frantically questing. It disappeared into the hole again. A moment later, a bloodshot eye rose from the blackness and peered out the hole.

"Mommy!" Lucinda called. She looked up at Mommy, and with a gasp of realization, she saw what had happened to Mommy.

Mommy wasn't sleeping. Her eyes were open and glassy. Between and above her eyes was a small red and black bullet hole.

"Mommy!" Lucinda shrieked.

The eye looking through the hole in the upholstery swiveled down in Lucinda's direction, where she still lay on the seat. A voice rose on the other side of the seatback.

"Oh, there you are!" it said, and laughed. It was Raymond's voice, but it sounded full of phlegm and hungry.

"Mommy!" she screamed again, and Mommy's head stayed immobile, resting on her chest, but her shiny, dead eyes rolled in Lucinda's direction.

"I couldn't do it, Cinda-girl," Mommy said, her voice a dark whisper. "Raymond died, and Deke killed me...I couldn't help Raymond..."

"No, Mommy, look! He's not dead! He's not! Look!" Lucinda pointed toward the hole in the upholstery.

From behind the seat, a half-swallowed chuckle came from Raymond. His face was pressed hard against the cloth of the seat, stretching it forward.

"I'm sorry, girlie-girl," Mommy said with a tired, resigned smile. "I couldn't help him...and now I can't help you." Mommy's dead hand rose and smoothed Lucinda's hair, and Lucinda pulled away.

"No, Mommy, no! He's alive! He's right there! Help me, Mommy! Help!"

Mommy smiled, exhaled a sigh, and closed her eyes. The red-rimmed black hole in her forehead leaked a single fat drop of blood, which rolled down her face and left a dark red trail. Mommy's hand fell, lifeless, to the seat.

Raymond's wild red eye retreated back into the darkness, to be replaced by the finger again. It bent around the edge of the hole, and another finger came through the hole and bent the other way. They pulled in opposite directions, and the hole in the upholstery stretched.

Lucinda pushed herself back from the seat and onto the floor of the car.

With a thick burring sound, the edge of the hole widened and tore. A tiny filament of dust sprouted from the tear in the old cloth as it grew longer. The fingers shifted then tore it more, until the hole went from the top of the seat to the bottom.

Raymond's bloody, shaggy head poked out of the ripped hole in the upholstery. One eye looked straight at her, and the other looked off disinterestedly. He grinned, his Adam's apple bouncing in his throat.

"I'm not a bad guy, am I?" He cackled at her screams and reached out of the hole. "Come on back here and see, little girl. We can lie back here and be good to each other...don't mind the blood, we'll be good to each other...*so* good to each other." He caught hold of her arm in a sticky, viselike grip.

"No! Mommy!" She struggled, pushing against the bench of the seat as he inexorably pulled her back into the trunk. "Mommy!"

Mommy sat, unaffected, with a sad smile on her face and her chin on her chest, a red line stretching from the bullet hole, down between her eyes, then around her nose to her mouth.

"...I can't help..." Mommy whispered, and Raymond pulled Lucinda harder. The black hole grew wider around her as she was drawn into it. Wider.

"Mommy!"

Lucinda jerked awake, her head still on Mommy's lap. Mommy slept, her head on her chest and her hair shining in the sun. The small hole in the upholstery wasn't torn open, and Raymond wasn't trying to drag her back into the darkness.

She panted, feeling the blood rush through her heart as it hammered in her chest. Her panicked breathing subsided after a few moments, and she sighed in terrified relief.

It had been a dream. She cuddled closer to Mommy, trying hard to keep from crying. She held Betty tightly in her arms, the dolly's hair whisper-tickling her neck. She looked up into Mommy's face.

Mommy's eyes rolled open and she smiled a sad smile. A black-rimmed bullet hole in her forehead wept a single drop of blood.

"I'm so sorry, Lucinda...I couldn't help..."

As Lucinda's lungs filled with air to scream, she heard the unmistakable *burring* sound of old upholstery tearing.

21

Oh, my sweet little baby, how the hell did I get us into this mess?

Sharon looked down into her lap at Lucinda's sleeping face, framed by her sweaty blonde hair. Of course the child had fallen asleep. Sleeping was one of the body's best defensive mechanisms, and if Lucinda needed anything right now, it was a little defense. Sharon ground her teeth together, frustrated by her own helplessness. Today's events were probably enough to mess with her mind forever. Sharon supposed it might help a little to let Lucinda's body shut down for a couple of hours so that her mind could try to make sense of what had happened.

She saw Lucinda's tiny involuntary sleep jerks and watched as her daughter's eyes rolled from side to side under their lids. Lucinda's brow furrowed, and the corners of her mouth suddenly turned down in a look of dismay. Sharon hoped she wasn't having a nightmare, but thought it perfectly understandable if she was.

Sharon smoothed her daughter's sweaty hair, wishing that the two of them were somewhere else. Anywhere, as long as they were together and safe. Her eyes drifted shut.

Maybe they could go back to Georgia. She could show Lucinda all the places she grew up loving in Caledonia. She remembered Sunday picnics under the pecan trees in high summer, with her mother and father and little sister. Mom laid the blanket out on the ground, unpacking the potato salad, the sliced tomatoes, and the cold fried chicken she'd made the night before. The iced tea she'd poured from the gigantic Mason jar was always so cold, even long after the ice had melted. Dad had always brought out the Frisbee and they'd toss it around in a rough square, from Dad to her, from her to Mom, from Mom to Pearl, and then from Pearl back to Dad. Pearl wasn't very good at it since she was so much smaller, so Mom was always careful to throw gently, and Dad always ended up spending more time running after Pearl's wild tosses than actually throwing the disc. He didn't mind; he ran and laughed at the same time.

The field where they'd usually had their family picnics was right next to a set of railroad tracks and on the verge of the tracks a weedy blackberry bramble grew. Mom always warned them not to go after blackberries without her or Dad because a train might come, or there might be a snake curled up under the bramble.

They'd never listened, of course. They were children, and as such, they were about as obedient as cats. Sharon remembered looking back for her parents once when she and Pearl had gone for blackberries. She'd seen Mom and Dad smiling at each other and kissing as though they were the only two people on earth.

Thankfully, no snake ever menaced them at the picnic spot, and they'd never seen a train on those tracks either, though Dad confided to her once that a freight train came through every night on its lonely way up to Atlanta.

Those were good days in a good place. Sharon wondered if that field was still there, or if something had eventually gotten built there.

So many things had changed. Dad now lived in The Piedmont, a place advertised in its pamphlets as a "secluded spot for extended reflection and meditation," but was in actual fact a "low security mental observation facility." At Dad's advanced age, it boiled down to little more than a nursing home. For years the administrators had expressed grave doubts that he'd ever be capable of reintegrating into society. Sharon didn't care. The state took care of the expenses so other than Dad's absence, it never affected her. She missed him, but she was terrified of him.

Mom had more or less worked herself to death after Dad had gotten taken away. She'd been forced to go back to work after several years of being a homemaker, and as a result had had to take what menial jobs she could find. That had been hard on her and Sharon, but the worst parts had been those times when Mom got caught in the snare of her own memories. She'd sit down on the sofa in the living room and stare off into space. Sharon thought she must've been watching and rewatching every scene she could remember from the movie that was Pearl's short life.

Pearl had gotten killed when she was about Lucinda's age, victim of a horrible accident which had probably been the key event that had driven Dad out of his mind and Mom to her early grave. Sharon supposed that if she wanted to turn the self-pity card, it might also indirectly account for all the screwed up relationship choices she'd made in her life.

She opened her eyes and looked up at the back of Deke's neck, at the sweat running in rivulets out of his hair into the stolen tan Army t-shirt he wore. He seemed to be humming along with some toneless gospel hymn on the radio.

She sighed and looked back down at Lucinda. Her beautiful baby girl still slept. In so many ways Lucinda was a mirror of the sister Sharon lost so long ago.

Sharon still remembered it like it had happened only yesterday.

* * *

It was the first weekend of April in 1984, and the first sunny day after three days of rain. The air was warm and humid. Sharon was eleven and was in the backyard shooting cans with a pump BB gun she'd gotten at a yard sale. Mom was out shopping for new clothes for the family, in order to make a good impression in church tomorrow, which was Easter Sunday.

Mom had always fought a losing battle for "reverence before the Lord" with Dad. She'd been raised Baptist, and he'd come from a Catholic home, but when he'd seen firsthand the night and day differences between the two denominations, he'd become disillusioned with the whole thing. Both called themselves Christian, but beyond that, any similarity between the two modes of faith was completely accidental. He'd told Mom soon after that he'd decided to give up religion for Lent. She'd not found it very funny.

Mom generally didn't argue about it much, but she did put her foot down when it came to Christmas and Easter Sunday. They always attended church for those two events, and Dad behaved himself. He usually made whispered side comments to Sharon and made silly faces at Pearl. Sometimes Sharon had to grab her own thigh and pinch really hard to keep from laughing out loud.

Mom had gone to the shopping center to try to find something to make them look respectable. Dad had poked a little fun at that when she was on her way out, asking her if Jesus was going to wear a new seersucker suit for Easter, too. She'd told him to watch his blasphemous mouth, but she'd smiled a little when she'd said it.

Since Mom pulled out of the driveway, Dad had been in the workshop that had once been their garage. He'd told the girls that he was making them something, and that they should occupy themselves for about an hour while he finished it up. Sharon found out much later that he'd been making them matching pairs of stilts.

Pearl was out front, playing under the gigantic fir tree with a pair of Barbie dolls.

The fir tree dominated the entire front yard, a huge green gnome's hat with its lowest branches spreading twenty feet across the ground and the top of the tree high above and tilting off to one side. They'd put a silver garland and a long string of lights on it during Christmastime, but with the top of the tree bent off at an angle, a star on the top had been impossible. Dad said it had probably been forked into two treetops when it was much smaller, but one half of it had been pruned back in order to make it look nicer. It actually looked lopsided, but it gave their yard such character that Dad had never considered removing it.

The last time Sharon had walked around the house to check on Pearl, her sister hadn't even noticed her. She was thoroughly engrossed in her imagination. She stood near the trunk of the tree, and her dolls, a boy and a girl, were acrobatically dancing from one low-slung branch to another while Pearl sang the little song Dad always sang to them at night.

It wasn't a whole song, only a chorus, and it had lullaby lyrics but an upbeat rhythm. "Little sister don't you cry, Doo be doo be doo be doo, Ev'rything'll be all right, Doo be doo be doo be doo..." Dad said it was an Elvis song from a long time ago, and he had sung them to sleep with it since Pearl had been born.

Sharon had a secret, though. She'd heard the song on the radio, and the real words didn't match what Dad sang.

Sharon returned to the backyard and her makeshift shooting gallery. She'd tied kite strings to a few Coke cans and attached the other ends of the strings to a branch of the magnolia tree in the backyard. The cans hung down right about eye level for Sharon, and the shed where Dad kept the lawnmower and the bicycles served as a good backstop. Sharon had been instructed by Dad to never shoot at anything alive, and to never pump it more than ten times. She was willing to abide by the safety rules, and knew if she hadn't been, Dad would've taken the rifle away, but she still wondered how much of a difference a couple of extra pumps would make. She told herself she'd get Dad to let her try it once she was a better shot.

She pumped the lever under the barrel a few times, lined up the sights, held her breath, and pulled the trigger. With a musical *plink!* one of the cans went spinning, a red, white, and silver blur bobbing back and forth at the end of its string.

"Nice shootin', Annie Oakley," Dad spoke from behind her. "Before long you'll have the rifle pointing back over your shoulder and you'll be aiming through a mirror."

She snickered. "No time soon, though."

He came closer, his eyes full of unspent mischief. "Well, maybe not right away, kiddo, but you're doing good. I watched you hit three out of five just now, which is pretty good when you're using a toy gun."

He was about to say something else when a huge sort of *crump CRUMP!* sounded from the front of the house. When she looked, Sharon saw the lopsided top of the fir tree over the roof peak, swinging back and forth like a giant green metronome.

"Oh shit," Dad said, the color draining from his face. He ran around the house. Sharon dropped the BB gun in the dirt and followed. When she reached the corner of the house by the driveway, her ears were assaulted by Dad's raw-throated cry of anguish.

Mr. Wilcox, the postman, was staggering out of his truck, his forehead bleeding. His pith helmet was knocked to the back of his head, the front of its brim crushed. The windshield of the white mail truck was spiderwebbed with silvery-green cracks where his forehead had hit it. He wiped the blood from his eyes and looked dazedly at Dad, who was screaming at him.

"Mr. Tibbedeau..." the mailman began, but got no further. Dad grabbed him by the uniform shirt and practically threw him back into the mail truck.

"Back this thing up, you dumb sonofabitch!" he barked to the mailman then he spoke to Pearl, pleading. "Hang on, Pearl! Hang on, honey!" He turned back to Mr. Wilcox. "Back it up, back it up, don't you know you're parked on my daughter! Move, goddammit!"

Mr. Wilcox finally realized what Dad was saying and restarted the stalled out vehicle. He ground the gears of the mail truck until he found reverse. The truck rolled backwards onto the driveway, and Dad dove into the broken boughs of the tree, his voice frantic and terrified.

Sharon didn't see Pearl until Dad backed out from under the branches on his knees, his tears pouring onto her broken body. He cradled her in his arms, weeping and roaring. Pearl's dirty knees dangled over one of his arms, her sandals swinging with his every movement. Her pale blonde hair, littered with green sprigs of fir, fluttered over his other arm. Between his arms, her body bent in a limp, grotesque curve. There was a small butterfly-shaped spot of blood between her collapsed shoulder blades.

"Sharon! Go inside and call for an ambulance! Go!"

Sharon sprinted into the house and called, yelling into the phone, and the ambulance came within minutes.

By the time it arrived, Pearl was already dead. They had no chance to resuscitate her. Her heart had stopped, punctured by thin shards of little girl rib bones. The technicians loaded her onto a stretcher, and Dad went back under the boughs of the tree for a moment and retrieved the pieces of the dolls Pearl had been playing with. They, too, had been broken by the impact of the truck, their plastic arms and legs popped loose from their plastic shoulders and hips. Dad held the pieces for a moment then put them on the trunk of the car. Sharon never remembered seeing them again.

Pearl had been crushed against the trunk of the tree by the mail truck, completely hidden from Mr. Wilcox by the heavy fir branches. The mailman stood beside the driveway tearfully explaining that he'd been distracted by a yellow jacket that had flown into the mail truck. He was very allergic and didn't have his bee sting kit with him. He was trying to shoo the insect out with a K-Mart sale circular, and he lost control of the puttering little truck. If Pearl hadn't been there, the whole episode could even have been funny. Dad didn't respond to him, and his explanations dried up.

Sharon returned to her father's side while the paramedics put Pearl into the back of the ambulance. The stretcher seemed much too big for her tiny body. Mr. Wilcox simply stood in the grass, ashen and horrified, while the blood dried on his seamed face. The paramedics looked him over and dismissed his injuries as minor. They dampened a gauze pad with peroxide, handed it to him, and pointedly ignored him after that. He didn't speak, and the gauze fell to the ground. His light-blue uniform shirt grew dark sweat rings around his collar and armpits. His pith helmet with its crushed rim sat far back on his head in a way that would've been comical if not for the look of abject misery on his face. The mail truck stood crookedly on the asphalt driveway, its appointed rounds forgotten.

"I'm so sorry," Mr. Wilcox said in a strangled whisper to everyone and no one. Still, he received no answer from Dad, Sharon, or the emergency people.

Mom arrived before the ambulance pulled away. She didn't say anything but ran straight to Dad. He took her in his arms, held her tightly, and whispered into her ear. She shrieked as she crumpled in his grasp and he took an awkward step forward to hold her steady.

The next few days that passed were an odd sort of contained emptiness, where Mom and Dad were islands of still mourning in a chaotic, screaming sea. Sharon could tell that they wanted to comfort each other, but they had no comfort to give. The well was dry, and with all the agony they suffered, their hearts had no solace to give. Mr. Wilcox was not charged with any crime. Pearl's death was, simply and terribly, a tragic accident.

The funeral passed in a blur of uncomfortable black clothes and tears, with a small swarm of well-meaning people continually buzzing among Sharon's parents. Mostly other neighborhood families and distant relatives whose hugs and platitudes often fell monstrously short of sincerity. At times, beneath the, "Oh, sweetheart, she's in a better place now," Sharon thought she heard a hideous under-echo of "Thank God it wasn't *my* daughter."

The days passed with a horrible, tortured slowness, and Mom and Dad were gradually pulled apart by the silent floods of their private grief. Some of the strained conversations they shared ended with an exchange of hateful blame-throwing and recriminations that both knew were untrue. As disturbing as it continually seemed, accidents happened.

Mr. Wilcox, the mailman, took his own life a few days after Pearl was buried. His wife found him in the bathtub, long razor cuts tracing the insides of his forearms. Though the law forgave him, the question of whether he could forgive himself was another matter entirely. Sharon was unaffected by the mailman's death, almost as if it had happened to a complete stranger. A new mailman came to their neighborhood, and she never learned his name.

Sharon was adrift in her own sad sea of loneliness, and wept herself to sleep almost every night. When she finally did sleep, she woke even more tired, her dreams haunted by the horrible metronome movement of the fir tree, ticking back and forth above the roof peak.

Mom was unable to offer any comfort to Sharon. She, too, seemed lost in her own dark hell.

Dad took to his shop. The door from the laundry room into the garage was always locked tightly, and although Sharon was curious, she was never allowed in. He went to work before daylight, a Tupperware lunchbox under his arm then he returned home around dusk. He went straight to the mausoleum-silent dinner table that Mom dutifully stocked and set, then out to the shop. Some of the time he came home from work with nothing more than the lunchbox, but on other nights he came home with unidentified bags and packages that went directly into the shop.

He never sang to Sharon any more at bedtime. It was a little thing, maybe, but it meant a lot to her.

It wasn't until after they took him to the hospital that Sharon had been allowed to enter the shop. She'd found doll heads and plastic parts hanging from the rafters, hundreds of "Daddy loves you" notes scribbled all over the walls, and stacks of spiral notebooks. The notebooks were all numbered, and stacked on the drafting table. They were filled with indecipherable rubbish, the ravings of someone who'd fallen too deep down the well of his own mind to ever come out.

In the shop, she found herself surrounded by long eyelashes on eyes that rolled closed when the doll's head tipped back, fat-dimpled knees on legs, and little rounded doll torsos with gaping sockets for doll arms and doll legs.

* * *

Sharon was jerked from her dreaming remembrance as she felt the car slowing.

It was strange to finally remember that the "Little Sister" song she whispered to Lucinda at night had originated with her father. She was sad that she'd blocked it out for so long.

Ahead of them, silhouetted by the late afternoon sun, a blue roadside sign welcomed them to San Angelo, Texas, home of Fort Concho.

22

No way to make the goddamned border today.

As much as it pained him to have to do it, Deke knew it only made good sense to stop. Get a room in one of these little shithole motels, get Raymond out of the trunk and into an actual bed, and get some rest. If the mileage signs were to be believed, he should be able to make it to the Mexican border pretty easily if he drove south tomorrow. Del Rio, down on the border, was about the same distance from San Angelo as Killeen had been, so a day's drive would see them deep into Mexico and beyond the reach of the Texas police. Deke wondered what would be on the TV news tonight about this morning's heist, and if he'd been identified yet.

He slowed as he steered the car into town. Ahead, the Heart O' Texas Motel beckoned, a pink neon VACANCY light buzzing at the bottom of the sign. The sign also advertised that all rooms were air conditioned and offered free HBO. The fact that air conditioning was considered such a bonus implied that the place had precious little else to offer, which was exactly the way Deke wanted it. Nice, quiet, and anonymous, and the lack of niceness wasn't a deal breaker. The motel was the best Deke was likely to find, and they could request a room in the back, away from the road. As he slowed the car, he heard Sharon and her kid shifting around in the backseat, and Earl snorted as he, too, came awake.

He thumped Earl in the shoulder. "Wake up, fatass. You gotta watch the kid while I take Sharon in yonder to get a room for the night.

"Oh no, hell, he won't!" Sharon piped up, and Deke dearly wanted to punch her teeth in. When was she gonna fucking realize that she wasn't making the goddamned rules? Jesus fuck! She wanted him to get caught; hell, she was probably trying to figure out a way to sabotage him.

"Yes, hell, he will. He'll do it to make sure you keep your fuckin' trap shut. I'm going in there to get a room, and I'm not leaving you out here with Earl. You'll get to talking, and you'll flutter your eyelashes at him, and next thing I know you'll have every goddamned cop in the state grind me into hamburger. Fuck a buncha' that! You're comin' in with me, and you're not gonna open your goddamned mouth even once unless I give you the go-ahead. Come on."

They got out of the car, looking as rumpled and used as any road-weary travelers. Sharon wore the shorts and tank top in which she'd started the day, and Deke still wore the soldier's stolen uniform pants and t-shirt. He balled his fists and stretched his arms up until the little bones at the base of his spine creaked.

They went across the pavement to the tiny lobby of the motel, Deke watching Sharon as they walked. From the defeated look on her face, he figured some of the previous sullenness had finally drained out of her. He wasn't sure whether to be relieved or suspicious. Either the silly bitch was finally seeing reason, or she was saving her energy for some other jackassed plan. Either way, she'd better mind her Ps and Qs or he'd kick a mudhole in her ass. The visual almost made Deke grin, despite the goddamned headache.

Behind them, Earl sat in the passenger seat of the Nova, his eyes glassy and dead. Now *that* motherfucker was cowed. Deke was pretty certain that Earl would do whatever Deke said in an effort to stay alive and in Deke's good graces. On the other hand, Deke didn't see Earl surviving too far past the Rio Grande. It was a tough old world after all, and he couldn't drag a bunch of dead weight around with him forever. And he damn sure couldn't turn Earl loose. Count on him to get drunk and start bumping his gums to complete strangers about what they'd pulled off. That kind of shit was begging for trouble.

The lobby of the motel was nothing more than a glassed-in front desk and a plywood easel holding stacks of old tourist pamphlets. "See the Caverns of Sonora!", "Del Rio—A Fisherman's Paradise!", "Come to the Hill Country Cabrito Cookoff!", and "While in San Angelo, Visit Historic Fort Concho!" competed for the attention of travelers. The curled corners of the pamphlets and the sun-faded inks of the photos told the real story. Sightseeing tourists were not likely to lay their heads on Heart O' Texas Motel pillows, despite the air conditioning and free HBO in the rooms. The Heart O' Texas Motel was simply a place meant to keep you from sleeping in your car.

The Hispanic kid behind the glass had dark eyes and deep acne scars. He didn't ask any questions, but passed the registration card and a pen along the formica-topped counter under the elongated rectangle cut into the glass. Deke filled it out with completely bogus information then passed it back through the hole with a hundred dollar bill and a smile.

"We were hoping to get a little privacy," he said to the attendant with a knowing wink. "She's kind of a screamer, if you know what I mean. You got something around back, away from everybody else?"

One glance at the wall, with keys dangling from nearly every peg, suggested that everybody else wouldn't have been worried. The attendant complied with the request anyway, passing Deke a numbered chip of plastic with a heavy pair of keys on it.

"All the way 'round back, sir. Checkout time is noon, okay?"

"We'll be long gone by then. Gotta get down to Del Rio for a fishin' trip. We get down there early enough, maybe I'll be able to drop a line in the water before dinner."

He walked out of the office, Sharon following close behind.

"You repulsive son of a bitch. A screamer? Ugh, you're disgusting."

Deke grinned and said nothing as he strolled across the lot to the car. Earl was sitting as if he'd not even breathed while they were inside the Heart O' Texas lobby. In the backseat, Lucinda sat with her face against the window.

They got in, and Deke pulled the Nova around to the back of the motel, where only a few parking spaces were occupied. Tired-looking cars that had rolled too many miles through the west Texas desert sat in the lot, heat rippling off their hoods and roofs.

Deke put the car in Park and shut it off. He grabbed a six pack of beer and growled at them.

"Well, get out. Let's go on inside. I got to get some rest."

He opened the motel room and was met by a hot raft of scent, a harsh smell of bleach and mildew, riding on currents of Texas summer swelter.

They all went into the room, and Deke cranked up the air conditioner wall unit beneath the window. He flicked on lights as he walked through the room, pointing to beds without turning around. "That bed is Raymond's, and that one is mine. Earl, you're getting one of the chairs over there, putting it by the door, and not letting anyone leave the room unless I tell you to. Got it?"

He disappeared into the bathroom without waiting for a response and took a long, satisfying piss. He returned a few moments later, awkwardly buttoning the uniform trousers.

Sharon started right in on him, and Lucinda stood by her side, protectively huddling under one arm.

"Deke, do you honestly expect me an' Lucinda to sleep on the floor?"

"I don't give a good goddamn where you and her sleep." He grinned his mirthless smile again as he leered at her. "You come crawling into my bed, though, we won't be sleepin'."

"Don't you wish, you pig."

He dismissed her look of repugnance with a wave of his hand. "Come on, let's go bring Raymond in here. Get him cleaned up and into bed. You gotta start earnin' your keep, woman."

Earl chose this moment to finally speak. "I don't think that's such a great idea, Deke."

"Since when did brains become your long suit, Tubby? And who asked you, anyway?"

"I'm saying it looks like we could get caught if we try to move Ray in the daytime. It ain't crowded, but people are out there who'd see us."

Deke pulled back a corner of the heavy maroon curtains and looked outside. Sure enough, even though the Heart O' Texas Motel wasn't any competition to the big chain hotels in the area, there were cars and people enough to make him nervous about lugging a gunshot victim from a car in the parking lot into a room.

"Well, you might be right, at that." Deke then spoke to the ceiling. "Raymond, hold on for a couple more hours, boy. We'll come out and get you real soon. As soon as it's dark."

Deke turned on the television from a remote control that was bolted to the nightstand. He stacked the pillows of his bed behind him on the headboard and flipped channels until he found the headline news channel. He sat through the full report without a word, but half an hour later, when it started to repeat, he abruptly turned it off.

Surprisingly, he'd heard nothing of the bank robbery or the police shooting. All that had been reported was the usual infuriatingly regular news. Gas prices were rising, politicians were spewing crap about helping the middle class, the Middle East was still going to hell, and some angry Tennessee senator was getting a ration of shit because he finally said out loud that "we need to pave over the whole damned region."

Hell, I coulda told 'em that years ago.

He was annoyed that his morning's work didn't at least make the little tickertape thing that ran across the bottom of the screen. A bank robbery and a cop-killing might not be news in New York City or Los Angeles, but in rural Texas? It had to get some play, didn't it?

Deke sighed, disgusted. He thought for sure that they'd have had at least a quick sound bite about the brazen bank robbery that had taken place, even if it wasn't a feature story complete with artists' sketches or blurry photo stills from security cameras. It'd make a good news day, though, showing the story of the Killeen man who'd gone berserk and left only dead bodies, sadness, and a cleaned out bank in his wake.

He turned on the television once more and changed the channel, hoping for better luck on the local evening news. Again he sat through an interminable report on how the storm coming up from the Gulf of Mexico wouldn't solve the local drought, a quick, bitchy editorial complaint about foreign oil prices, and one completely dumbass "triumph of the spirit" story of a local boy who collected bottles and cans from the shoulder of the highway every morning and every night in order to pay for the feed and stabling of his horse.

Not a single whisper of Deke's outlawry crossed the airwaves. He thought about this for a moment, and then the truth dawned on him.

They're keeping it quiet, a voice spoke in his head. *They want you to feel cool and safe so they can pounce on you when you least expect it...they're coming for you, Deke, and no mistake about it...don't worry about the news, what the fuck do they ever know?...they might be on your ass even now, and they didn't give the information to the media so that they don't tip you off that they're closing in...Fucking hurry up, Deke, and get your ass across the border, where you really can be safe, and let this crazy shit storm blow over.*

DEV JARRETT

A profound mental itch suddenly begged for a good scratching, but Deke's intellectual muscles had no ability to reach it. He had a glimmer of an idea of what he needed to do to control what was going on, but he couldn't quite grasp it. He sat with his eyes closed, reaching out with his mind. He almost had it...he could get away with it if...

But no. His headache closed in again, throbbing like a bad tooth. Deke groaned, pressing the heels of his hands into his eyes.

A whisper of that same voice echoed from the back of his mind.

They're all against you, Deke.

He pressed the button to turn the television off, stood, and went to the window. In the parking lot, a family was getting into their pale gray station wagon, likely going to dinner. They drove away, leaving the parking lot quiet. The orange parking lot lamps were on, and beyond them the western sky was the plum color of fresh bruises. In the east, a few faint stars glittered.

"There ain't no more sense in waitin'. It's dark. Ain't nobody out there to see nothin'. Let's bring in Raymond."

142

23

This was precisely what Sharon had been dreading. She'd been amazed that Raymond had still been alive earlier when they'd checked on him. He'd needed a hospital, but dumbass Deke seemed to think Ray could get some rest and then walk it off in a day or two. Because he was usually on the giving end of it, Deke knew nothing of suffering or real pain. He'd consistently been the type of guy who, when watching a football game on television, would scream, "Get up, you goddamned baby!" at the player who'd nearly gotten his head ripped off. He was all about television-toughness and cowboy-ammunition, where the guns never run out of bullets and misfires only occurred when the hero had a gun pointing in his face.

She went with Deke to the car while Earl kept an eye on Lucinda. She hoped and prayed that Lucinda would find some means of escape. As for herself, Sharon didn't think Deke would keep her around for long after they opened the trunk.

She fully expected Raymond to be dead, but when Deke popped open the trunk, what they saw went so far beyond expectations that it was sickening.

Not only had Ray died from the gunshot wound, but in the stifling heat of the Nova's trunk, he'd begun to cook. His skinny frame looked swollen and rubbery, but the swelling collapsed like a sinkhole around the gunshot wound in his midsection. His mouth hung open and his eyes were rolled back, showing only the whites. His drying blood on nearly every surface of the trunk was a shiny, thick, half-congealed syrup.

"Yeah, you're awesome, Deke," Sharon muttered. "Such a good friend."

The high smell of blood, shit, and spoiling meat hit her like a sledgehammer, knotting her stomach and making her eyes water. As soon as Deke was sure that Raymond was dead, he slammed the trunk shut, grabbed Sharon by the upper arm, and dragged her back to the rented room.

"God damn God damn God damn!"

He slung her into the room. Before she was able to get her feet under her, she was flying across one of the beds. Her head hit the front edge of the nightstand anchored to the wall between the two beds, and knocked the phone receiver off the hook, and the little round tin of tobacco onto the carpet. A wave of blackness washed over Sharon and only receded when she realized she heard Lucinda screaming.

"Shut the hell up before I knock you through the wall!" Deke's voice growled at Lucinda, which changed the sound of her voice from the upper octaves of fear to the strident registers of terror.

Sharon staggered to her feet and faced Deke. "Don't you fucking touch her, asshole." Hot stars of pain throbbed in her head where she'd struck the nightstand, and warm wet blood flowed down her face. She tasted salt as one rill of it found the corner of her mouth. "Come here, Lucinda. He won't hurt you. I've got you, baby girl."

Lucinda rushed to Sharon, hugging her mother's legs and further unbalancing her already shaky equilibrium. "Mommy! Your head! It's bleeding."

Sharon began to feel her actual pulse thumping in her forehead, and as she moved through the room to the bathroom basin, her view of her surroundings seemed to trail slightly out of sync with her movements.

"It's okay, baby, just a little cut," she said, unsure if she was truly downplaying her injury to Lucinda, or if she was trying to convince herself. She lurched to the bathroom counter as behind her Deke started ranting about how everyone was against him and how they were all out to get him. He screamed and threw everything he could find that wasn't bolted down; he'd gone completely nuts. Sharon looked into the mirror and saw a deep, bloody gash in her forehead.

Despite what she knew of head wounds bleeding more freely than wounds elsewhere, Sharon could tell the cut was bad. It was deep, and at least two inches long, about an inch above her left eyebrow.

Lucinda stayed as close as she possibly could without getting in the way of Sharon's ministrations, watching wide-eyed as Sharon soaked a washcloth with warm water and pressed it painfully to her head. One of Lucinda's hands stayed in contact with Sharon, while the other held her Betty dolly by one arm. Sharon wet the washcloth again and wiped the blood from her skin, then replaced it on the cut. She looked into her own eyes in the mirror. The pupils seemed to dilate properly, and she hoped that meant she didn't have a concussion.

Concussion or not, it hurt like hell, and she thought she'd chipped a tooth as well.

She gingerly lifted the washcloth and inspected the cut more closely. Reflexively, she raised her eyebrow, but she immediately regretted it. The bleeding began again, and a hot lance of pain shot through her head and down into her neck. She figured she probably needed about a dozen stitches, but she was absolutely sure she wouldn't be getting them.

She doubted she'd need to worry about the unsightly scarring. If Deke had his way, she and Lucinda probably didn't have much longer to live.

Deke was finally running out of wind, and everything in his reach had already been thrown. He looked at her, foamy saliva flecks hanging from his bared teeth like he was some huge rabid gorilla. His eyes were red with anger and strain, and his growling voice sounded even more hoarse than usual.

Earl still sat in the chair by the door. He'd not moved a muscle since they'd reentered the room. He wasn't relaxed in his stillness, he was fucking petrified. He looked like he was afraid to even blink. His mouth was pursed into a strange pucker, and Sharon saw the horror in his expression. He must be horrified by what he'd done and seen, by what he'd been through in the past fifteen hours, and by his vision of what he'd become. He was misery personified, and he had no means of escape.

Deke's raving had disintegrated into something tired, overwrought, and assuredly insane. It looked like he was talking to the television with unshed tears standing in his eyes.

"You don't goddamned keep Raymond alive, and you don't fucking let anything happen the way it should. Nothing can ever be easy, and go the right goddamned way! That useless fat bastard over there fuckin' sits on his ass and grows bigger man titties, and the dumb bitch and her dumb fuckin' kid keep fuckin' wearin' me down!"

Sharon looked down into Lucinda's eyes then pointed to the bed closest to the door. Lucinda crossed the room as quickly as she could. When Lucinda was clear, Sharon smiled, despite the pain in her head.

Even though she knew it would only antagonize Deke more, she couldn't help asking, "Who are you talking to, Deke?" The mildness in her voice declared her mockery of him. A quiet voice far down inside her mind cheered for her defiance, but another, more familiar, voice, closer to the surface of her mind, asked her what the fuck she thought she was doing. Sharon focused on that first voice. Even though she rarely heard that voice, the simple, pragmatic strength of it was empowering. Even though her defiance was a miniscule victory in the greater scheme of things, it was still a victory.

Deke jumped when his name was called in such a derisive tone, and he lunged for Sharon.

"You shut the fuck up, bitch!" he screamed, spit flying from his mouth. His mammoth fist looped around and probably would have smacked her into the mirror if he'd hit her squarely. Instead, his thumb hit her cheekbone a glancing blow before his fist shattered the mirror. Sharon still saw stars, though, and reality lurched drunkenly to one side.

Deke stared stupidly at his fist. It was speckled with tiny silver-backed glass shards and bleeding in several places. He inhaled with a hiss, but didn't move the bleeding fist from beneath his eyes. Cursing, he shoved Sharon away from the sink with his uninjured hand, and she barely kept her feet under her as she stumbled through the doorway toward the bathtub. Deke bent his hand to the sink basin where he ran water over the injury, and Sharon watched with a miserable joy as his thick fingers did a terrible job of drawing the mirror splinters from the back of his hand.

She found a hand towel to replace the washcloth she'd dropped. When she leaned over the tub spigot to wet the towel, the added pressure in her head threatened to overwhelm her. She stood too quickly, and she again grayed out for a numb couple of seconds. She placed the cold compress on her stinging forehead, certain that the compress itself had reopened the wound. She briefly considered trying to rip the aluminum towel rod out of the wall, then discarded the idea. He was going to kill her anyway, but she still harbored the hope that she could get Lucinda free of him before that happened.

She edged past Deke, who was still trying to pinch the tiny grains of glass from his flesh while a thousand distorted reflections of his crazed face stared up at him from the countertop and the bottom of the basin. Turning the corner into the main room, at first she didn't see Lucinda.

The girl was huddled in the corner, past the bed closest to the window, with her Betty dolly held tightly in her lap. She had one of the bed pillows, probably retrieved from the floor after Deke had thrown his little piss-fit. Sharon crossed the room and sat with her daughter, and Lucinda clutched at her in a panic, starting to cry.

"Shh, shh. It's going to be okay, baby. Little sister, don't you cry. Ev'rything'll be all right." The words were meaningless and untrue, but they came to Sharon's lips before anything else could. She'd grown so used to saying those words without any evidence to back them up that saying them had become automatic. She continued to coo to Lucinda until the child's sobs melted into hitches and hiccups, and finally disappeared altogether. Sharon looked down to see if Lucinda was asleep, but found her wide-eyed and staring into space. Sharon hoped her daughter wasn't going into shock.

After a few minutes, Deke turned from the bathroom and sat on the other bed.

"Well, what the fuck are we gonna do now?" he asked, as if picking up some inane, everyday conversation where they'd left off before being interrupted. His voice sounded almost happy, but at the same time it was strained, as if the last shreds of his sanity were being burned up to fuel this false good humor.

"What I could do—hell, *should*, probably—is take you both out into the desert and blow your fuckin' brains out," he said, maintaining a conversational tone. "The cops would probably never find you. Shit as far as I know, they're not even looking for you." He let that gruesome threat hang in the air for a moment, then continued.

"But what I'm thinking now is that I still might need you. Earl and I have got to get across the border. If the cops try to stop us, I'm going to need a little bit of insurance. They wouldn't shoot me if they might accidentally hit a little girl, would they? And Earl can use you as a shield. It's perfect."

He kept talking, rambling disjointedly, but Sharon ignored the rest of his little speech. She focused instead on the fact that she and Lucinda weren't going to be killed right now. They still might have a chance to escape. That chance was growing fainter all the time, but it was still there and better than nothing. It was a thin hope to hold onto, but it would have to do.

"Before we worry about getting any sleep tonight, though, we've got to take a little field trip. Let's all go out and get back into the car so we can take care of a little business. After that, we can pick up a little something to eat on the way back to the room, then come straight back here and get some sleep. We've got miles to cover tomorrow before we get to the border and more besides that on the other side of the line."

The false cheer drained out of his face and voice as his hate refocused. "You get what I'm saying, bitch? Get to the fuckin' car. We gotta go dump Ray somewhere. The threat from earlier still applies. You try anything stupid, and I'll put a bullet hole in your daughter's little blonde head."

They went outside and got into the car. It stank of death and corruption, and for a moment Sharon wondered when it had gotten this bad. After thinking about it, she realized that the smell was probably about the same as it had been when they'd gotten out of the car. Their noses had grown accustomed to the odor as it had grown so they had not noticed it. Now that they'd spent a few hours out of the car, their sense of smell had returned, and the air in the car was putrid. Lucinda sat beside Sharon on the backseat, holding her nose with one hand. She made her dolly beside her hold its nose with her other hand.

Up front, Earl wasn't holding his nose, but his larynx bobbed up and down in his throat as if he could be sick at any second. Deke didn't respond to the scent at all, seemingly immune to it. He played the radio and sang along with any of the hymns he recognized and followed the car's headlight beams through the small Texas town.

Finally the car began to slow. Apparently Deke had found what he'd been searching for. The car approached a bridge, the small white sign announcing that they were crossing the Concho River. At the middle of the bridge, he pulled over into the breakdown lane and turned off the lights and the engine.

They waited in the darkened car. A pickup truck passed them going the other way. After a few moments of silence, Deke opened the door and Sharon watched him get out of the car through the sudden glare of the dome light. When he closed the door, green dots swam before her eyes. He was a hulking black figure barely visible against the night sky. The dim illumination was cast by the thin radiance of a gibbous moon and a net of stars, changing blackness into a dark blue whisper. Deke walked around the front of the car and leaned over the concrete barrier of the bridge, peering down to the surface of the river. He stood there for a few moments, unmoving, then pushed off from the barrier.

He tapped on the glass of Earl's window. Earl opened the door, bringing the dome light to life again, and Deke growled at him from the outside.

"Shut that fucking door, asshole!"

Earl shifted his bulk and got out of the car, and the old Nova leveled noisily on its springs. He shut the door quickly, then walked to the back of the car with Deke. He came back and spoke to Sharon through her open window, the pitch of his haunted voice a half-step above the monotone of catatonia.

"He said for you to come on out."

Sharon looked into Lucinda's wide, apprehensive eyes.

"It'll be okay, baby. I'll be right back."

Lucinda's grip slowly loosened enough that Sharon was able to free her arm and get out of the car. She walked around the back, where Deke had already reopened the trunk and backed a few steps away. Earl stood beside him, and Sharon could see the trunk light reflected in Earl's eyes. She saw that Deke was holding his pistol, not pointing it at anyone. It looked like a toy in his huge hand. In his other hand he held an unopened beer.

Sharon read his intentions, and spoke.

"Deke," she said, "when is this crap going to end? Everything you do is only digging your hole deeper and deeper. Doing this is—"

He jumped forward, the oily tip of his nose pressing against hers.

"Don't even *think* about saying it's crazy, you stupid bitch. You do that, and you'll join his dead ass down in the river. You'd best watch what the fuck you say. Your life is barely hanging by a thread as it is." His breath stank, soured by wintergreen chewing tobacco, stale beer, bad hygiene, and madness. Sharon couldn't see the look in his eyes, but she didn't have to. If he were a cartoon, his eyes would flash the word "TILT" in bright red neon letters.

He'd lost his mind.

He gestured at the trunk of the car with the pistol. "All right, you two. Come on. Lift him out of there and throw him over. He was always a skinny little shit, shouldn't be too hard."

Sharon swallowed, and the voice inside her head spoke. It was that same voice of steel strength that cheered when she'd defied Deke earlier. Sharon let it convince her.

You can do this. It's worth it, if only to keep Lucinda safe for a little while longer. Even a few more minutes. Do it for Lucinda, and keep looking for a way out of this mess.

She moved to the side of the trunk, with Earl beside her. In the odd shadows cast by the yellow trunk light, Sharon could see the sparkle of sweat on his broad slab of forehead. The stress of this night was even starting to eat through his morose numbness.

"Get under his shoulders," she whispered. "I'll get his legs. It'll be quick, and then we can get out of here."

Raymond's body was positioned so that he was almost spooning with the spare tire. One of his arms stretched forward toward the backseat of the car. Sharon put her hands under Ray's bent knees and lifted. His body, though no longer warmed by the circulation of blood, was still warm from having been closed in the greenhouse heat of the trunk. His joints were stiff with rigor mortis, and the blood partially dried on every surface was almost like glue. Moving Raymond was difficult.

Holding her breath, Sharon yanked up and backward. With a Velcro rip, Raymond's trousers came free from the lining of the trunk. An old page of newspaper clung to the side of one tan boot. Earl had not had the same result and was still trying to wrestle Raymond's torso loose from the spare tire. He leaned back with a grunt, and a wet sound of sockets popping signaled that Raymond's spine was finally free of its curl around the tire. Earl's grunt of effort changed midstream into a whimper as the repulsive deadweight of Raymond sagged in his arms. Behind them, Deke cracked open his beer and took a long drink.

"Ready?" Sharon whispered through clenched teeth. "Okay, one... two...three!" They lifted together, and Raymond's body reacted like a side of beef. Despite the fact that he was little more than skin and bones, Ray was heavy. Sharon and Earl scuttled away from the trunk and to the edge of the bridge as quickly as they could.

Deke stood out of the way, the pistol at his side. Sharon thought that the loss of Raymond was probably affecting him more than anything else in this monumentally screwed up day. She and Earl made a final straining effort to lift Raymond's body over the edge of the cement railing, then pushed the body off and down.

A second later, they heard the flat slap of Raymond landing in the river. Sharon grasped the railing and peered down. Either a sandbar had grown in the lee of the concrete abutment, or the water level was incredibly low. Although she couldn't make out the details in the dimness, Sharon saw Ray's curled body below, unmoving. She smiled, knowing that if the body didn't get moved away from the bridge, it'd more likely be found. As she backed away from the railing, she also noticed a smear of Raymond's blood on the cement. She mentally crossed her fingers, hoping that in the light of day, the police might see the smear and investigate. If they found and identified the body, they could get a better bearing on where Deke was headed.

Deke had apparently noticed the smear of blood as well. He poured the remainder of his beer on the blood, then scrubbed it barehanded until it faded. He stood, spitting a thick brown stream of Copenhagen spit onto the pavement.

Fuck! Can't we catch even one break? she thought.

"Get back in the car. Let's go."

On the way into town, they stopped at a drive through and picked up a few burgers and drinks. They ate while Deke drove back to the motel, Lucinda barely finishing her burger before she fell asleep with her head on Sharon's lap. Sharon finished her daughter's citrus punch and continued to fruitlessly flip through possible escape plans. None of them were even remotely feasible and only added to her growing frustration.

When they got back to the motel, Sharon lifted Lucinda's sleeping form in her bloodstained arms and carried her from the car. The Betty dolly slid to the seat. Sharon took her daughter into the room and laid her on the bed previously intended for Ray. She looked at Deke.

"Ray won't be using this bed, and Earl's guarding the door. This is where Lucinda and I will sleep."

She thought he would come up with something new and hateful to say, but after a moment, he simply turned away. "The fuck should I care?"

She smiled. This small victory over Deke's earlier pronouncement of sleeping arrangements was so petty it was hardly worth declaring, but she secretly reveled in it. The assertiveness felt good, no matter how small a reward it afforded. That voice in her mind was quiet, but she knew it was pleased. She looked down at her daughter's face, dirtied with road grime and flakes of dried blood off a dead man.

Oh, Cinda-girl, how the fuck did I get us into this mess?

She pulled the blankets up over Lucinda's sleeping body and crept in beside her. Sharon's forehead still blazed with pain, and Deke left every light in the room on. Despite that, she was asleep almost as soon as her head struck the pillow.

24

As the hot Texas wind hisses through the spindly pine trees of the Concho Valley, the cool whiteness of the moon is distant and comfortless. To the southeast, a hurricane lands at Corpus Christi and begins a lumbering overland march northwest. The night sky over San Angelo is clear, and the wind smells like a subtle mixture of cinnamon and sand.

Inside the dim and dismal motel room, the girl Lucinda sleeps deeply, safely wrapped in her mother's arms. The girl's mother also sleeps, though her slumber is marred by hopeless dreams of sadness and loss. The other two in the room attempt to evade sleep. They succeed for only minutes then drift into their own disturbing dreams. One is tortured by dreams of guilt, and the other is menaced by nightmares of indifference.

Very different nightmares. In the end, though, all nightmares are the same.

In the old car, a soft plastic body in a dirt-streaked dress sits up and pulls the plunger of the door lock with a hollow *clunk!*

The girl Lucinda needs the dolly's help.

Inside the room, the one sitting in the chair by the door snorts as he shifts his bulk. The television is on, its volume set to a low drone. The squeak of the old car's door as it opens penetrates the room, but the occupants do not respond. They continue dozing, each in the deep, echoing canyons of REM sleep and dream.

The door handle of the room, centimeters away from the head of the one in the chair, turns with a near silent whisper of metal on metal, slowly rattling against the lock. It turns back and forth several times as the dolly attempts to open the door, to no avail. The dolly must protect the girl from the two who are, in the girl's mind, *bad guys*, but the dolly's efforts, this night, are thwarted.

The sleepers are left in silence for a moment, then another sound comes muffled through the wall of the room. It is the familiar sound of an old car door thumping solidly closed.

The noise is followed a moment later by the sound of the lock plunger being pushed down.

The dolly must wait. It lies back down on the Nova's backseat in the same position as before and listens to the melancholy song Lucinda's sleeping mind sings.

25

It had happened while Sharon had been away, spending the weekend with Aunt Claudia and Uncle Herbert.

In dimly remembered overheard conversations, Sharon found out that Mom was focused on a last-ditch effort to rekindle the embers of her love with Dad. Since Pearl's accident, he'd retreated into a strange, quiet existence, and Mom not only knew that she was losing her grip on her husband, but also that he was losing his grip on reality.

She sent Sharon out to the farm that weekend. It had always been "the farm" because it was the only farm Sharon knew. It was owned by their closest relative, Mom's sister Claudia. Aunt Claudia and Uncle Herbert's farm was down in Talbot County, where Uncle Herbert grew a mixture of corn, field peas, and summer squash on a few humble acres. They had chickens, a pair of pigs, and a milk cow as well, but no children.

Sharon used to enjoy going to the farm, with its rich smells, the chores, and the simple pleasure of listening to crickets serenading the moon after a long day. On this visit, though, all her activities were wrapped in mourning black. She couldn't truly have fun doing anything without thinking how much Pearl would have liked it, too. Still, she stuck it out. She knew with the simple wisdom of a child that Mom and Dad needed some time together, in the hopes that they might find each other again after the last few months of loneliness.

It was July, and the newest crop of field peas was in. Sharon sat with Aunt Claudia in the front parlor, shelling peas and drinking lemonade. Uncle Herbert was out on his tractor, trying to clear some ground for a neighbor. The old box fan set in the window buzzed, pushing the muggy heat around the room as Sharon and Aunt Claudia each dug a handful of peapods from the bushel bag between them, shelled the peas, then discarded the hulls into a large paper sack from the Piggly Wiggly.

The purple-hulled peas were dry and dusty on the outside, and after they'd shelled the first few of them, their index fingers and thumbs were stained a purple so dark it was almost black. They'd been putting up peas all morning, and had done several batches already. First the shelling, then rinsing and sorting, then drying and bagging them in big gallon freezer bags and stacking the filled bags in the gigantic chest freezer on the back porch.

The phone rang, and Aunt Claudia laughed.

"'Bout time the good Lord sees fit to give me a break! Thank you, Jesus, for getting someone to call me." To Sharon she said, "You should take a break, too. I don't want you to get too far ahead of me."

As Aunt Claudia reached for the phone on the side table, Sharon looked down into her bowl. She compared her meager pile of peas to the nearly full bowl in Aunt Claudia's lap. Her aunt had only been pulling her leg.

"Hello?" Aunt Claudia's purple fingers held the tan telephone receiver up to her ear, and her smile vanished as the person on the other end started talking.

"What?" Aunt Claudia's entire bowl of peas fell to the cracked linoleum floor, and peas bounced across the parlor and under the furniture.

"He did *what?* Oh my Lord! For God's sake, get out of that house! Call the police! Right now! We're on our way."

She quickly hung up the phone, leaned over further, and picked up the gray microphone to the CB radio.

"Herbert, this is Claudia. Come in, over."

Sharon heard the click of Uncle Herbert keying his microphone, followed by the growl of the tractor in the background. "Hey, girl, how you doin', over."

"Herbert, come on back in. We gotta get back into town right now, over."

Perhaps he heard the unusual tension in her voice over the radio. Perhaps he was nearly finished for the day with the ground clearing. Either way, he didn't ask any questions. He said, "On m' way, sugar. Out."

Aunt Claudia put the CB mike down on the table then looked off into space for a moment. She blinked then refocused on Sharon.

"We've got to get you home, young lady." She paused for a moment as if hunting for the right words. "There's been a...well, something's happened back at your house. Let's get your stuff packed and get ourselves cleaned up while we wait for your uncle to get back." She spoke sweetly enough, but when she stood and stepped away from her chair, she crushed handfuls of peas underfoot. She paid no attention to the mess but strode across the room to the hallway. Sharon knew, looking at the pulped peas on the linoleum, that something serious had gone wrong.

They scrubbed as much purple as they could from their fingers, and Sharon's pajamas and change of clothes were packed in her overnight bag by the time Uncle Herbert arrived, red-faced and sweating. Aunt Claudia pulled him into their bedroom, spoke to him, then helped him change out of his work clothes. In ten minutes they were on the road back to Caledonia, a good thirty-five mile drive northwest into town.

When they arrived at Sharon's house, it was all over but the crying. The police had already come and gone, as had the man from the county coroner's office. The police had taken Sharon's dad away.

Mom wept in Aunt Claudia's arms, and Aunt Claudia whispered kindnesses to her. They all went inside. In the living room, Mom sat in the recliner, but forward, as if sitting back would distance her too much from her sister. Aunt Claudia sat cater corner from her at the end of the sofa. She leaned over the sofa's arm so that she could cradle Mom's hands in her own. Uncle Herbert sat beside his wife, silent but present. Sharon sat on the other end of the sofa, smothered by her anticipation of what Mom would say. She also feared that Mom would shoo her away from the living room while the grownups had their conversation.

Mom, in a choked, halting voice told Aunt Claudia about her husband's behavior since Pearl's accident.

"I should've known, I suppose," she said, dabbing at her reddened nose with a wad of tissue. "John doted on that little girl. When she died, it killed him, too."

Aunt Claudia picked up Mom's hand and held it tightly. "You can't blame yourself, honey. No one can ever really know what's in another's mind. There's no way in the world you could'a known that John was so tore up by Pearl's death."

"He cut us off," Mom began again. "He went to work and came home every day like some sort of robot, and his life was nothing human. Lifeless. He never talked with us, he didn't play with Sharon, and he didn't even smile anymore. Grieving sucked him dry. When he finished his dinner in the evening, he went straight to his workshop, locked himself in, and we didn't know what he did. He never talked about it, and he never left the door unlocked. He stayed there until he came to bed, nearly always after midnight. Sometimes he didn't come to bed at all. I guess he slept in the garage those nights if he slept at all. He was tormented, and I should've helped him."

Claudia reached out to the box of tissues on the coffee table and drew a couple out. She handed them to her sister, who pressed the tissues to each eye to blot away new tears. Mom sniffled again then continued.

"I thought he might be out there drinking. I was really getting worried about him so when I called you to see if you could take Sharon for the weekend, I was hoping we'd be able to reconnect. Maybe we could start to get our lives back on track.

"We had dinner last night, and I tried so hard to draw him out, to get him to talk. It was like throwing stones down a well. One little bubble of response then he'd shut right back up. He was running on autopilot. After dinner, he did the same as always. He pushed away from the table, stood up, and went straight to the garage. He locked himself in there, and that was it. I went to the bedroom, put on the nightgown I'd bought especially for the occasion, and I sat up reading, waiting for him to come to bed.

"I waited and waited, and I tried to stay up long enough, but he didn't ever come to bed. I waited..." her voice rose into a higher register as another sob forced its way out, and she struggled to continue talking. "I waited as long as I could, but I fell asleep."

Mom stopped again, wiping her eyes and breathing deeply to try to control herself. Dread chilled Sharon despite the heat of the summer afternoon.

"I woke up this morning in bed alone, and I thought he'd fallen asleep in his shop again. I was sad because I thought I'd missed another opportunity to get him back out of the funk he's been in so I got dressed, came into the kitchen, and I made a huge breakfast for us. It was one of those times that I purposely fixed too much food, expressly so we could sit and be gluttons, reading the paper and playing Scrabble while we munched on bacon or toast, the way we used to. Those were always so nice. Sometimes we didn't finish breakfasts like that until nearly lunchtime...oh, it was disgusting to be such pigs, but it was so much fun!" her voice cracked.

Sharon noticed that the blue shadows of dusk had begun to crawl out of the corners of the room. They seemed threatening, promising that a close suffocating night was on the way. Sharon remembered Mom fixing those gluttonous breakfasts, too, where the four of them had all laughed and played together and ate like breakfast was a feast, and Mom was right. It was fun. The last time they'd had such a breakfast was before Pearl's accident, though.

"I made breakfast and brewed a pot of coffee then I listened at the laundry room door to the garage. I expected John to smell the coffee and the bacon and come on out, but he didn't come, and didn't come, and I started to get worried. The doorbell rang and nearly scared the life out of me, but it was only Mr. Milliken from next door saying that he noticed that the headlights of the car were on. That was odd so I went out, got into the car, and turned them off. John's keys were in the ignition so I brought them in.

"I really didn't know what to think about that. There was no way that John had left the lights on from yesterday. The battery would've already gone flat by then, and besides, it'd still been daylight when he'd gotten home. No reason for him to have even used the lights. I went back inside and poured a fresh cup of coffee, still listening for any sound from the workshop."

Uncle Herbert stood. He went around the living room, the dining room, and the kitchen, turning on lights in each room. Sharon was glad he was there to push back the darkness. He soon returned to Claudia's side, and Mom continued.

"When the phone rang, it was getting on about lunchtime. It was the Glenwood Memorial Cemetery where we've got the family plot. They were calling to apologize and offer their condolences for what happened. They said the police had some leads, and they'd be able to catch the sickos that did that to our daughter. Well, I didn't know what in the world he was talking about, and the grounds manager was about to explain it to me when a police officer snatched the phone from him. The policeman told me that a car was on the way to the house right now, and that we shouldn't go anywhere.

"It didn't take but a second for the car's headlights to come back to my mind; that, and John's keys left in the ignition. I went outside to the car, and I really looked at it this time. I don't know why I didn't notice it before, but the trunk wasn't all the way closed. I lifted the lid, and I saw the dirt- and red clay-smeared tarp folded open in the trunk like a sleeping pallet.

"One of the pink sandals we buried Pearl in was lying loose in the tarp.

"I screamed and damn near fell out. I ran into the house to get John, begging God for mercy. It terrified me, but I had to find out what he was doing in that garage. I went to the door and started beating on it, yelling his name over and over. He never answered.

"That's when I called you, Claudia. I didn't know what else to do.

"The police got to the house a few minutes later, and they ran straight in when they heard all the ruckus I was making. They knocked down the door into the garage, and they found John sitting on the floor by his drafting table, holding a doll. It stank to high Heaven in there, smelling sour and rotten at the same time. One of the policemen threw up his breakfast on the floor right there in the doorway.

"The doll was over three feet tall, with blonde hair and brown eyes, and wearing a white dress. It looked exactly like Pearl had looked. John sat there on the cement floor, rocking this doll back and forth, whispering lullabies to it, and crying.

"The police asked him where he'd put Pearl's remains, and he looked up at them like they were crazy. He said that Pearl was okay, that she wasn't dead no more. She was right there, and he patted the doll on the head.

"That's when they noticed all the mess on the floor. Withered up, wrinkly skin and dried out muscle, drawn off in strips. Long, dirty hair. Whole fingernails.

"One of the policemen yanked the doll away from him in horror, and John scrabbled for it, sobbing and fighting against them. Another policeman held him while the first one took the doll. He touched it, squeezed its arms and legs, then flicked open his pocketknife. John started screaming that they were going to hurt her.

"After all those long weeks of silence, I thought his ragged, desperate screaming had to be the worst thing of all.

"I was wrong, though. It wasn't.

"The policeman with the knife sliced into the rubbery plastic of the doll's mouth and tore a big hole in the face.

"Beneath the heart-shaped, rosy pink plastic face was a skull. Pearl's skull, stripped clean and all hollowed-out. Her baby teeth were gray-brown and mossy looking, and the white cotton ticking he'd stuffed into her head was sticking out of the eye holes of her skull like escaping clouds of steam."

"Oh my dear sweet Jesus," Aunt Claudia whispered, her face as pale as cheese. She looked like she was going to be sick at any moment.

"When I saw that, I really did pass out. When I woke up, I was lying right there on the couch. I think I bumped my head when I fell. One of the men from the coroner's office waited till I woke up, keeping the police from trying to get me up too quickly. They all gave their contact information and their condolences, and they took John away. For the second time, the coroner has my baby girl. It's like she died all over again."

Mom's pleading expression as she looked at Aunt Claudia broke Sharon's heart. "I'm so lost. What would make a person do such a thing? What did I do to drive him to that?"

Mom's resolve collapsed again into a storm of tears, and Aunt Claudia held her. At the far end of the couch, Sharon sat, stricken. As the enormity of what her father had done to her little sister sank in, Sharon was by turns revolted, terrified, and sickened.

More than that, though, Sharon was furious. How could he even claim to have loved Pearl if he took her apart and made her into a doll? What sort of messed up psychopath even thought that way? As much as she wanted to hate him for it, Sharon couldn't picture Dad doing such a disturbed thing. She couldn't associate it to him and couldn't hate him for it.

Sharon got up from the sofa and went into the kitchen while the grownups continued to console one another. She got herself a glass of water then looked into the darkened laundry room. The door was open, as was the far door into the garage. The mildewed smell of rot and earth was more noticeable in the kitchen, and it made swallowing the water difficult.

She put the glass down on the counter and stepped forward into the laundry room. The garage beyond was black, and she wondered if the coroner's office had cleaned up everything. Sharon suddenly saw an image of Pearl's desiccated, peeled skin coming together in patchy chunks, building itself into a Pearl-shaped husk like the cicada shells they pulled from the bark of pine trees. She wondered if it would meet her in the dark, and if it would touch her with its cold, boneless fingers. The dry, whispery skin touching her face and her hands and—

When Uncle Herbert's hand fell upon her shoulder, she screamed.

"I don't think it'd be a good idea for you to go in there, little lady."

Sharon turned to him suddenly. It seemed that the second of startlement opened the floodgates for everything else. Sharon held onto her Old Spice-scented uncle and sobbed. She cried and cried until late at night her profound sorrow finally pulled her into a shallow sleep full of horrible monsters, all named Dad.

She'd gone to live with Aunt Claudia and Uncle Herbert for the rest of the summer while Mom trudged through the forced march of police interviews, lawyer interviews, and psychologist interviews. Sharon lived at the farm, and her aunt and uncle helped her focus on the life and hope before her instead of the death and horror behind her. When summer ended, though, she had to go back to school. She had to go back home.

Sharon found that the idea of *home* had lost its meaning, and that Mom had changed into some kind of shambling zombie. She'd become a strange, unfathomable fixture of the house. She worked and worked until she practically crippled herself, and when she wasn't working, she was absent—even when she was at home. She'd disappear down her internal rabbit hole and sit and stare at the wall. All Sharon could do was wait out these episodes of emptiness and hope that Mom would return. Sharon began keeping the house straight, cleaning up inside and outside. She sometimes found Pearl's old toys, and each discovery brought hot tears to her eyes and fresh pain to her heart.

One evening Sharon forced herself to go into the workshop. She saw all the doll body parts floating in midair above the drafting table. Two of the doll heads were different and hung lower over the worktable. Sharon wondered why and looked at them more closely. Finally she remembered. They were the heads of the dolls Pearl had been playing with when the mail truck hit her. Dad had saved them. They were the last things Pearl had ever touched.

Sharon saw that the doll heads were not actually floating, but suspended on monofilament threads above the table. They all hung at precise angles, and Sharon imagined that they were tilted in such a way that whenever Dad had sat on the stool before the table, he could look up and see any reference angle he needed to see.

Her father's workshop. Her father, long gone to the hospital where they sent crazy people. The tabletops in the workshop were thick with dust. Stacks of ragged spiral notebooks sat on the drafting table. Sharon opened one and saw her father's strange writing about how love was magic and life was the product of love. The writing wandered across the pages, not guided by any lines or enclosed within any margins. Sharon closed the notebook and looked at the rest of the room. The corners were stitched with cobwebs. Mom had not cleaned out the garage after he'd left. She couldn't even approach the door.

Sharon was still confused by how she felt about her father. She thought she should despise him, hate him for what he'd done, but she couldn't. Not really. No matter what horrible thing had happened to his mind, he was still her dad.

She loved him and pitied him and still had horrible dreams that he was some kind of monster. Her hopeless feelings made her sad, but her dreams deepened her sadness to abject misery.

How could love get twisted into something so sick and terrible? Was there some fundamental flaw in her father that made him unable to cope with the loss of Pearl, or did he love her too much? Was love itself flawed, bringing with its delicious fruits of happiness? The hard black seeds of insanity?

The cement floor of the workshop still bore the errant sweep stripes of the police investigators' brooms and the coroner's dustpan. Sharon wondered how much of the leftover dust was actually dust. Some of it must surely be leftover particles of Pearl. She found herself breathing more shallowly so as not to inhale molecules of her sister.

Sharon looked up at the strange galaxy of plastic doll anatomy still hanging on its threads like some child's mobile of dismemberment. The parts all hung unmoving except for one.

A brunette doll's head slowly turned around on its thread and looked down at her. Its flat, dead eyes swiveled open almost soundlessly. The tiny pink lips, sculpted into a pout, opened. It spoke with Deke's harsh hateful voice.

"Hey, you dumb bitch! Get up already! We gotta get out of here!"

Sharon opened her eyes, and as she became aware of her surroundings, all of yesterday's pain woke in her body. Her ankle and her head were the worst. She rolled over, waking from her nighttime dream and falling into her daytime nightmare.

26

Mommy rocked the bed as she got up, pulling Lucinda from the shallow end of sleep. When Lucinda opened her eyes, she could tell that something new was wrong. Deke was pacing around the tiny room, red-eyed and fuming like a caged animal, and Earl was sitting in front of the TV with his brow furrowed and his mouth hanging open. A red banner at the bottom of the screen had white letters scrolling across. After it went past a few times, Lucinda was finally able to decipher the words. They said "Late Breaking—Unidentified Body Found in Concho River."

A man with a microphone was standing outside on a bridge talking into the camera.

"For KLST, I'm Josh Ford reporting live from South Chadbourne Street, about a mile from the front gate of Goodfellow Air Force Base. We're on a bridge over the Concho River, where this morning a group of joggers made a grisly discovery.

"The joggers, Air Force students here at the Firefighter tech school, were performing their daily Physical Training when one of them noticed a stain on the road that looked like blood. Upon investigation, they found a body down on the riverbed that appears to have been thrown from the bridge.

"Despite the fact that the body was found wearing a military uniform, none of the units here at Goodfellow have any unexplained absences. The matter is being investigated jointly by both the San Angelo Police Department and military authorities. One officer expressed his thanks to the firefighter students for being so observant, saying that tomorrow's predicted rain could have washed the body downstream where it wouldn't have been noticed until it reached the Lake Nasworthy Dam, if even then.

"As more information becomes available, we at KLST 8 News will keep you up to date. We now return you to your regularly scheduled programming." The newscaster's face disappeared and was soon replaced by a morning talk show host in the middle of a laugh.

Lucinda looked at Mommy. Her forehead was swollen and black, horribly bruised around the cut Deke had given her last night. There were even bruises beneath Mommy's eyes. Mommy's expression was strange as she watched the TV. She looked tired, hurt, and haggard, but beneath that Lucinda saw something else. Righteousness? Hope? Anger?

Lucinda got out of the bed, noticing that something personal was out of place. She looked around the room, uneasy and deep in thought, but was unable to put her finger on what was missing.

Fat Earl was in the chair by the door breathing through his mouth. She'd dreamt of him last night, and now she'd decided that he was a bad guy too, even if he wasn't crazy like Deke.

Deke was repeatedly checking his gun to make sure it was loaded all the way up. He shucked the clip thingie that held the bullets out of the gun's handle, looked at the bullets, then slid it back in. A few paces later, he did the same thing again, the same way. Mommy stood between the two beds like a deer on the road, tense and waiting to see if she needed to jump one way or the other. Mommy was pale, except for the crusted black spot surrounded by purple-gray on her forehead and the bruises under her eyes. Lucinda hoped Mommy wouldn't say anything that would make Deke angry again. Last night he'd thrown her across the room then shattered the mirror with his hand. This morning, though, he was holding a gun. It made Lucinda think he wouldn't bother with hitting Mommy with his fists this morning. It scared Lucinda badly.

Deke clicked off the television, then crossed to the window. He peeked through the slit in the curtain, then looked out the peephole of the door. Earl had his chair cocked back on two legs, and Deke shoved it farther back as he passed. He snickered as he watched Earl struggle to regain his balance. Deke was even mean to his bad guy friends.

Lucinda jumped when she realized what was missing. *Betty!*

"Mommy, have you seen my dolly?"

"Oh, baby, you fell asleep in the car, and she dropped out of your arms onto the seat when I picked you up."

"But, Mommy, I need her!"

"I know, baby, I know, but she's safe in the car." Mommy's glance wandered over to Deke. "I'm sure we're heading out there soon, and you'll be able to get her then."

Lucinda fretted, hoping Deke didn't go outside and tear up Betty for no other reason than to be mean. It was too easy to picture, and once she'd imagined it, she couldn't push the thought from her mind. She stepped toward the window to see if she could see Betty in the car.

"The fuck are you doing, you little shit? Get away from that window!"

At the sound of his voice, Lucinda yelped. She watched him as she backed up, her spluttered apologies tripping over themselves as they tumbled out of her mouth. Her eyes never left Deke's gun-holding hand. The gun, with its tiny black hole, promised thunder, fire, and death.

"Leave her alone, Deke."

"Leave her alone? Leave her alone? You're lucky I'm not leaving her ass in a ditch!"

Mommy's nostrils flared. "Yeah, we all saw the TV, and we all know how well that's working for you."

Oh, Mommy, don't! He'll get even madder! And he's carrying around that gun!

But Deke didn't make any response to her comment. Instead he stepped over to Lucinda. He grabbed her by the arm, pulled her to the bed he'd slept in last night, and forced her to sit down beside him. He looked at Mommy.

"Come here. You've got a job to do. You haven't outlived your usefulness yet. Be happy about that."

"What?"

"Ain't no way me an' Earl can go around lookin' like GI Joe anymore. You gotta go to the store for us."

"You're out of your mind."

"No, no. What I'm out of is *patience*. You're gonna do this, and you're not gonna give me any of your goddamned lip about it. Little Lucinda's gonna stay right here with me and Earl—"

No! No, Mommy, please don't leave me here! Please!

"—and the second you go out the door, the clock starts ticking. If any cops show up, the first gunshot they hear will be the one blowing Lucinda's brains all over the wall. If you're gone even a minute longer than I think you should be, that'll lead to trouble, too."

"Deke, no, don't...she's just a little girl."

"If you're gonna start fuckin' arguing with me, you're only gonna make me start hitting her before you leave. Know this: you're going. I'll give you my sizes, Fatass will give you his, and you'll go out to wherever and pick up some jeans, a t-shirt, and a pair of shoes for each of us. You need a shirt for yourself, too. Try anything cute, and I'm telling you, Lucinda will bleed for it."

"Goddamn it, Deke!" Tears sprang to Mommy's eyes. "Why do you have to be such an asshole?"

"That's the way shit is. You'd better dry up and get on the road, girl. You've only got an hour. And if you start thinking about actin' up," he put the cold, dirty muzzle of the pistol to the center of Lucinda's forehead and pressed, tattooing her skin with a faint smudge of burnt powder, "I want you to stop and think about the consequences."

They gave her their sizes, a fat wad of money from the bank robbery, and the keys to the car. Mommy knelt before Lucinda.

"You know I wouldn't leave you like this, don't you, baby girl?"

"Yes, Mommy." Tears threatened, and Lucinda's lower lip trembled.

"Can you be brave for an hour? I'll be back as quick as I can, I promise."

"Please hurry, Mommy."

"Remember what I always tell you: little sister, don't you cry," she said then she looked at Deke once more. "I'm going to the store, like you said. But if you touch a hair on that child's head, I'll kill you."

Deke grinned at her around a little knob of tobacco under his lip. "Oh, you got me trembling in the traces now, whore. Move your ass."

Mommy wiped her eyes then used the tears to wipe the powder-smudge from Lucinda's forehead. She stood then hurried from the room, closing the door behind her. Lucinda's stomach began to hurt. She heard the car start up then the tires screech as it rounded the corner of the building and headed toward the road.

Lucinda wasn't sure what to expect from Deke and Earl with Mommy gone, but nothing happened. It was as if, without Mommy there to protect her, she stopped existing. While that made her thankful, it also made her a little sad.

Deke turned on the TV again, found ESPN, and soon fell under the spell of highlight reels, while Earl stared at the stippling of the ceiling. Lucinda changed beds to get farther away from Deke, and she curled into a ball around a pillow. She watched the digits change on the clock and she cried a little, scared for Mommy and scared for herself.

She was brave, but not *that* brave.

Eventually, he eyes drifted closed and she slept.

27

Sharon drove as quickly as she could, the speedometer needle hovering beneath the posted speed limit all the way there. She could picture all too easily Deke using the butt of the pistol to tap out Lucinda's teeth, for no other reason except to relieve his boredom. Earl was still a little human, but Deke seemed to have finished his total transformation into a raving psychopath.

She parked the car, then glanced in the rearview mirror. She looked like death warmed over. She pulled her hair down across her forehead to hide the tender gash there, then got out. She yanked a red plastic cart from the chromed aluminum pen and speed walked. She found the jeans, t-shirts, and shoes for Deke and Earl then stormed to the other side of the store. She picked out a set of clothes each for Lucinda and herself then added in some underwear and shoes.

Satisfied that she'd gotten everything on the list, she began moving to the checkout at the front of the store. She slowed for a moment as she passed through the Sporting Goods section. A large glass case displayed knives of every shape and description. From huge, sheathed machetes (ostensibly for yard work, not mass murder), to tiny, polite little penknives that might only be useful for cleaning the bowl of a smoker's pipe.

Sharon considered the possibilities. If she purchased a knife, and Deke didn't notice right away, it was possible that she'd find the opportunity to use it. On the other hand, if she bought the knife and Deke did catch her, he'd kill her and Lucinda.

He's going to do that anyway, isn't he? That voice of anger told her to take whatever she could get to save Lucinda and to swallow her fear.

Still, she wavered. Even if she was able to conceal the knife somehow, hiding it until a chance to use it revealed itself, would she really be able to use it? She hated Deke and was terrified of him, but could she kill him?

If Lucinda's safety depended on it, she could. *Lucinda's safety does depend on it. Get the knife, and use it.*

As revolting and irredeemable as it made her feel in her soul, yes, she could kill Deke.

She picked out one of the smaller knives, with a brand name she didn't recognize. It didn't need to be one of those "Never needs sharpening!" knives. After all, Sharon thought grimly, she only needed it to last for one use. She certainly wouldn't get a second chance to use it. The knife was a folding type, with a black plastic handle and a three-inch blade that locked open, and she figured that she could easily hide it somewhere in the car before she returned to the motel room.

She pushed the shopping cart to the checkout.

"Jesus, lady, what happened to you?"

The kid running the cash register was staring at her. She'd noticed the furtive stares she'd gotten the entire time she was in the store, but she'd chosen to ignore them. Now, though, the question she'd seen in all those eyes had been asked. Sharon struggled to come up with a reasonable explanation.

"It's, ah, not as bad as it looks. I was in a car accident last night, and cracked my head open. I guess they could make me the poster-child for an 'Always Wear Your Seatbelt' campaign. Instead of Click it or Ticket, maybe it should be Click it or Bash Your Head into the Windshield." She tried to smile and look embarrassed at the same time.

The young man's expression looked suspicious, as if he didn't totally buy her explanation. *Think I'm trying to bullshit a bullshitter, genius?*

"Hmph. You sure you're okay?"

"Oh, yeah. I'm fine. I mostly hurt my pride and my car, so now I'm driving my neighbor's piece of junk—and that poor old thing is barely held together with Bondo and prayers."

The stern, dubious expression evaporated completely and the young man smiled as he bagged the items she'd selected. "Hey, that sounds like my car, too." They went through the ritual of exchange, and Sharon made sure she purchased the knife separately, in case Deke decided he needed to check the receipt. The young man thanked her and wished her a speedy recovery.

Sharon made her way to the exit and looked at the clock over the door. She had about twenty minutes left to get back to the room. Cutting it so close made her nervous, but she didn't dare go over the speed limit driving back. If a cop stopped her, her world would end.

Once in the car, she sorted the items in the bags. One bag for Earl, one for Deke, and one for her and Lucinda to share.

Sharon took the knife out of its plastic template packaging and secreted it in the car. She tossed the plastic out the window then opened the knife and made a small cut in the back of the front seat upholstery, near the floor. She folded the blade closed and stuck it into the hole. Lucinda's dolly was hanging off the edge of the seat. She pushed it back so that it wouldn't fall to the floor then closed the back door.

Sharon got into the driver's seat and pulled out of the mostly empty parking lot. She headed straight for the Heart O' Texas Motel, silently praying for all the stoplights to be green.

As she drove, Sharon briefly considered Lucinda's dolly. After the dreams she'd been having of her dad and his strange obsession with dolls, the one he sent to Lucinda made her feel uncomfortable all over again. Lucinda had already grown so attached, and in this situation, if Sharon were to take it away, Lucinda would be left even more adrift than she was presently.

She remembered that after her father had gone to the hospital, his break with reality became permanent. He began to send home strange constructions of plastic forks, crayons, and twists of paper, insisting that they were "dollies" for Sharon. The doctor suggested that Mom and Sharon accept them, not as toys, but as evidence that her father was reaching out to them in love. Compulsively fashioning the dollies out of whatever materials he had at hand could be a kind of emotional penance, symbolically attempting to make something beautiful from rubbish. The doctor believed at first that the penance would eventually lead him out of the twisting forest of insanity back to the straight roads and avenues of reality. Until Dad could bring himself to search for a more concrete absolution, the doctor figured he would keep sending Sharon the dolls he created.

He did, and over time he grew better and better at making them look like actual dolls, but they were never anything that Sharon could love. The dollies scared her. When new ones arrived, Sharon put them into the closet until she could dispose of them without Mom finding out.

After Mom died and Sharon was on her own, she stopped even pretending to keep the dolls. They'd go directly from the mailbox to the trash can. Even after years of knowing that Dad had fallen sick and could not be blamed for what he'd done, the very idea of keeping a doll he'd made was ghastly. The dolls themselves made her uncomfortable as well, with their creepily eager, fervid eyes and the smiles that were too broad to be real.

Through the scratched and smeared lens of time, Sharon had haltingly begun to understand her father. He'd loved Pearl, and he'd lost Pearl. After that, everything he did was simply a reflection of that loss. The love and the loss burned him from the inside out.

Betty was the first dolly he'd sent to Lucinda. Sharon didn't want to think about the significance of that. She realized uncomfortably that Lucinda was now the same age Pearl had been when she'd died.

Sharon sighed. If they survived this surreal mess with Deke, it might be time for her and Lucinda to go back to Georgia and start mending fences with Dad. She knew he loved her and that he'd loved Pearl. He'd simply forgotten how to show it.

While all the lights didn't cooperate with her prayer, Sharon still made good time getting back to the motel. She arrived and parked in the parking space directly before the room with five minutes to spare. She grabbed the bags of clothes, and, as an afterthought, opened the back of the car. She reached in and picked up the dolly, which was on the floorboard by one of Deke's discarded beer cans.

She held her breath as she approached the door, knowing that Deke had already strangled Lucinda to shut her up. Positive that he'd pressed a pillow over her face to stifle her cries. Certain that he'd throttled her and hidden the body in the box springs beneath the bed.

Earl opened the door before she knocked and stepped out of her way. Sharon saw Lucinda's dead body crumpled on the bed.

With a cry, she dropped the bags and rushed to Lucinda. She dove to her daughter's side, and the dead girl sat up, rubbing her eyes and yawning.

"Oh, Mommy, you're back."

All the air rushed out of Sharon's lungs. *My baby, my baby, my baby.* Lucinda was alive.

"Are you okay, sweetie? Did they do anything to you?"

"No. They left me alone, and I took a nap. I was brave, like you said. I missed you, though."

"Oh, Lucinda, I missed you, too, honey. You did so good! You always make Mommy so proud."

"Mommy! You brought in Betty!" Lucinda reached out for the dolly, and Sharon passed it to her. Lucinda hugged it to her cheek.

"Yeah, she was out there crying because she missed you so badly. The poor dear. I couldn't leave her out there any longer."

From behind Sharon, Deke spoke, his voice cutting between them like a backhoe cutting through tree roots.

"Yeah, yeah, yeah. How fuckin' sweet. Course we didn't do anything to her. You got back in time without screwing around. See, I'm a man of my word. You'd best keep that in mind."

"Deke, look, you've got everything you need to get away clean. You don't need me and Lucinda anymore. You and Earl can get down to Mexico before suppertime, and then you'll be free. You don't need us slowing you down. Just leave, and Lucinda and I will go in the opposite direction. We've got nothing to gain by going to the police. You're free, and we're free."

Sharon could tell that she'd pushed too hard. She'd seen the thought go out of his eyes suddenly, replaced by nothing but darkness. It was like a set of window blinds ratcheting all the way out to their limits and banging on the windowsill. She watched him absently shift the fat knob of tobacco in his lower lip.

"Shut up. You're my insurance. We went over this last night. If you act right, I might let you go after we cross the border. Now get ready to go. We got to make tracks."

Deke and Earl changed out of the stolen Army uniforms they'd been wearing. They put on new, starch-stiff jeans and shirts then pulled on the cheap sneakers from the discount store. Lucinda and Sharon went into the bathroom and changed as well, discarding everything they'd been wearing before. They bathed as much as they could in the five minutes they were given then Lucinda used the corner of a damp washcloth to wipe some of the grime from Betty's face and hands.

"Come on, now. Let's go," Deke called from the other side of the door.

They went outside and got into the Nova, and Sharon found her eyes were constantly drawn to the cut she'd made in the back of the seat. It looked so perfect, such a clean cut would never be mistaken for a tear. Surely it would eventually draw Deke's attention, or maybe he'd feel the knife through the seat like some kind of demented redneck version of *The Princess and the Pea*.

After traveling a few miles south, Sharon's paranoia faded back into the regular acidic menace her life had been for the past million years that had barely lasted twenty-six hours. The broad sky in the south was dark before them, a curdled wash of purple- gray violence that promised much more than rain.

They were headed into a storm.

28

Deke didn't know what the hell she was thinking with, but it for damn sure wasn't her brain. Let her *go*? What kind of friggin' sense would that make?

They couldn't stay with him, and he couldn't kill them yet. He still harbored the cinematic fantasy that he'd have to use them as shields while he dodged the hail of bullets from the police, the Texas Rangers, and the Border Patrol. Granted, according to the television, police had not yet pieced together yesterday's events so there was a good chance that they weren't even looking for him yet. The only related news they'd seen was the finding of Raymond's body in the low water of the river. Maybe by now the police had connected the name on Ray's uniform to the soldier at Fort Hood, which was only one step away from connecting the bank robbery and the cop-killing. Maybe they were calling out the Rangers and the FBI right this second.

Deke pictured himself crashing through barriers and making a mad dash to the Mexican side of the fence, where fellow banditos, wearing bandoliers of bullets and wide, pale sombreros, would meet him and accept him as one of their own. They'd cheer him on with toasts of tequila and cerveza and give him his choice of senoritas for the night.

Letting Sharon and Lucinda go free now would certainly screw that idea all to hell.

It went to show, that vindictive bitch would do anything to make sure he failed. Her and her snot-nosed kid. That fat bastard Earl was probably in on it, too. He acted like a goddamned zombie during the day, when Deke was watching him, but what about when Deke slept? That's when Earl was probably making his moves on Sharon, swinging his dick around and telling her he'd save her and Lucinda. Of course he'd betray Deke for a used up piece of ass like Sharon.

Deke knew, suddenly and without a doubt, that he couldn't trust anyone else. No one that was left was on his side. No one except himself. They all wanted him to fail.

Well, he'd have to show them. He'd show them all who was boss.

They drove south from San Angelo toward Del Rio. According to the road atlas in the glove box, Del Rio was half in Texas and half in Mexico, where they called it a different name. Cue-dad A-coon-ya. Whatever. It sounded like something you'd catch from forest animals. Something that would make you itch.

The big hurricane that had been all over the news this past week was causing all the overcast today. Deke hoped they'd be able to get past it before they crossed the border, but he wasn't confident that would be the case.

As every mile passed the land became more forbidding. What started as low, rolling hills with thick wildflowers had transformed into dry washes and flint gravel arroyos whose only vegetation was beavertail cactus, yellow clumps of dead or dying weeds, and thorny mesquite trees.

They traveled through San Saba then Eldorado, and the clouds looked like they were growing darker. They passed a green road sign telling them that Del Rio was only sixty more miles when the first fat, heavy raindrops landed on the windshield.

Suddenly, it was as if the clouds simply unzipped and dumped every drop of rain in the world onto the road they were traveling. Even at their highest setting, the windshield wipers were no match for the pouring rain.

Immediately following the sudden downpour, the hail started. It was loud, and Deke could imagine what the car would look like afterward, pocked, puckered, and dented all over the roof, hood, and trunk. That dumbass kid started screaming about it, scared and crying. Deke made Sharon try to shut her up, lying down in the backseat and holding her, but not even that worked. Being in the car in the midst of the hail was like being inside a giant steel drum.

When they drove under a highway overpass, Deke stopped the car and parked there until the worst of it blew over. A pickup truck going in the opposite direction had the same idea. The dark-skinned driver wore a cowboy hat, and he tipped a quick salute to Deke when he made eye contact. Deke sneered at him and looked to the sky again. He began to get antsy to get back on the road but made himself wait. He wanted to get across the border sooner rather than later, but driving in a storm like this was begging for trouble.

He turned on the radio, then spun the dial from the Gospel group grope station to the bullshitters in Washington station in the slim hopes that he'd get a weather report. Instead, the droning talk radio horseshit went on and on, the Nova's radio hissing with the spotty reception. Finally the news came on, and when he heard the report, it took all the self-control he had not to jump out of the car and dance under the thundering overpass.

Authorities had identified the body found in the Concho River this morning as one Raymond Edwin Carter, a suspect in a string of crimes in Killeen. The reporter continued, saying that Carter's partners, Earl Billings and Deacon "Deke" Satterwhite, were also being sought. Satterwhite was perceived as the probable leader of the group, and it was believed that the three escaped with a sum well over twenty thousand dollars. Carter had been fatally wounded in the bank robbery. A description of the remaining suspects followed. Listeners were cautioned against attempting to apprehend Satterwhite and Billings, as they were armed and dangerous. Instead listeners were encouraged to call Crimestoppers if they spotted either remaining suspect. In addition to the bank robbery, they were also being sought in connection to the murder of a Killeen police officer and for a home invasion of one Sharon Ingram, who, with her daughter, was currently listed as missing. It was believed that the mother and daughter were being held hostage by the two bank robbers still at large.

Once again Deke's mind soared with fantasies of some wild shootout with police as he sprinted for the Mexican border. He grinned at Earl, whose face had paled.

"Deke, we need to go," he whispered.

"Relax, Fatty. We're practically home free. You might better start bonin' up on your Es-pan-yol."

Deke's eyes found Sharon's in the rearview mirror. "Hey, how 'bout that, sugartits? You're now officially hostages."

When the hail finally blew itself out a few minutes later, the rain seemed to slack off as well. Deke pulled the car onto the road and continued south, and he soon began to see billboards inviting them to stay at this hotel or that motor lodge when they arrived at Del Rio and others that tried to convince them that they needed to buy "Mexico Insurance."

It was either related to some kind of panic response, or Earl was actually taking Deke's advice to relax, but for the first time on this trip, Earl seemed like he was actually calming down and livening up. He started bringing up stupid wetback jokes and some of the nasty sex stories he'd heard about Mexican border towns. Deke found it strange that he was acting that way, but some of the jokes were pretty funny and everyone who'd ever heard about Mexican border towns was familiar with the stories of donkey shows and underage hookers.

When they stopped in Sonora for lunch, they ordered from the car and a teenager on roller skates brought them their food.

Deke stayed buttoned-up, still trying to figure out what to do about Sharon and Lucinda. Sometimes, with Earl's unnatural and newfound relaxed attitude, he was convinced that fatass was trying to trick him. *Oh, sure, act like we're on the same team now, you fat sack of shit. What's the deal? You feeling scared because we're so close to freedom with the cops on our asses, and you want me to be your friend? Or are you finally running out of time to catch me flat-footed so that the police can stomp my ass?*

Whatever the truth, Deke wouldn't allow himself to be taken in. He snickered at the childish wetback jokes, but kept his distance. Earl could turn on him at any time, and he had to be prepared. Deke knew there was no way Earl could be left alone in the same room with Sharon. She, too, must be growing desperate. And their conspiracy already showed, didn't it?

Though the hail had not returned, the rain continued to pour steadily from a sky still heavily clouded and dark. The clouds were almost the same color as the bruises Sharon wore, even down to the greenish color at the edges. He figured more rain was coming. Heavy rain, and maybe even a tornado or two on the way as well.

The green reflectorized signs telling of shrinking mileage to Del Rio finally gave way to the much smaller blue sign that told Deke they were crossing the city limits, and his anticipation rose. *Mexico, here I come! I'm almost there!*

He pulled into a gas station to top up the tank, and he dragged Sharon into the store with him when he paid for the gas. He struck up a conversation with the attendant, asking the old guy where they should cross the border into Mexico. The attendant, a tall, leathery man with sparse white hair and eyes the washed out blue of a winter sky, tipped his ball cap back on his head. The bill of the cap had a roof-peak crease right up the middle of it.

"There ain't but one crossing spot, young fella. Right there at the Border Patrol station. If you got all your papers in order, you can drive through there any time you want."

"What all do they want you to have?"

"Well, if you're taking your car, they want you to have some Mexico Insurance and the registration and all the other shit you've always got to have with a car, and if you're going for more than a day-trip, you also gotta have passports for whoever's going over yonder. 'Course, if you ain't staying long, you can park your car on this side of the border and walk through. Still gotta have either passports or one of those day-trip passes, though."

"Passports? For Mexico?"

"Yeah. New policy. Where you been the last ten years? 'Fore 9/11, we used to go across the river for the night, get us a—" his eyes ticked over to Sharon, who was on the other side of the store at the soft drink cooler, "—a little drink and a little La-tina lovin', if you catch my meanin'. These days, though, the Border Patrol works for those Homeland Defense jokers, and they're making everyone who wants to cross get a passport or a passport card. Takes two or three months for the application to go through, and they make you pay through the damned nose for it, too. Buncha shit, if you ask me."

"Sounds like it to me, too. I guess we'll stay on this side of the river, then."

"Now, if you're still lookin' for a little taste of mescal, or maybe a tumble with a senorita, you can still find it here. Plenty of fun to be had this side of the border, too." He winked knowingly at Deke, snugged his ball cap back down on his head, and went back to restocking the Lotto scratcher tickets under the cloudy glass countertop.

Goddamnitall, one more fucking thing keeping me from getting away.

Deke sighed as they left the store and headed back to the Nova, where Earl was waiting with the same dead eyes he'd had for most of the trip. The earlier animation he'd shown seemed to have faded. Lucinda had the back window rolled down and was watching for Sharon to return to the car. He noticed, too, that there was no hail damage on the car. Seemed these old cars actually had something going for them. If Deke had been driving one of those new cars, made out of that shitty fiberglass epoxy junk, the hail would've made a pitted mess of the hood.

For a moment, he thought about making himself a wetback. Instead of leaving Mexico, though, he'd be leaving the United States. Would the Border Patrol even bother with him then? They'd probably poke each other in the ribs and say, "Hey, look at that dumbass. Illegally entering Mexico. What a fucking dipshit."

Deke drove farther into town, still considering his options. The overcast day was giving way to an early, overcast night. The clouds spun, looking like poisoned cotton candy in the sky.

He made a decision. Despite the fact that he instinctively knew the police must be right on his ass, he needed a chance to figure out his next step. He decided they needed to stop for the night. He began looking for a place to go to ground.

The border crossing, when they approached it, was unmistakable. It was a huge building with a road leading right through the middle of it. There were automatic lift gates, poles cemented into the ground to channel the traffic into two narrow lanes, and Severe Tire Damage spikes that rose out of the road surface. Huge fluorescent lights banished all the shadows and well-armed guards stood around looking bored. The long-handled mirrors for inspecting the undercarriage stood leaned against the wall. Along the far left, Deke saw the pedestrian walkway, with large bilingual signs pointing to the Customs counter. Beyond the building was the bridge which stretched over the Rio Grande. It was a lighted concrete span over a black gulf. Beyond the bridge, a similar fluorescent-lit building marked the gateway on the Mexico side.

A block away from the harshly lit border crossing station, Deke found this town's answer to The Heart O' Texas Motel. It was called Rancho Del Rio.

"We're staying here tonight," he said to them.

"But Deke," Earl began, "what about the news report? The police are looking for us. Come on, now, the border's right there."

"Earl, I told you to fuckin' relax. With all your little jokes and shit, I thought you were finally coming around, but I guess you're still a dipshit. Sit down and shut up. Keep an eye on that kid. Sharon, get your ass out the car. You're comin' with me."

He stuffed his pistol into his front pocket, and he and Sharon went into the lobby of the motel. They got an anonymous room away from the street, and Deke drove the car around the building.

Other than a half-assed wave toward fake Old West decorating, it could've been the exact same place as The Heart O' Texas. Two beds, a bathroom, a television with the remote control bolted to the nightstand, and a wall unit air conditioner squatting below the window. Somewhat interesting was the white circle on the window where a bullet had been shot into or out of the room. Even more interesting was the boot print on the outside of the door, right beside the doorknob. *Holy shit, we're actually in the wild west.*

They went inside, Deke holding the last six pack of the beer in one hand. He took the pistol from his pocket with the other so that he wouldn't accidentally shoot his own dick off. He'd heard of that happening before.

As if they were returning to a set of assigned seats, Deke went to the bed closest to the bathroom, Lucinda and Sharon went to the other bed, and Earl took the chair next to the door.

Deke clicked on the TV and found that half of the channels were in English while the other half were in Spanish. It was past time for the network news so he flipped channels until he found the headline news channel in English.

Again, nothing. He'd gotten some local radio airplay, but still no national coverage.

Soon, he told himself, soon. Like Billy the fuckin' Kid.

"Awright, here's the deal. To get across the border, we've got to have passports. All four of us. I'm going to go out and get 'em for us, and then we'll stroll across the bridge tomorrow morning like regular tourists. Only difference is that we'll have a few thousand dollars stuffed into our pants. Sharon's coming with me to get the passports, and Earl's stayin' here with the brat."

"Deke, damn it, enough! You and Earl go! We won't stop you, and we won't try to get anyone else to stop you."

In one move, Deke lunged from one bed to the other, and his fist made a meaty smack on Sharon's cheek. She flipped backwards over the edge of the bed with a muffled cry, and Lucinda's eyes grew to the size of saucers.

After a moment, Sharon lifted her head over the side of the bed. Blood was seeping from the reopened cut on her forehead and tears wet her cheeks.

"Tired of your shit," Deke said. "You keep on talking to me like your opinion means anything, but goddamn. Haven't you realized the truth yet? I'm in charge. Me. Deke. If I fuckin' tell you to stop breathin', you damn sure better do it. If you don't, I'll make you. If I tell you you're going with me tonight to get these passports, fuckin' guess what? You're goin'."

Without making any sort of response, Sharon went to the bathroom sink. She pressed a washcloth to her face, and after a moment, the bleeding stopped.

Goddamned stupid bitch thinks she can tell me who's runnin' the goddamned show...she's got another think comin'...

"I'm not staying with him again!" Lucinda suddenly screamed. She was so quiet most of the time that the vehemence in her voice was a shock. "He's fat and stupid, and you're mean!"

Deke paused for a moment then laughed at her outcry. He turned to Earl.

"How's that make you feel? I mean, it's one thing if *I* say you're a worthless fat ass piece of shit but a little kid? To think, a tiny little girl can talk shit not only about you but *to* you."

Red-faced, Earl stood still with his eyes closed, almost hyperventilating through his nose.

"God damn, Earl, are you gonna take that shit?" Deke continued to goad him. "Next thing you know your fat ass will be steppin' and fetchin' for that little brat!"

Earl trembled, his face growing darker.

"Stop it, Deke," Sharon said, still leaned over the sink.

Deke ignored her. "Why don't you go ahead and bend over and kiss her ass, Earl?"

Earl's trembling increased, and he turned toward Lucinda, whose wide eyes said that she was probably as surprised as anyone else at her outburst.

Deke snickered again. "Yeah, big tough fatass called out by a little snotnose! What are you gonna do about it, you stupid, fat bastard?"

Earl's growl finally broke free of his restraint like some under-water mythological beast breaching the surface of the ocean, and he roared. He backhanded Lucinda with one hand and pointed to Deke with the other.

"Just shut up!"

As soon as he released his anger, Earl reeled it back in, ashamed. Lucinda shrieked on the pillow, holding both hands to her face. Sharon jumped from the sink, but Deke caught her in midair by the throat and slammed her backwards into the wall.

"Don't even fucking think about it, bitch. That little shit had it coming, and so did you. You'd better calm the fuck down right now, you understand me?"

She scowled at him, and a grin split his face. "It's about time the fat boy grew a set of balls and let his animal side show a little bit." Deke released her throat and turned away from her.

Earl stood in the middle of the room, holding his face in his hands. Lucinda sat up in the bed, tears in her eyes and a red handprint rising on her cheek. She looked fearfully at Earl and held her dolly close.

"Lucinda, I'm sorry," Earl said into his hands. "I didn't mean it."

Sharon slapped his hands away. "I don't give a goddamn what you meant, asshole. You hit my daughter."

Deke grabbed her by the upper arm and shoved her toward the door before she could hit Earl again. "Yep, and I'm gonna hit her too if you don't get your ass back out to the car. Right now. Earl, give me your gun."

Sharon bowed her head with a growl as she left the room, and Earl handed over his piece.

Goddamned right, bitch, you do what you're fucking told.

29

Could she bring herself to use the knife?

Oh hell yes.

Sharon walked out of the room, Lucinda's sniffles hurting her far more than the swelling knot under her eye or any of the other abuse she'd sustained. She went out to the car.

I'm so sorry, baby, she thought toward Lucinda.

"I saw a place to check out," Deke said as he opened the driver's door. "Steakhouse or somethin'." He started the car then turned to her. "You mind your fuckin' manners, and you and Lucinda might get out of this alive. Soon as me an' Earl are on the Mexico side, I plan to turn y'all loose. Go do whatever you want. The Mexican cops won't be after me, and Earl and I can ride off into the sunset, a couple of hard-case desperadoes."

Her anger growing, Sharon snorted. "Is that what you think? You're some kind of tough guy? You trying to be some wild west gunslinger?" Listening to herself, she noticed that her voice was beginning to sound more and more like that hard voice that spoke to her inside her head. She didn't know whether that was a good thing or bad, but it felt right. "Some tough guy, beating up on women and children."

Deke didn't answer her. Sharon looked out the passenger side window as he pulled out of the motel parking lot. The orange streetlamps seemed to give less illumination than the neon tubes of honky tonks, restaurants, and bars, but everything fell under the heavy shadow cast by the buildings surrounding the border crossing. From several blocks away, she turned and looked back at the crossing station, covered in its pearly dome of light, a huge bubble of blue-white fluorescence that marked the gateway to Deke's freedom. If she were to believe what he'd said, it was also the gateway that led to her own freedom.

Deke turned the car into a parking lot that was mostly full. More neon tubing in shades of yellow and red proclaimed that they were at the West of the Border Family Steakhouse. Deke parked the car and they went inside.

West of the Border was one of those places where steel pails of roasted peanuts sat on the tables, and the patrons were encouraged to throw their peanut shells onto the floor. The rafters were all exposed, with turquoise-painted ventilation ducts stretching back and forth overhead like the veins of an old man's hand. The primary decorations were old, buckshot-riddled advertising signs, taxidermied snakes, armadillos and jackalopes, and a collection of about a thousand farm-themed baseball caps hanging from hooks all over the room. Sharon could also immediately tell that the place was only a family steakhouse until the tourists took their kids back to their hotel rooms. After that, the jukebox volume would get cranked up, the kitchen would close, and the two-stepping and line dancing would begin.

The real question was why anyone would bring their kids to a Tex-Mex border town for vacation. What were they doing, literally slumming? It's not as though Cuidad Acuna was any sort of resort destination. Sharon expected that it was like any other border town: Texas on one side of the river, and a Third World country on the other.

It was creepy to contemplate, but at least ten of the booths had families in them. Two of the booths even had high chairs set up beside them.

A pretty, young Hispanic woman with her hair pulled back in a short, thick braid approached them with a pair of menus. When she looked at Sharon, a questioning look briefly displaced the plastic friendliness of her smile. For a moment, her face took on the same puzzled expression the cashier at the Target store had worn earlier: *Jesus, lady, what happened to you?* Sharon smiled and repeated the same lame-ass story of the car accident. Deke shrugged and nodded, and a vapid flash of sympathy crossed the girl's face.

"Aw, you poor thing," she said, and then the sympathetic crease between her eyebrows disappeared and was replaced by the previous vacuous expression. She seated them at the last unoccupied booth and gave them each a slightly sticky, laminate-sheathed menu. "Can I get y'all somethin' to drink?"

Deke scowled and looked like he was ready to yell at the waitress. Instead of letting this girl fall under the guillotine blade of Deke's anger, Sharon cut in. "Could you give us a minute, please?" she said.

"Aw-right, y'all, I'll be right back for your order!" The woman smiled then hurried away, loudly greeting a regular customer as he walked in the front door.

Instead of looking at the menu, Deke started craning his neck around, probably looking for a likely family of tourists so he could steal their passports. Sharon wondered what Deke's plan was. Would he take the tourists out back and rob them? If he did that, they'd go straight to the police, and Deke would be blocked at the border. If he took them outside and pistol whipped them, they'd be found, and they'd go straight to the police when they woke up. So what did that leave?

Murder? Shoot them and hide the bodies then skip the country on their identification? As cold-blooded and horrible as that seemed, it was probably Deke's best chance for success.

The waitress came back and asked if they were ready, and the look that briefly flashed in Deke's eyes was savage. *Lucky for you Deke's already got a punching bag, Chiquita.*

If the girl noticed his expression, she didn't respond. Deke asked for a Lone Star and a steakburger for each of them, and two more burgers to go, and the girl hurried away again. She returned immediately with the beers, and Deke cracked open a peanut and munched on it while he tossed back half of his beer. He left the shell halves on the table round side up like little brown beetles.

Sharon took a sip of her beer, found it bitter, and passed it across the table. Deke finished his then picked up hers, alternating more peanuts with each swig.

The waitress brought the plates out shortly, along with a plastic bag with two Styrofoam to-go plates inside. Deke looked up at her and told her to go ahead and bring the check, too.

The food was a standard burger with fries. Sharon ate, but the worry gnawing at her gut kept her appetite to a minimum. Deke's words kept bouncing back and forth in her head. *I plan to turn y'all loose...* Could she trust that? Was there any way, really, that Deke could let them go? She doubted it, and that voice in her head was yelling at her again, telling her to step up and assert herself, telling her to *make* things happen instead of *letting* them happen to her and to Lucinda.

After a moment, Deke leaned over the table. "The couple over there with the grown son and the younger daughter. That's the ones."

"Deke, they don't look anything like us."

His eyes flashed at her. She knew he wanted to hit her again. Apparently, he'd grown used to beating her up already. "You got a better idea, bitch?"

Sharon rolled her eyes. No matter what she said, Deke had already made his decision. He would get the passports from them, and if they resisted, they'd get killed. Deke had killed before and clearly felt no remorse about it. If anything, Sharon thought it made him feel more powerful.

He'd kill again with no problem.

He'd kill again and he'd *like* it.

Her inner voice suddenly overrode her common sense again, if only to save some stranger from what would most likely be a violent death.

"I'll do it," she said.

"How?"

"I don't know. I'll figure something out."

"Don't start cuttin' up now," Deke warned. "You're so close to getting out of this with your heart still beatin'. Don't fuck it up now."

Sharon ignored him. She had hope, but she knew better than to believe anything he said. She got up from the table and walked over to the family in the other booth. Based on the amount of food remaining on their plates, they were nearly finished.

She sat down beside the father, surprising him into scooting over. The son, beside him, was getting pressed into the wall of the booth.

"Hi, my name's Sharon," she said. "How y'all doin' tonight?"

The father and the children said nothing, but the mother started spinning right away.

"What do you think you're doing? What's the meaning of this?" Her eyes left Sharon's, her attention grabbed by the purple goose egg with the blood-black split in it on Sharon's forehead. The mother looked like she was someone who needed things to go according to plan, with no room for improvisation. Too bad for her. If it came to a test of wills between Sharon and this woman, Sharon had no doubt who'd win. Sharon didn't want this family to get hurt, but if they caused a problem, Deke would certainly hurt them, and she wouldn't be able to do anything to stop it. And, not to put too fine a point on it, she wouldn't do it anyway. To look at it in another light, if it came down to a choice between these strangers and her daughter, tough shit for them. She'd pick Lucinda every time.

"You folks look like you're getting ready to go south of the border. I've got two words for you: don't go."

"What?" The father had finally found his voice. It was reedy and thin. Based on the sound of their voices, Sharon knew who was the boss in that house.

"These Mexican border towns are full of nothing but crime, drugs, and trouble, and you'd be better off not going. In fact, why don't y'all turn around right now and go back home?"

"Are you out of your mind? I'm getting the manager!" The mother got up, but Sharon grabbed her wrist and yanked her back down into the seat. The mother pulled her hand back like she'd been bitten by a snake, and Sharon smiled. She pointed toward Deke, who was putting a wad of rumpled bills on top of the receipt at the table she'd recently vacated.

"You see that guy?" she waved to him, and he lifted his hand with a puzzled, angry look on his face. Sharon turned back to the mother. "He's the one who's been beating the shit out of me. Just because I didn't do what he said a couple of times." She pushed back her hair to give them the full effect of the gash and knot on her forehead, and the beginnings of a fresh bruise below her eye. The little girl beside the mother let out an impressed, "Ooooh."

"Now he wants us to go across the border into Mexico, but we don't have any passports. Now I could tell him tough shit, but that'd mean more trouble, right? So he saw y'all, and he thought we'd be perfect substitutes for y'all. You're obviously tourists, and you've got money, and there's four of you. There's four of us, too, but his asshole friend is holding my daughter hostage back at some fleabag motel." She paused, but before they could speak, she got to the point.

"So, bottom line, what I'm saying is that I need your passports, all four of them. After that, I need you to go away quietly."

"No. No way."

Sharon gestured to Deke, telling him to lift up his shirt. As soon as no one was looking at him, he did so, showing the two pistols stuck into the waistband of his jeans.

"I'm asking you for help, to save me and my daughter. But since 'No' is your answer, I'll give you a choice. Would you rather be shot with the Colt or with the Beretta?" Sharon had no idea what type of guns Deke was carrying, but spat the first brand names she thought of. The threat seemed to make an impression.

"Wait a minute, wait a minute. Hold on," the father said. "Steff, give her the passports."

The mother looked like she was about to object, but then she looked into Sharon's eyes. Sharon was suddenly vulnerable, as if this woman could see the pain and fear inside her, despite her tough veneer. Sharon held the woman's gaze even though the tears welled up in her eyes.

"Oh my God, you're telling the truth," the woman whispered. Her discovery wasn't the jumping around shouting "Eureka!" sort of discovery. It was a discovery more along the lines of a kid turning over a rock and finding something dead and jellied under it. It was a discovery she'd rather not have made.

"Yeah."

The mother took the four blue booklets out of her purse and passed them across the table to Sharon.

"Can we help you? You want us to call the police?"

"If you do, he'll kill my little girl." A tear rolled down her cheek and she wiped it brusquely away, shocked by the sudden pain of rubbing the bruise where she'd gotten punched earlier.

"What else? Do you need anything?"

"No. I wouldn't want you to put yourselves in danger as well. He said he'll let us go as soon as he gets across the border, but I really don't know if he will. The only thing I can do is wait and see. If he does, I'll try to get these back to you. I promise."

"Don't worry about it. After tomorrow, we'll call them in as lost. You just worry about getting yourself and your daughter away from that maniac."

The back of Sharon's throat tightened. "It's so hard to do...I've got no place to go."

The mother, Steff, squeezed her hand. "You could go to a women's shelter. Even if you're living on the street, you're away from him. Trust me, I know. Anywhere is safer than with someone like that."

The father was silent. Sharon thought the mother probably watched too many Lifetime channel movies and that she was having some kind of *sisterhood* moment. Sharon didn't care. She wanted to leave, to get back to her Lucinda. She thanked them and stood.

She went back to the other table, got the to-go plates, and followed Deke outside. She felt the family's wide eyes on her all the way to the door. Heavy rain met them in the parking lot, and they ran for the car.

"What did you say to them?" Deke asked when they'd shut the doors.

Sharon was drained, wiped out. This was too much. Death, robbery, body disposal, and now illegal border crossing. She didn't know how much more she could take. The strong voice inside her head rose, lending steel to her own voice.

"I told them the truth, Deke. If they didn't hand over the passports, you'd shoot them."

Goddammit! The first thing they're gonna do is call the cops!"

They're not, Deke. They looked at me, and I told them that if they went to the cops, you'd kill me and Lucinda."

Sharon thought again of the knife hidden in the car's upholstery. If she took Deke out now, the problem would be solved. She and

Lucinda could easily get away from Earl. His petulant, childish anger was nothing compared to the rage Deke nurtured in every cell of his body. There would be a chance to use the knife on Deke sometime during the night. He had to sleep eventually, right?

While Deke tamped out a dip of Cope', Sharon lifted Lucinda's and Earl's dinners over the seat, making a big production of putting them on the floorboard behind Deke. She hung over the back of the seat, pushing beer cans and other trash to one side of the floor, and suddenly the lights in the parking lot went dark.

"Shit," Deke's voice spoke over her shoulder. "Power went out."

While Sharon settled the bag onto the floor with one hand, with the other she reached into the hole she'd cut into the vinyl. She dug her fingers back and forth in the slit, hunting. Panic rose in Sharon's heart.

The knife she'd hidden so carefully earlier wasn't there.

30

In the dimly lamp-lit motel room, the television drones through yet another infomercial. The television volume is turned up in order to be heard over the rain outside. The salesman's voice buzzes at certain pitches, as though in the past someone had turned the volume too high and blew out the television's tiny speakers. The one called Earl watches the flashing pictures of the television blearily, his thoughts not on the exercise machine being praised as the next best thing to abdominal crunches, but somewhere else, deep inside his mind.

The girl Lucinda sleeps heavily. The redness has faded from her cheek, but the shock and pain will color her thoughts and actions for a long time. Her last conscious thoughts before sleep had been sad, fearful images of Earl hurting her again.

The dolly wriggles loose from the clutching arm of the girl, careful not to rouse her. It moves to the edge of the bed in silence, then leaps lightly to the carpeted floor. It lands silently on rubber feet that are encased in cloth slippers. Outside, lightning strikes with a flash that whites out the window momentarily. Seconds later, thunder growls and crashes. The dolly pauses, for a moment feeling Lucinda waking and struggling toward the surface of awareness. The thick, warm arms of slumber gently take hold of Lucinda and drag her down again, and the doll moves.

The doll reaches into its bodice and withdraws the black-handled pocketknife that Lucinda's Mommy hid in the car. Tiny, soft plastic fingers lever the new, razor-sharp blade from the handle. The only sound other than the television and the rain is the muted click as the blade locks open. The blade is virginal, unblemished, and perfect.

Earl does not turn at the sound of the blade. It is possible he hears nothing but the echoes of his own humiliated rage. The dolly, catlike, approaches him on the silent feet of approaching fog. It stands directly behind his chair, considering. The dolly must protect the girl Lucinda. At all costs.

It leaps into the air, landing on Earl's shoulder. Before he can react, one tiny hand wrenches a handful of hair back. The other plunges the knife into Earl's thickly-padded throat then rips across it. His exclamation of surprise does not make it to his larynx before his throat is opened, and his scream is nothing but a low, bubbling exhale. Blood leaps into the air, splashing the ceiling and walls in hot wet spurts. The dolly saws the knife back and forth, intent on killing the man who hurt the girl. The fresh blade slices vessels, fat, gristle, and the tendons holding the bones together. Lucinda, in the bed behind Earl's chair, is liberally splattered but does not wake. The television picture is covered in a dark translucent red as arterial sprays fountain into the air almost gracefully as his heart pumps its last beats.

Earl does not move from the chair, and as his heart fails, the aerial arcs of blood shorten, then stop. He bleeds out in impotent silence. Still holding the knife, the dolly hops backward from the reclining dead body. The dolly, too, is red, covered in blood.

Another bolt of lightning strikes outside, and the room is plunged suddenly into darkness. Thunder rolls again, but the sound is more subdued now. Occasional flashes brighten the room like a photographer's bulb, but the brightened scene of carnage lasts only a second before the darkness takes hold again.

Outside the rain continues to fall. Inside, there is only a slow dripping sound accompanied by the quiet sibilance of the dolly moving against the counterpane of the bed, scooting back into the sleeping girl's embrace.

31

Sharon was confused.

Where could the knife be? Had it somehow slipped farther down into the padding of the seat? She didn't think it could've been jarred loose. The opening she'd made had been snug.

God forbid, had *Deke* found it?

Less than three feet from her, he sat on the driver's side of the bench seat. He didn't seem any more or less threatening than he had earlier in the day, but that meant nothing. He'd given her a fresh black eye only three hours ago, after all. He'd been doubtful about the people who'd surrendered their passports so easily to her, but currently he was fully engaged with trying to get back to the motel with none of the Del Rio traffic signals functioning. All the roadside neon was out as well due to the power surge. All he had to find his way were headlights and lightning flashes.

Deke was hunched over the steering wheel, peering into the rainy darkness while the racing wind made the tip of the car's radio antenna thrum. The headlights mostly reflected the glare of the pouring rain. Eventually Sharon began to notice landmarks she recognized and saw a vague outline of the Rancho Del Rio sign approaching.

Deke pulled the car into the parking lot and drove around the side of the building. He parked and turned the car off.

A block distant, Sharon saw the neon sign of a cantina flicker back to life. She turned and leaned over the front seat to retrieve the dinners for Earl and Lucinda, checking one last time for the hidden knife. Her pulse throbbed achingly in her forehead. Convinced that it must have fallen out of the hole earlier in the day, she let her hands sweep the rest of the floor but found only trash. She hissed with frustration, getting out of the car with the bag.

Her interior voice raged at the stupid injustice of it all. She'd decided to step up and take charge of matters, to the point of killing Deke, and now even that decision was taken from her. She stalked along beside Deke, hoping her fury didn't show. It seemed Deke was distracted by his own thought processes, preoccupied by his harebrained escape plans.

They walked across the asphalt to the room, and the Rancho Del Rio sign began to shine again with the telltale waspy buzz of neon. Deke stuck the key into the keyhole, turned it, then turned the doorknob as he pushed the door open.

The lights of the small hotel room flickered to life, and the TV clicked on as power was restored. Sharon saw the psychotic funhouse chamber before her and Deke and dropped the to-go containers, spilling greasy fries across the sidewalk. She gasped.

Red. Tons of red. Gallons of red. Earl had been sitting with his back to the door, obviously facing the television. Now on the television, through a red haze of wet blood, the newscast showed a video still of a masked Deke barking orders at someone in the bank in Killeen—*holy shit was that yesterday?*—as Earl's upside-down rictus of pain grinned at her; it bobbed on the last rubbery shreds of connected neck flesh. There was bright red blood on the white stippled ceiling like some terrible modern art painting, and broad, red fans stretched across the walls like a mural of wild, vine-covered jungle trees. The same thick maroon braids looped across the sand-colored carpet, on the bedspreads, and on the imitation wood finish of the furniture.

206

The heavy ammonia and metal smell of the blood overpowered the hydrocarbon stink of the air conditioner. Earl's broad head dangled backward on a stretching piece of red-splashed yellow neck fat, his dead eyes staring at them as they stood in the doorway.

Worst of all was Lucinda lying on the bed and covered with thick gouts of blood, completely unaware of the abattoir the hotel room had become. Sharon saw her chest rise and fall as she slept. Her dolly was a gory clot in her arms, completely covered with blood. The dolly's eyes were open, and in its small hand was the knife Sharon had hidden so carefully in the car. Its blade was open and gummed with blood and shreds of excised flesh.

The dolly winked a blood-sticky eye at Sharon and then was still.

Not possible...Dad's dollies never did that...

Sharon screamed, long and loud. Her scream was the only thing that anchored her to consciousness.

Deke only stood, wide-eyed like a highway deer, in the doorway. He looked stunned.

Sharon's scream woke Lucinda with a start, and when the child looked around at all the blood, she screamed as well. Sharon rushed into the room, her shoes squelching through the spilled blood that soaked into the carpet and the pad beneath it, and scooped up Lucinda. As she did so, the pocketknife fell to the bedspread, but Lucinda held tightly to her dolly. Sharon ran from the room with her daughter in her arms, her scream migrating down from her throat to her chest, becoming a roar.

Their mingled cries brought the motel to wakefulness, beginning a general alarm. The manager, an older gentleman with steel-gray hair, glasses, and a dinner plate-sized rodeo belt buckle riding low under a round bulge of gut, came around the side of the building. At every open door he came to, he told people to go back inside, that he had everything under control.

Before the manager made it to their room, Deke regained his composure. He swung his arm into the old man's charge, clotheslining him and laying him flat out. The old man's head sounded like a ripe winter squash hitting the pavement, and after that he didn't move.

Sharon backed away from the room, drawing a deep breath so she could scream again. She barely noticed Deke pulling one of the pistols from the waist of his jeans and turned away as he drew down on her. The furious voice in her head was finally burning through her terror, and she heard it screaming at her to run.

Behind her, Deke's voice roared. "You'd better stop right goddamned now!"

She kept moving, knowing her chances were growing slimmer every second.

He squeezed the trigger. Asphalt chips exploded behind her, and she felt something like a bee sting as either a piece of pavement or a bullet fragment tore through her jeans and into her leg. With a cry of pain, she faltered, nearly dropping Lucinda. She stood again and took a tentative, painful step forward.

"I won't miss again, bitch!"

Sharon stopped and turned, limping to face him.

"Stay put!" he barked at her. He kept the gun trained on her as he strode forward to the car. He opened the trunk, grabbed the blood-smeared plastic grocery bags, and approached her through the pouring rain.

Sharon's mind was still trying to make sense of what she'd seen. All that blood, all over the room. Earl dead, his head practically cut off, and little Lucinda asleep on the bed. And she would swear that the dolly had winked at her and had held the knife in its tiny hand.

How could that be?

Was she imagining things?

Deke got close to her, his hair plastered to his skull in the driving rain. A siren began to howl in the distance.

"I don't know what the fuck happened back there, but we're not waiting around to find out. Earl was such a fuckin' idiot, he probably figured out a way to do that to himself! He couldn't turn on a light switch without fucking it up. All bets are off! Move your ass! I'm crossing the border right now, and you're coming with me!"

He shoved her in front of him toward the border crossing station, and though Lucinda was heavy in her arms, Sharon continued to carry her. Lucinda was still sobbing. Although the sound of the rain drowned out most of the cries, Sharon hugged her close to stifle the sound.

Even though most of the lights were coming on throughout the town of Del Rio, the border crossing stations on both sides of the river were still blacked out, and they were only visible in the occasional white flashes of lightning.

The border guards, most of them younger men, stood across the outside of the building in a line, a few double arm spans apart. In addition to the holstered pistols on their hips, they wore rifles slung over their backs and held large black flashlights. From inside the station, Sharon heard one voice say, "You got six Honda generators in case the power went out, but you didn't get any gas for 'em? Jesus Christ, Hal!"

Deke stopped her before they came within range of the guards' Mag-Lites, but given the rain, they were already very close to the line of guards. Without a word, Deke transferred both of the money bags to one hand and turned the pistol around so that he was holding it by the barrel. He strode up to the guard at the end of the line and bashed him in the head with the pistol grip. The guard slumped to the ground, and Deke quickly picked up the dropped flashlight and began shining it around in the same semicircular pattern. Sharon was sure it wasn't an effort to avoid taking another life. Deke didn't care about that. He was only trying to be quiet.

He pointed the pistol at her again, motioning her forward. She came, staying close to the fence. Once she was within reach, all pretense he'd made at posing as a border guard was dropped, and he yanked Lucinda and the doll out of her arms.

"Noooo!" she screamed.

The guards reacted immediately, drawing their weapons and ordering Deke to halt. Sharon watched him sprint into the building. The guards began to advance, but they were slow and cautious. *If I wait for them to get their thumbs out of their asses, Deke and Lucinda will already be in Mexico!* Sharon bent to the fallen guard Deke had knocked out and pulled his heavy pistol from its holster then she ran after Deke.

He ran through the dark building, past the shut down customs checkpoint, and out onto the pedestrian bridge to Mexico. Sharon followed as quickly as she could.

Lucinda screamed for her, reaching over Deke's broad shoulder. Sharon limped forward, trailing them onto the bridge.

With a flicker, the pedestrian bridge lights came back to life. Deke stopped, facing Mexico. Before him in the rain-swept night, the river roared. The footbridge was long and narrow and dipped in the middle of its length. The heavy rain fed the Rio Grande torrent to the point that in the middle of the channel, the surface of the river was a few inches above the level of the pedestrian bridge. Brown water rushed through the chainlink upstream of the walkway, flooding it. While only a few inches deep, the surge was powerful enough to bulge the fencing in on the upstream side and out on the downstream side. Metal fence posts on the upstream side barely stayed in place, but the ones on the downstream side had begun to come loose from their moorings. Sharon saw Deke look back to see if he was being pursued then turn again and walk forward on the bridge. Several feet above them and thirty or forty feet downstream, the closed vehicle bridge was only a black smear across the river, dimly outlined by the meager lighting of Del Rio's returning electricity. Beneath her feet, Sharon felt the walkway tremble.

Sharon looked ahead. Mexican land was less than a hundred yards away from Deke, at the end of the bridge. He would run away into freedom, and she'd never see Lucinda alive again. Sharon couldn't allow that to happen.

"Stop, Deke!" she screamed. "Put Lucinda down!"

He didn't react.

Sharon lifted the pistol into the air and fired. With the roar of the rain and the thunder of the river, the sound was pathetic, but he heard it. He looked back at her, grinned savagely, and waved. Lucinda renewed her screaming and struggling and elbowed Deke in the back of his head. *Good girl!* Her dolly fell from her grasp, landing in a heap on the pavement.

From behind her, a border guard yelled to be heard over the tumult of the river and the rain. "Ma'am, please put down the weapon or we'll be forced to shoot."

"But he's got my daughter!" she screamed.

"Ma'am, please put the weapon down."

You goddamned fucking robots! Shoot that asshole, not me!

She threw the weapon down in disgust and moved forward along the bridge. She saw Deke shift his grip on Lucinda and heard him yelling at her.

"Goddammit! Be still, you little shit!" he barked then he brought the pistol up in a short swing. It hit her head soundlessly, and her small body slumped limp in his arms.

"Nooo!"

A hand fell on her right shoulder, while another grabbed her left arm.

"Ma'am, please step back."

"Let go of me, asshole! He's got my daughter!"

The border guard pulled her left arm behind her back. In front of her, Lucinda's slack weight was causing Deke to lose his balance. She was a solid child, a good forty pounds, and Deke was trying to hold her in his left arm while holding the two sacks of wet money in his left hand. He also had to keep the pistol free in his right hand.

Closer to her, Sharon saw the crumpled form of the dolly start to move.

32

It sits up in the driving rain then stands on wobbly legs. The dolly must protect the girl. The girl loves it, and it loves the girl.

The bad guy Deke stands on the walkway, river water rushing around his calves. Lucinda hangs bonelessly over his arm. The fence to his right bells inward, the bottom edge of the chainlink pushed in by the flooding river, while the left bells outward off of the walkway. Brown fans of water spray upward around Deke's legs.

The difficulty of balancing in the rushing water with arms full finally proves too much for Deke. Rather than set the child down, he simply stretches out his arm. She falls heavily to the pavement, splashing in the muddy torrent. The dolly runs to the unconscious girl as the rushing water rolls her over, pushing her toward the downstream edge of the walkway, where the fence has been pushed away from the cement. The girl's face is under water, and the flood forms fat brown rooster tails over her body.

The one called Deke moves forward, no longer encumbered by the child.

The dolly arrives at Lucinda's supine form. The current threatens to pull both the dolly and the girl over the brink, but the dolly grabs the girl by the belt loops of her trousers and pulls her backward until she is clear of the surging brown water and white froth.

When the girl is safe from the water, the dolly looks up at the bad guy's form staggering forward through the water. Because the upstream side of the fence is being pushed across the walkway almost as much as the downstream side is being pushed away, he is holding the upstream side of the fence as he walks. Chunks of flotsam from miles upstream are collecting in the links of the fence: blackened agave stalks, flat yellow beavertails of dead prickly pear, a thin pine bough, and a dead, swollen goat.

33

"Let me go, idiot!" Sharon yelled. She drove her right elbow up and back, smashing it into the border guard's face. His grip on her loosened, and she lunged away from him. His muffled, "You boke by doze, bitch!" swirled off in the cacophony of the flooding river, the driving rain, and Sharon's cries to Lucinda.

After all she'd gone through to get to this point, when she finally dug deep and found the strength to face impossible odds, she had no means to do it. She'd surrendered the gun already. The knife was gone. She had nothing else. She wanted to kill Deke, that hateful son of a bitch, and save Lucinda.

She hoped she wasn't too late.

She raced forward on the footbridge toward her fallen child. Lucinda lay on her side, bent in the middle. Her head and feet were closest to the rush of the brown Rio Grande water, but clear of it.

Sharon had seen her, face down in the water. She'd seen the dolly moving of its own accord and pulling her daughter out of the water. Sharon saw it chase after Deke as he waded through the flooding river. *How is that possible? It's a doll!*

Sharon fell to her knees and picked up her daughter, rolling Lucinda onto her lap. She was breathing, but an angry purple knot was already swelling at her temple where Deke had hit her with the pistol.

Sharon looked into the rain and saw the red-stained dolly spidering across the chainlink fence like a small, pissed-off monkey.

34

The dolly jumps onto the belled-in upstream fence and scampers after the bad guy's retreating figure. It springs from the fence, a furious thing. Its raw, righteous hatred of Deke, born from its love for Lucinda, drives it. It lands with a slap on the back of Deke's head, knocking him off-balance momentarily. He falls forward onto one knee, but immediately regains his footing. He swats backward at the dolly with his pistol, first thinking that Lucinda is attacking him from behind. The pistol makes contact with the dolly, bludgeoning a dent into its head. It soundlessly screams but maintains its grip on him.

It reaches its small plastic hands forward around his head, holding on with one hand while digging into his eye socket with the other. His reaction is too slow, and by the time he, screaming, brings his hand up to his face, his left eye has been removed from its cradle and sits loose on his cheek in a nest of torn muscle, tethered only by its optic nerve. He howls, clawing at his head and face in order to remove his tormentor. The bags of money are dropped, forgotten in the wild lightning of his pain. The bags fall into the rushing water and slide off the footbridge into the current. The gun, too, drops into the water with an inconsequential splash.

Deke staggers on the walkway, shrieking and holding a cupped hand over his dangling eye and its bleeding socket. He is disoriented and unbalanced from the agony and the strange twist in his vision, and as he finally grabs hold of the dolly on his back, he stumbles over the edge of the pedestrian bridge. As he falls, the dolly grips the chainlink fence in both of its tiny hands, catching the mesh and hanging on tightly. Deke maintains a hold on one of the dolly's legs, ripping it from the small body as he falls away into the raging flood of river. Deke's splash, as the river consumes him, is diminished by the fury of the water, the ripples caused by his thrashing body elongating for an instant before being obliterated by the rushing brown river.

He is visibly thrown into the air by a surge of the river then he disappears finally into its dark depths.

The bad guy is gone.

The dolly creeps its stuttering way along the rippling fence to Mommy, who sits on the concrete with Lucinda on her lap. The girl does not move, and her clothes are plastered to her pale skin. The dolly moves slowly and awkwardly. Its leg is missing and its vision is distorted from the dent in its head. The dolly looks at Mommy, who weeps as she holds the limp body of the little girl in a tight embrace. It burrows between Mommy and Lucinda, clinging to the girl. It feels the shivery sorrow of Mommy and feels the young girl's mind as it moves behind a heavy, soft curtain.

The knot on the child's forehead continues to swell and blacken.

35

The border patrol guards surged onto the pedestrian bridge, surrounding Sharon and Lucinda with uniformed safety. They swarmed over the two of them, and Sharon couldn't help but think, *Where the fuck were you guys five minutes ago?* She held Lucinda, rocking back and forth and crying.

Once the guards had assured themselves that the dangerous asshole who'd started all the trouble had been swept away by the river, they calmed down. They called for an ambulance for Lucinda and for helicopter support to search for Deke. The ambulance arrived in less than five minutes, and the EMTs loaded Lucinda onto a backboard and a stretcher. They carried Lucinda and Sharon walked as quickly as she could beside them. They went back through the customs area of the border crossing station, and the bright white light of the fluorescent tubes was a welcome brightness, but it did nothing to dispel the darkness in Sharon's heart.

Lucinda wouldn't wake up.

In the ambulance, Sharon sat in the cramped space beside the gurney holding Lucinda. They raced toward the Del Rio Medical Center. One of the EMTs cut open the leg of her jeans, cleaned and dressed the cut on her calf, then put a handful of butterfly bandages on the reopened gash on her head. Sharon held onto the wheeled stretcher beside her as the vehicle bounced through potholes. The siren serenaded the night. By the time he was finished, the ambulance was slowing and pulling into the hospital lot. Lucinda was strapped onto a backboard with an oversized oxygen mask on her face. Her dolly, its head now shaped almost like a gourd or some sort of pod, lay loosely in the crook of one of her arms.

When they got out of the ambulance, Sharon saw that the rain had stopped. The EMTs hopped out of the ambulance onto the wet pavement, unlocked the wheels' brakes, and lifted the stretcher out of the ambulance. The legs extended on their own weight, and the techs rolled the stretcher into the building. Sharon followed closely, certain that she wouldn't let Lucinda out of her sight. With a frown of distaste, one of the nurses passed Lucinda's dolly to Sharon. She took it hesitantly, almost expecting it to wriggle away from her grasp. The emergency room personnel took Lucinda into a trauma room and examined her then a nurse came to Sharon and asked a series of questions about Lucinda's medical history. The doctors decided that Lucinda needed surgery right away, and they banished Sharon to waiting room limbo. Del Rio police showed up, but after taking her statement, they mostly kept their distance from Sharon. The perpetrator had, after all, been washed away in the flood, and his chances of survival were next to nothing.

The hours passed slowly, reluctant to reveal the future. A hatchet-faced doctor came and talked to her about Lucinda. He asked about allergies, family history of illness, and if their captor had ever abused Lucinda sexually. Then he told her that, due to the blow to the head Deke had given Lucinda, she was bleeding in her head and pressure was building up around the child's brain. *Subdural hematoma.*

"We don't like to use the terms coma or comatose state, because at this point, it's an advanced state of unconsciousness," the doctor explained.

Whatever. *Calling it something more clinical doesn't change the fact that my daughter's brain won't let her wake up.*

The doctor continued and explained that they needed to open her up and install a drain before the cranial fluid pressure cut off the blood supply to her brain, causing a stroke. Without hesitation, Sharon signed the consent. The hatchet-faced doctor disappeared into a set of double doors marked, "No Admittance," and Sharon turned to the television mounted on the wall, where a man in shirtsleeves was giving a weather report in Spanish.

A few moments after the doctor left, the detectives approached her: a Del Rio police officer, a Texas Ranger, and an investigator from the Border Patrol who only introduced himself as "Agent Pollard, Homeland Defense." They each spoke to her individually, asking her to repeat her story again and again, from the beginning in Killeen, through San Angelo, and into Del Rio. They asked about Whistler, Whistler's dog, the bank job, the Killeen police officer, Ray, and Earl. They spent a long time on Earl, since they had a team dispatched to that actual crime scene and the evidence left many unanswered questions.

In the interest of not sounding like a crazy lady, Sharon told the investigators as much as she could but said nothing about the dolly that she currently held on her lap. Crazy ladies got put away for "observation" and got their daughters taken away so the bloodstained dolly stayed out of the narrative. In reality, she'd seen the dolly in action, protecting her daughter and sending Deke to his death. Having seen that, she believed it really could have been the dolly that killed Earl. Only hours earlier, Earl had struck Lucinda. From there, it was only a short jump to Whistler's dog. The pit bull had terrorized Lucinda one day and wound up dead the next. The doll had been filthy and blood-spattered, but she'd attributed it to the events of the playground, not anything else. Now, though, she wasn't so sure.

Logical in terms of cause and effect, but she still didn't see how any of it was possible. Holding Betty now, Sharon could feel the weight and balance of it. It was a dolly, nothing more. No gears or servos to make it move on its own. No high-tech circuitry.

A doll. Cloth, molded rubber, and stuffing. Nothing more than that—and yet something much more, beyond her understanding.

How did you do that, Daddy?

Sharon, distracted by her own wonder, began to grow bored with the questions when they started repeating themselves. They could tell she was leaving out a few facts, and they were hoping to catch her in some minor inconsistency to make her spill the truth. Like the guy in that movie, she didn't think they could handle the truth. She turned over the stolen passports, and they retreated with some satisfaction.

Can't you guys see? I'm a little busy right now! My daughter's life is hanging in the balance, and you want details about things I didn't even witness?

Every time the double doors to the operating suites hissed open on their automatic hinges, Sharon looked up. She hoped to see the hatchet-faced doctor, to get an update on Lucinda. She imagined Doctor Hatchetface striding out through the double doors with a grin, wheeling an alert and smiling Lucinda before him in a wheelchair. Lucinda would see her, jump from the chair, and sprint into Sharon's arms. It was a ridiculous idea, and she knew it, but it helped keep her hopes high.

Sergeant Cowdrie, the Del Rio policeman, approached again, and Sharon sighed, her anger simmering. If he asked her even one more stupid question, she would bite his head off.

"Ma'am? There is one other thing."

"What's that?"

"Is there anyone we can call for you? A family member or a friend? Even a close neighbor?"

Sharon had none of these. Her father back in Georgia was locked up and probably would be forever, and Ronnie, Lucinda's father, was either deployed or getting ready to deploy again. Neighbors? *Oh hell, no.* Who did that leave?

"I've got no one. It's only Lucinda and me."

"Really? No one back home in, ahh—" he flipped through the pages of his notebook, "—Georgia?"

Sharon mentioned that the only other relatives she'd known as a girl were her Aunt Claudia and Uncle Herbert, but that she'd lost touch with them years ago. The policeman jotted that down, offered his concern for Lucinda, and left his business card with Sharon. She watched him walk away from her. By the soda machine, he stopped an eager-looking kid with an open steno book, pulling him by the elbow to the exit.

"No press, Sam. Leave her alone for now. If she wants to talk to you, she'll find you." The kid looked at Sharon as if she were the one snubbing him, robbing him of his news story. Sharon was grateful to the policeman. He was right. She had nothing to say.

Sharon was finally able to go to Lucinda. When she came out of surgery, they put her in ICU for observation. The tiny girl wore a huge turban of bandage on her head, out of which snaked a plastic tube filled with red-tinged liquid. Lucinda's nostrils were plugged with two thin oxygen tubes. Sharon put the dolly on a chair and stood by the bed. She held her daughter's hand and wept, asking Lucinda for forgiveness and to please come home. She sang to her daughter like she always did, every song she could think of that Lucinda liked—from the old Motown stuff to Christmas carols to the old butchered Elvis song. Afterward, she stood there in the whispers of the ICU for a long time, careful of the disorderly tangle of tubes, sensors, and IV bags hanging all around her child.

"I love you, baby girl," she said. Time unrolled, punctuated by the chirp of the EKG machine.

Finally Doctor Hatchetface came in, and Sharon noticed that his actual name was Garza. He was the resident pediatric neurology specialist and the doctor assigned to Lucinda. He looked tired, but his expression was guarded. He approached and spoke to her in low tones, saying they'd installed the drain successfully and had relieved some of the pressure in Lucinda's head. Hopefully she would stabilize and regain consciousness soon.

"We need to keep her in ICU for at least a day or two more. After the first forty-eight hours, she should show some improvement, and then we can reevaluate. Thus far, we've gotten no physical response other than the standard stuff. Her pupils are dilating normally, and her muscle reflexes are good, but her EEG is not showing the spikes we like to see, the ones that would indicate that she's coming around. For now, her body is resting while her brain takes some time to heal itself."

"Okay. Thank you, doctor."

"I'd recommend you getting some rest as well. Your daughter's condition will likely stay the same for some time. You can leave your contact information with the front desk, and we'll call you as soon as anything changes."

She thanked the doctor again and he disappeared through the double doors. She picked up the dolly from the chair and stepped back out to the waiting area.

All around her, the hospital bustled. The harsh yellow light of dawn splashed through the windows and advertised not only the passage of the night, but also the passage of the storm.

Sharon found herself a strangely immobile object in the midst of an intricate ballet of moving hospital employees, as if she were a still life photo in the movie of their lives. The hospital's night shift was gathering up emptied dinner containers, dog-eared paperbacks, and empty soda cans as they prepared to leave. The day shift was coming on, bringing their respective paraphernalia of travel coffee mugs, crossword puzzle books, and breakfasts.

One of the nurses going off-shift came by on her way out. Her oversized purse hung from one shoulder, her glasses rested on her ample bosom by a necklace chain, and in her hand was a cup of vending machine coffee. She touched Sharon's arm and handed her the paper cup.

"Good luck, honey. We're all prayin' for you and your little girl."

Sharon thanked her and the nurse left, escaping finally from Sharon's inertia into the rest of the animated world. The exit doors closed behind the nurse with a pneumatic hiss as she left. Where, though, did Sharon have to go? Nowhere.

Sharon sipped the bitter black coffee, not really tasting it at all. She mentally took inventory. Self and daughter both alive? Check. Deke gone to hell or Mexico? Check. Those were the important items, but other than that, what did she have? She was broke, in a strange place, and all alone. Her torn jeans were filthy and blood spattered, as was her shirt. The doll in her hand, comforting and alien at the same time, was also soiled with a variety of blood, tears, and stinking river mud. Sharon was thankful the police hadn't found a way to take the doll from her as evidence.

She sat in the first chair of the first row of waiting room chairs and sat Betty on the seat beside her. The doll's formerly pretty dress was probably irretrievably stained and its carefully styled hair was now a complete rat's nest. One of the doll's legs was missing, the plastic socket leaking a coarse, purplish cloth stuffing. Every crease of the dolly's fingers and hands was etched with dirt, as was the dent in her now almost peanut-shaped head. Sharon looked at the dolly's painted eyes. Despite all the trials the dolly had been through in the past few days, the eyes were still a clear, vibrant blue-green. She put the dolly on her lap and looked into the painted-on eyes.

How did Dad make you? How could he? Was it some kind of magic?

No answer presented itself. No life, no intelligence, showed in the doll's features. Sharon tried to flatten the doll's hair to its head and straightened its dress. She picked the largest pieces of debris from the doll's clothes and hair, making it as presentable as possible. When Lucinda woke, Sharon thought she would ask for her Betty dolly first thing.

Sharon looked at the litter of dirt and tiny bits of trash around her chair. She realized that she didn't care that she was making a mess and continued to fuss with the doll's hair, braiding it, then unbraiding it; braiding it, then unbraiding it.

"Excuse me, ma'am?"

A young man behind the counter looked at Sharon. She pointed to herself and raised an eyebrow then winced at the soreness.

"Are you Sharon Ingram?"

She stood. "Yes?"

He held up a slim, white telephone receiver. "You've got a phone call, ma'am."

"Hello?"

"Ma'am, this is Sergeant Cowdrie, down at the police station. We met earlier?"

"Uh-huh."

"I wanted to let you know we were able to track down your aunt and uncle back in Georgia. Your aunt said to tell you to sit tight and that she'd be here tomorrow morning."

"Thank you, Officer," Sharon began, not really sure if she meant it. Her mind was already spinning off in six different directions. Tomorrow morning? That fast? When had she and Aunt Claudia last talked? Would her aunt have changed much? How much had the police told her of what had happened? Where would she stay when she got here? The questions buzzed in her head like angry bees.

"Well, ma'am, we know when you're going through a rough patch, it's always better when you have someone helping you out."

"Thanks again," she said. She hung up the phone and went back to her chair. She picked up Lucinda's Betty dolly, hugged it close, and wondered. Aunt Claudia had always said she'd rather look fat than old, and that if she ever got any wrinkles, she'd eat and eat until the loose skin plumped up and filled out with fat. Sharon tried to picture what her aunt would look like if she'd held to her threat. Round, probably.

She held the dolly on her lap, and although worry for her baby girl gnawed at her insides, exhaustion finally took over. She nodded off.

"Ma'am? You've got a phone call." The young man held up the receiver.

"Hello?"

"Miz Ingram, this is Ranger Tate. We found Mister Satterwhite downstream a bit. He's a little beat up and a little waterlogged, but he's all right. He ain't got but one eye now. I reckon the fish got the other'n. He sure is a ugly galoot. Anyway, since he didn't have none uh that money on him, and he said all that bank robbery shit was nothin' more'n a big misunderstandin', we done turned 'im loose. He sure was glad. You should'a seen him grin. He said he's headin' up yonder to see you."

The voice changed, suddenly and unmistakably, to Deke's.

"Yep. Comin' to see you, bitch. I'll get rid of the goddamned doll then I'll kill your fucking brat kid while you watch. Then I've got something extra special for you. How's that sound, you worthless cunt?"

She didn't hear her strong inner voice speaking in her head anymore, but she knew that when she spoke, it would be that voice, the one of steel and grit, that came from her lips. The voice she'd heard all along inside wasn't something strange and foreign after all. It was *her* voice, and she finally recognized it as such.

"Go ahead," she said. "Come and get me, you stupid fuck. Show your face anywhere near me or Lucinda, and I'll kill you. I'll kill you with whatever weapon I can find, and if I don't have anything, I'll tear you to pieces with my bare hands."

Deke's voice screeched in the phone receiver then faded away into sounds that might have been laughter or sobs.

Sharon jerked awake. She looked around to see if anyone in the waiting room was eyeballing her. Had she screamed? As her heart slowed, she realized that if she did, no one noticed. They all had their own tragedies to attend.

Sharon was still sleepy, and the knot on her head throbbed. She looked from the oblong rectangle of bright sunlight reflected off the waxed floor to the clock on the wall. Though the dream seemed to have lasted only seconds, she'd already slept most of the day away. She got up and stretched and picked up the dolly. As she walked around the waiting area, her protesting muscles, popping joints, and grainy vision told her that she wasn't merely still sleepy. She was bone-tired. Weary to her core.

Sharon pushed through the doors into the ICU and looked in on Lucinda again. Such a little girl in such a big bed. She lay on her back, with her mouth hanging open the tiniest bit. Her lips were chapped, but other than the strain of the last few days showing around her eyes, she looked peaceful. If not for the turban of bandage with its thin red snake trailing from it into a drainage bag, Lucinda could have been asleep. Sharon sighed as she watched the rise and fall of her daughter's chest. She was so small, so fragile, and so beautiful. Sharon was reminded of her sister, when the accident had happened with the mail truck. Pearl had seemed tiny on such a big stretcher, too.

For a moment, Sharon considered putting Betty into the bed beside Lucinda. She loved the dolly, and despite all sane logic, the dolly loved her, too. The ICU nurses would probably have a fit if they saw this filthy dolly in bed with their patient. For now, Sharon held onto Betty, wandering back out of the ICU and into the waiting room area.

She found that if she went down the hallway on the other side of the nurses' station, there was a different place to sit, furnished differently. This waiting didn't have the usual emergency room contoured plastic torture devices but a set of fat upholstered sofas and overstuffed chairs. This was the waiting room for those people settling in for the long haul. Sharon gratefully sank into one of the chairs, and with Betty firmly in her arms, she soon fell deeply asleep again.

After she fell asleep, she briefly dreamed that Betty returned her hugs then the dolly turned into Lucinda.

36

Lucinda was in a strange, scary place. It was dark without being any color, not even black, and sound echoed and dripped from the ceiling like a recording slowed and played back through syrup.

Her head hurt, and she saw through the darkness a swarm of horrible shapes that looked like dancing winter trees, trunks and branches that were all angles without leaf or blossom. Gnarled, knuckly sticks flexed and lunged to catch her. She tried to run, but found she couldn't move.

From behind those horrible trees, she thought she heard Deke's voice, and once she caught a glimpse of his face. He smiled a mean smile, and the diseased-looking orangey light on his face looked like he carried a torch. He said bad, ugly cusswords like he always did, but after a moment he went away, leaving only the colorless darkness and the ghost trees.

Why didn't Mommy come get her?

She couldn't see the rest of her body.

She remembered even though it hurt. She remembered everything up until the bridge across the river. Deke had grabbed her and tried to go across the bridge, and Mommy screamed and went after them. After that, everything changed to darkness and pain.

She saw something else in the gloom before her. The darkness lightened and shifted, and the ghost trees disappeared from that spot. A window opened in the darkness.

She saw a face in that window. The old man she'd seen in her other dream. Her granddaddy. He saw her too, and he smiled at her. The darkness retreated further. Behind her granddaddy, Lucinda saw a meadow as green as emeralds and a sky like a robin's egg with a yellow sun and fluffy white clouds.

"Little sister, don't you cry," he whispered, like Mommy sang to her sometimes. "Ev'rything'll be all right."

He smiled, and his smile was like Mommy's, too. His smile was everything that Deke's was not. Deke's smile was only ever mean and hateful. Lucinda felt the warm, sweet breeze from that place and smelled the clover in the meadow. It made Lucinda feel better. It made Lucinda's head stop hurting. No more dark ghost tree shadows to grab at her, and no more Deke. No more headache.

She looked again, and she saw something else in her granddaddy's eyes.

Tears.

37

In Sharon's dream, she was in her father's shop in the garage. All the dolly body parts floated over the drafting table, and she and Dad were talking about making dolls. He said it was like home cooking. Home-cooked meals always tasted better than going out and getting food at a fancy restaurant. Did she know why that was? When she shook her head, he'd smiled and told her it was because of the secret seasoning. The secret seasoning was love, of course, and when that was added to any recipe, the results were bound to be wonderful.

Behind her, Sharon heard Deke's hateful giggling voice coming from the laundry room. She heard him threaten Lucinda again: *I'll kill her while you watch, bitch*, and Sharon turned back to her father. His face looked grim. He pushed a shovel into her hand. Sharon knew it was the one he'd used to dig up Pearl. His eyes were intense but still filled with love. "Big sister," he whispered.

"Don't you cry," she finished for him.

She turned and ran through the doorway into the house where she'd lived, the shovel held high above her shoulder like a baseball bat. Around her the house looked old, as if it had fallen into severe disrepair. Where happiness had once lived, there was now only decay.

Comin' for you, bitch.

She swung the shovel toward the voice and hit the light hanging over the dining room table. It shattered into shards of brittle glass, flakes of rusted metal, and dry, rotten wood. As the fragments fell to the table, it, too, collapsed into dust.

Got something extra special for you.

The voice was coming from the hallway.

She turned. The walls of the corridor were scabbed with spreading black mold, the paint visibly peeling and curling on itself. At the end of the hall, Deke stood like a statue. He was huge, filling the hallway from wall to wall and floor to ceiling. A giant, hulking brute of the evil man he'd been. In the dim light, he smiled. His teeth shone.

Get over here, you stupid bitch, and let me show you who the fuck's in charge.

For a moment, Sharon's heart quailed and she faltered. She glanced at the wall again and saw a photo. Two sisters dressed in matching sundresses, giggling, and clowning before Dad's camera. Her and Pearl in happier times. Deke laughed, and the sound of his hateful joy made dust from the crumbling ceiling shower down on her. The photo's frame began to bend and sag, and the glass fell from it, shattering on the floor. The two sisters still smiled, one with the missing teeth of a six-year old, and the other with the thin, awkward limbs of pre-adolescence. The image of Pearl smiled with wide blue-green eyes.

Sharon knew what she had to do.

"You can't have her, asshole!"

Deke continued to laugh and larger chunks of the ceiling began to rain down.

"You can't have her! You can't have *either* of us!"

She raised the shovel and charged at the monster at the end of the hall. She roared, a sound of anger, of pain, and of pent-up hatred. She adjusted her grip and swung.

With a *clank!* the shovel struck Deke, and his hideous laughter broke off. She swung again and missed. She was swinging too high. Deke now stood at his normal height, blood pouring from his face. An uprooted tooth sat on his chin, lodged in bloody stubble.

He spoke again.

You'll never be free of me, bitch.

She swung again, and the shovel struck another metallic note. When she looked, she saw a bright white stump of cheekbone poking through a flap of skin.

He was still standing. And despite the ruin of his face, he was still smiling.

He snuffled blood, but before he could speak, she hit him again with the shovel.

When she looked this time, he was finally lying down, his head creased in the middle. Still he smiled up at her, sneering as she panted. He inhaled again.

I'm in charge, bitch, he slurred.

Sharon had had enough of his mouth, now and forever. Enough of any part of him. She rotated the shovel in her grip and swung again. She was no longer beating him with the flat of the shovel. She was chopping into him with the edge of the blade. She raised the shovel again.

And again.

And again.

And again.

Then the old house fell away to darkness.

"Excuse me, ma'am."

Sharon opened her eyes and tried to focus on the young face in front of her but found it difficult. Her eyes stung in the eternal fluorescent light. The windows were black squares. Night had fallen again. Time seemed to be passing so quickly. *Close my eyes for one second, and I go through a time warp.* With one hand, she rubbed her face, and with the other, she levered herself into a sitting position on the deeply-padded chair. She looked down at the spot on the cushion where her face had been. Wet. She'd been either crying or drooling in her sleep.

She hurt and was angry and terrified from the dream, but she felt more alive than she had in months. She again tried to focus on the person before her.

He looked familiar, but at first she couldn't place him. He was redheaded and thin, with a dark tan that probably covered a face full of freckles. She looked down and saw his press badge clipped to the breast pocket of his shirt.

No press, Sam, she remembered.

It was the reporter she'd seen before, the one that Sergeant Cowdrie had sent away.

"Ma'am, if I could just get a statement..."

Sharon was surprised at the sudden anger that roared through her heart. She was exhausted, waiting for word from the doctor about her daughter, and this kid thought he could zoom in and get a story out of her?

"You're waking me up for a *statement* for your paper?"

"Yes. I write for the Del Rio Telegraph, and—"

"Go to hell."

He seemed shocked. "What?"

"Go to hell. I've spent the last week having one of the most harrowing experiences of my life, and my daughter's in a coma, and you think I want to talk about it to a stranger? You must be out of your goddamned mind."

His face flushed. "Ma'am, it's news. It's a great story."

"You want to *entertain* your readers with my tragedy?" she accused, her voice rising.

"Ma'am," he said, his voice rising as well, "I think I've been more than patient, waiting for you. I'd hoped I could ask you a couple of questions."

"Go away."

He referred to his notes. "Based on police radio traffic, they haven't yet made the determination of who killed Mr. Billings. Do you care to make a comment on that?"

"Go away."

She saw the muscles in his jaw bunch as he gritted his teeth, and suddenly she saw this young man in a whole new light. Instead of trying to bully an interview out of her, she saw him bullying others. The girl in the office whose ass he ogled every time she walked past, the waitress who flirted to increase her tips but instead got cornered by him near the back tables at closing time, the high school girlfriend he'd threatened to leave stranded out in the desert unless she sucked him off right now. It was too much. This guy could be Deke. Better education didn't necessarily mean a better heart. Sharon turned away from him.

"I said *go away*."

He grabbed her shoulder and turned her back to face him. "Hey," he said, "look me in the eye. I'm trying to talk to you."

He'd touched her, and that took things *too* far. She'd been pushed around *too* long, and she wouldn't be pushed around anymore. Her fist lashed out, punching him squarely in the nose. He fell backwards, landing on his backside. He clapped his hands to his nose, and his spiral notebook slid across the floor.

Sharon stood. "I told you to go away and leave me alone! Now do it!" Despite her anger, inside Sharon was exultant.

He stood, mumbling curses under his breath. He grabbed his notebook and backed away. He passed Sergeant Cowdrie immediately inside the doorway, who stood with an older woman.

"Did you see that? She hit me!"

Sergeant Cowdrie smiled. "I didn't see anything, Sam, but if you don't move along, I'll knock you down, too."

The reporter looked disgustedly at the police officer, and the older woman spoke.

"She told you to git! So git!" She raised a large purse as if to swing it at him, but he hurried from the room.

Aunt Claudia. It had to be.

The woman before her was the same but somehow shrunken. She was older, certainly, and a little heavier, but time seemed also to have compressed her body. Her face was round and so pale it looked powdered. The eyes were young and bright and held nothing but love and concern for Sharon. For a second she wondered if this was how Mom would look today, and the thought nearly swept her away. She hugged her aunt and was fiercely hugged in return. Sergeant Cowdrie offered a small wave then disappeared through the exit doors.

"You came!" Sharon wept into Aunt Claudia's shoulder.

"Well, course I did, baby. We're family." The way her aunt said it, Sharon thought the sentiment was a talisman that could explain any action and answer any question. Sharon felt strange, but good, to be held in Aunt Claudia's arms. How long had it been since Sharon had been able to let someone else be the strong one?

Her aunt had apparently not held to her threat to "fatten out" all her wrinkles. Her face was rounder than it had been, but time and gravity had pulled seams and creases into the curves of her skin, and she looked a little road-weary. Her silver hair had probably been pulled back into a bun when she'd left home, but now several wisps corkscrewed down onto the back of her neck and her forehead. From the circles under her eyes, Sharon thought she'd probably not slept at all on the way.

"I caught a plane and flew out here as soon as I got the call from that policeman. He told me a little about what happened, honey. I got a rental car back in San Angelo and I drove down here as fast as

I could. It smells like someone's been totin' pigs around in that rental car if you ask me. I got into town, got directions here, and I found you. Now let's get in there and see that baby girl of yours. You know I haven't even seen pictures of her in a couple of years."

Sharon listened carefully for any sound of accusation in that statement but heard only pleasure and excitement at the prospect of seeing Lucinda. They went back to the nurses' station, Sharon still holding Lucinda's Betty dolly, and through the double doors of the ICU.

"Oh, the poor little angel!" Aunt Claudia whispered as they stood over the bed. "Bless her heart. She's so precious!"

Lucinda was still comatose, with the tubes still in her arm to feed her, in her nose to give her oxygen, and in her skull to draw off the fluids causing the dangerous buildup of pressure. To Sharon, the contents of the cranial tube appeared darker, as if it was now more blood than cranial fluid. A machine was monitoring her heart through a small clip attached to her index finger. A couple of stick-on sensors were attached to her forehead below her bandage, and their wires fed into a different machine.

Lucinda lay in the white sheets and blankets, not moving, not smiling, not laughing, and not playing. Sharon sighed, and attempted to push the sorrow from her heart. It didn't work.

"Oh, baby, how did I get us into this mess?" Her vision doubled with tears, and she allowed Aunt Claudia to lead her out of the room.

Claudia took her back to the more comfortable waiting area. She sat Sharon down, held both of Sharon's hands in her own, and she looked into her niece's eyes.

"Now you listen to me, baby girl," she said, her cracked voice stern. "Ain't none of this your fault. Sometimes things happen. You didn't make that Deke be some no good redneck. He just was. It was plain ol' bad luck that you crossed his path."

"But I never saw it!" Sharon berated herself. "At the beginning I should've seen Deke for what he really was! When he showed up driving a strange car and wearing strange clothes, saying he robbed a bank and that one of his partners was in the trunk bleeding to death, I was shocked. I didn't know what to do! I guess I knew he was a bastard all along, but I never thought he would do something like this!" Speaking became impossible as sobs clenched Sharon's throat. She let Aunt Claudia hold her while she weathered another squall of tears.

"No matter how well you think you know somebody," Aunt Claudia said, "there's always something else. Even between me and Herbert. We've been married over forty years, and we know each other pretty much as well as a couple can know each other, but to this day I'm sure we've got secrets from each other. He's a good man, I know that much, so I don't begrudge him any privacy he still thinks he needs. I think most of his secrets are things I wouldn't want to know anyway. There's no way you could have known everything about Deke, either."

When she was finally able to speak again, Sharon asked after Uncle Herbert. She was taking the opening that Claudia had given her so that they could move to a more comfortable subject of discussion.

"Herbert's about as hardheaded as ever. Still tryin' to be a farmer even though I told him he's too old. He's ornery, though. He'll probably drop dead in that tractor of his, cussin' and tryin' to put in a field of peanuts."

Claudia sat back, hesitating. Sharon feared she had bad news.

"Sharon, when's the last time you heard from your daddy?"

Sharon held up the dolly. "He sent Betty here to Lucinda for her birthday. Up to a few days ago, Betty was probably the prettiest doll I'd ever seen. She's had a rough week, though, like the rest of us."

Claudia looked at the doll with some distaste. "Lucinda's birthday was a week ago? I guess that's probably the last thing he sent to anybody, then."

"The last?"

"Yes, baby. Your daddy died in that hospital about a week and a half ago. They said he went in his sleep, peacefully. I reckon he's finally free of all that pain he's been totin' around for all these years."

Sharon sat on the sofa, unsure how to feel. She was sad, but the pain was buffered by time's distance and unfamiliarity.

"Herbert and I went up to the cemetery to watch them put him in the ground, right next to your momma and your sister. Wasn't anyone there except the nurse who'd been takin' care of him these last couple of years. We thanked her for comin', and she cried a little bit. She said he was always real nice to her. The hospital sent all his old belongings to us, but I didn't know what to do with them. Herbert put them out in the barn a few days ago. Maybe someday you and I could go through them together. If you want."

"I wish I could have seen him again, to let him know we love him."

"Hush, girl, ain't no need for that. He knew you loved him. He always knew that."

They went to the cafeteria and got some tasteless food on foam plates covered with plastic wrap, and after eating, Aunt Claudia said she needed to get out and run a couple of errands. She left, promising to be back in a couple of hours. Daylight had come again to Del Rio, and the sun hung low in a clear desert sky.

Sharon went back to the waiting room and picked up a magazine. She took the magazine into the ICU suite and read to Lucinda. She read stories of Hollywood celebrities behaving like idiots, an article on a single mother of four who opened her own catering business, and a recipe for a faux key lime pie that called for crushed saltines to make its crust. A putrid idea, Sharon thought, but Lucinda didn't seem to mind.

Doctor Garza came in and reported his findings. The EEG series they'd done was still inconclusive, but they were going to run another one today. He still wanted to wait before attempting to move Lucinda to a regular room. He smiled and sounded optimistic, and he again encouraged Sharon to go get some rest and said that he'd call if there was a reason to.

Around noon, Aunt Claudia returned. She'd changed clothes, and the bun on the back of her head had been reworked so that no wisps of hair escaped now. She handed Sharon a set of car keys and a hotel key card.

"Your turn. Go get cleaned up and changed and take a break. It's the Coronado Hotel. I bought you a few things to wear, and I left them in the trunk of the car. I guessed at the sizes, but they should be pretty close. You don't have to keep wearing those filthy clothes. I believe those jeans'd probably stand up all by themselves."

"But Lucinda—"

"Lucinda's gonna be fine. You need to keep your strength up, too. I'll be right here. You go on, now. It's a little blue car. Press the button on the fob and it'll flash its lights at you."

Aunt Claudia shooed her out the door, and Sharon easily found the car. She smiled when she sat in the driver's seat. The car *did* smell like it'd been used to move pigs. She put Betty on the passenger side seat and barely kept herself from buckling the dolly in.

She arrived at the hotel, parked, and got out. When she popped open the trunk, she couldn't help but flinch, thinking about Raymond's dead, bloated body in the back of the old Nova. She got the clothes and Betty then went to the room.

She didn't dare look into the mirror. She showered and changed clothes, her mind a fogged jumble. Her father was dead. The man who'd loved Pearl so much that it broke his mind when she'd died was now finally at peace. The psychotic break he'd suffered had grown its own obsessive behavior, the doll making. And Betty was the last of them. Betty was the strange, scary, but ultimately protective legacy. With her missing leg and a bulbous head, the dolly represented all

Sharon had left of her father and all the strength that Sharon had been unable to find in herself.

Lucinda's impossible little protector. A couple of times, Sharon tried to speak to the dolly, but felt foolish when it looked mutely at her with those strange blue-green eyes. The eyes were so arresting, and Sharon nearly figured out why when it slipped her grasp again. She was too tired to think straight.

She washed Betty as best she could, getting the dirt and blood out of the crevices in the plastic. The room was quiet, and Sharon had to force herself to get up off of the bed before she relaxed too much and fell asleep. The muddy, blood-spattered clothes she'd worn she tossed into the trash can then she carried Betty back to the car. She returned to the hospital and found Claudia at Lucinda's bedside.

"Well, you're lookin' better, honey."

"Thanks, Aunt Claudia. Thanks for everything."

Claudia dismissed her gratitude with a wave then turned back to Lucinda. The girl lay in the same tangle of wires, sheets, and blankets, her breathing even and slow. Lucinda's lashes were long and fine, and her closed eyes had dark circles beneath them.

Doctor Garza stepped into the room.

"Oh, good, you're here. I was looking for a phone to call you."

"Is there news?"

He stepped over to the monitor and pointed with a mechanical pencil to an area on the left side of the screen where one of the ghostly green lines stretched up from the middle baseline nearly all the way to the top.

"You see this spike? It indicates a possibility that Lucinda's higher brain functions are reasserting themselves. That means there's a possibility that she's on her way out of her unconscious state."

"So she's waking up?"

"No, not yet. But if this trend holds, she could. Even as early as tomorrow."

Aunt Claudia stepped forward, studying the screen. She pointed to another spot further along. "Uh huh. What about this spot, where it dips down like that?" Sharon had noticed it too but was too afraid to ask its meaning.

"That's a very good observation ma'am, but at this point we don't think that drop is operationally significant. It should clear up as Lucinda's higher brain functions continue to reassert themselves."

Claudia's face registered skepticism, but she said nothing more to the doctor. Sharon shifted a few tubes and leads around Lucinda, then put the Betty dolly under one of the girl's arms. Aunt Claudia took her from the room, and they sat down in the plastic chair waiting area, which was closer to the ICU.

"I wanted to talk to you about something, honey. Now, if you're not interested, that's fine; we won't mind. Herbert and I discussed this before I left. He thought of it, and I think it's a fine idea, but like I said, it's entirely up to you."

Sharon waited, looking at the eager smile of hope blooming in Aunt Claudia's face.

"When your mother died, we understood that you needed to get out on your own and give your wings a try. Now, though, with all that's happened, we were wondering if you'd like to come back home. Even if it's only for a short while. We've got more room than we need out at the farm, and we'd love to have you. You and Lucinda are the only kinfolks we've got on my side of the family, and Herbert's side of the family is all a bunch of no accounts that live and die by NASCAR and Bud Lite. You could come and help me keep an eye on Herbert, make sure he doesn't work himself to death on that farm."

"Oh, Aunt Claudia—"

"Don't answer now. You don't have to. Just know this: we love you, and you're always welcome."

"No, I was going to accept! It's perfect! I think a *home* is exactly what Lucinda and I need."

"Well good, then. It's settled."

The day passed slowly, with frequent visits to Lucinda's bedside. Still there was no visible change, but the monitor still showed the green spike on one side of the screen, and the trough on the other side.

Aunt Claudia asked Sharon tentative questions about what had happened, circling around the edges of the whole situation, and while Sharon didn't mind her curiosity, she did eventually get irritated with her aunt's weird sense of propriety. It was like Aunt Claudia was rubbernecking at a car wreck, but pretending she didn't see it. Eventually she was going to have to give the entire story to Aunt Claudia, so she took a deep breath and decided to get it over with. Sharon interrupted another obtuse question that wasn't really the question Aunt Claudia wanted to ask, and said she'd start from the very beginning.

Sharon told her the entire story, beginning with her meeting Deke several months ago. It seemed like it had been so long since that stupid water pump needed replacing on her car! A lifetime ago. Sharon only skipped the parts near the end that included a certain doll protecting a certain child. Even though the story had a few holes in it, Sharon hoped her aunt would chalk them up to Deke's craziness the way the cops apparently had.

The hospital's public address system clicked to life then a nurse's voice spoke. Despite the careful modulation of her voice, Sharon could hear the panicked urgency that crept into the nurse's tone.

"Doctor Garza, please report to ICU. Stat."

38

She had her Betty dolly. She wasn't sure where the dolly had come from, but she had it nestled securely under her arm.

Lucinda still saw her granddaddy's smile and the tears in his eyes as he looked at her. He was in a pretty place with green hills and blue skies, but she thought he might be alone. No matter how nice a place he was in, being all alone would be very sad.

Lucinda wondered if she should go to him. She'd be safe away from those nasty ghost trees, and her granddaddy wouldn't be alone anymore.

Betty floated up to her ear and whispered something to her.

Up in the colorless darkness overhead, Lucinda heard an echo of Mommy's voice. It was slow and it dragged, but she recognized it as Mommy's. She couldn't understand what Mommy was saying, though.

She saw Granddaddy raise his hand to her. He beckoned to her with his loving, sad smile. She understood his gesture, and moved toward him.

As Lucinda approached, she could feel the sweet, clover-scented warmth of the bright place where he was. The sun warmed her face and banished all her pain. The fleecy clouds turned slowly as they drifted across a perfect, late-spring sky.

His arm went around her shoulders, and she felt warm and safe. She looked up and saw his lips purse then he lay a soft kiss on her forehead.

Mommy's voice rose again in Lucinda's mind, swooping into her consciousness like a big bird diving after unsuspecting prey.

Mommy's voice pulled at Lucinda.

She realized then that she couldn't go to Granddaddy. Mommy needed her, and she needed Mommy. Instead of going to Granddaddy, she raised Betty to the window and gave her dolly to him. That way maybe he wouldn't be lonely anymore.

As Granddaddy took Betty with a smile, the dolly stretched and grew. The dolly became a pretty girl who was Lucinda's age, a thin little girl with bright blue-green eyes and a smile like Mommy's.

The little girl and the old man hugged each other then they both waved to Lucinda.

Then the noises crashed in on her.

39

Sharon raced into the ICU in time to panic.

beeeeeeeeeeeeeeeeeeeeeeeeeeeeeeeeeeeeeeeeeeeeeeeeeeeee-

Through the open doorway to Lucinda's room, she saw a nurse frantically squeezing a plastic bag, using it as a bellows to push air into Lucinda's lungs. Another nurse rushed past Sharon with a defibrillator cart, and Doctor Garza barked orders at the nursing team in furious street Spanish.

eeeeeeeeeeeeeeeeeeeeeeeeeeeeeeeeeeeeeeeeeeeeeeeeeeeee-

Sharon watched as they worked, her heart in her throat. They sped up their efforts and raised their voices when they spoke. The defibrillator hummed as it charged then Doctor Garza discharged the tiny, child-sized paddles onto Lucinda's narrow, pale chest. Her body bucked like a landed fish each time, and each time, Sharon cried out.

They continued their efforts for several minutes, and still the electrocardiogram wailed its long, high alarm—

eeeeeeeeeeeeeeeeeeeeeeeeeeeeeeeeeeeeeeeeeeeeeeeeeeeee

--until finally, panting, Doctor Garza waved them off of Lucinda and stood over her bed, his eyes bouncing back and forth between the girl and the flat-lining monitor.

"Nooo!" Sharon screamed. "Don't stop! Bring her back! Hurry up! Bring my baby back!"

She lunged toward Lucinda's bedside, fighting Aunt Claudia's restraining embrace. She shrieked, she wept, she kicked, she hit out at anything within reach.

"My baby my baby my baby oh God!"

Doctor Garza held up his hand, one finger raised toward Sharon. She stopped. She stopped screaming, stopped fighting, she even stopped breathing.

Doctor Garza's eyes were on the monitor.

The heart monitor chirped once, the wave spiking up from the baseline.

After a pause, it chirped again.

Then again and again. The rhythm restarted itself, and everyone in the room heaved and gasp of relief. The nurses smiled at each other and touched each other on the shoulder.

On the bed, Lucinda's chest expanded with a sudden inhale. When she sighed it out again, her eyes were open. They found Sharon immediately.

"Mommy?" she asked drowsily, more a groan than a question. "What happened?"

40

A few days later, Sharon and Lucinda returned to Georgia with Aunt Claudia. They never went back to Killeen. Anything left in their ratty little single-wide trailer was presumably either scavenged by others in the trailer park, or taken to the dumpster at the end of the road, where a new steel chainlink fence with a gate now enclosed the children's playground.

Aaron Whistler may have nursed dreams of vengeance for a short time, but he was quickly forgotten. He still visited Sharon's nightmares, but in the grand scheme of things, he was a comparatively minor threat. Sharon hoped that Dusty, his kid, would escape the vicious cycle of redneck cultural heredity, but she suspected that the apple, in the end, wouldn't fall far from the blighted tree.

In Georgia, Sharon, Lucinda, Aunt Claudia, and Uncle Herbert found that they got along okay. Through the rest of the summer and into fall, they all enjoyed sitting on the front porch listening to the songs of the cicadas and the crickets in the evenings, and watching the yellow dance of lightning bugs hoping to find mates.

Over a few evenings in October, Sharon and Aunt Claudia went out to the barn and sifted through the returned belongings of Sharon's father. Some of the boxes held clothes, a few letters and pictures, and various writing implements. At least thirty of the large boxes held notebooks. Stacks and stacks of dog-eared, ragged, spiral-bound notebooks, packed with John Tibbedeau's perfect penmanship. The cheap cardstock covers were puffy and worn at the edges by use and by the sweat from the palms of his hands.

Sharon made herself read his every tortured word, his every self-destructive emotion, the intangible hole in his heart made tangible by transcription. Though she pored over every page, she found no recipe for what her father had done to make Betty dolly.

In the end, she thought what he'd done would likely have been as much a mystery to him as it was to Sharon. She found ten thousand declarations of love and five thousand more poems from a grieving father. Every page was a haunted cry for help, a plea for forgiveness.

Other boxes held doll parts: plastic heads, arms, legs, tiny tubes of paint, swatches of cloth, thread, plastic grocery bags of soft purple lint. Sharon didn't spend any time inventorying these. It seemed somehow obscene, and looking at the parts made Sharon feel more like a voyeur to her father's insanity than reading the notebooks he left behind.

In the beginning, when they first moved to Georgia, nightmares haunted both Sharon and Lucinda. With love, understanding, and patience, the nightmares, after a time, lost most of their power over the two of them.

Sharon helped around the farm as much as she could, and Uncle Herbert finally learned that he could slow down. Sharon picked up the slack, and the more she did, the more he let her do. She found that farming suited her fine, like the farmyard chores she'd performed as a child. Uncle Herbert taught Lucinda how to fish, and she reminded him what little girls were really made of. The sugar and spice of the poem was often leavened with a measure of snips and snails, much the way Sharon felt about her own makeup.

Lucinda's Betty dolly was played with less and less, until finally it sat in a corner of the room and began to gather dust. Sharon had never been able to make herself mash the doll's head back into shape, or replace the leg Deke had ripped off. On the other hand, she'd never been able to throw it away, either. After what had happened, she worried that it might feel pain if she fixed it or might be sad if she threw it away. Despite the events that were so clearly imprinted on her memory, she never saw the doll move on its own from the corner of Lucinda's room. She supposed there was no need for it to move now. The two of them were safe.

Sharon once asked Lucinda why she didn't play with her Betty dolly anymore, and Lucinda looked at her like she'd grown a second head.

"I don't need her anymore, Mommy. I've got you. She went back to Granddaddy."

Sharon wasn't sure she understood all of that answer. She had beliefs and vague suppositions of spirits inhabiting the doll, but nothing concrete to back them up. That is, nothing concrete except the fact that she and Lucinda were still alive and still drawing breath.

For one thing, she realized why Betty dolly's eyes were so arresting. They were the same color as Pearl's eyes, a bright blue-green—the color of the ocean where the coastal shelf drops off and finally gives way to deep water. Nothing else about Betty dolly even whispered a resemblance to Pearl, but the similarity of her eyes was haunting.

Sharon's father might have been treated for his problems for decades, but he still wanted his Pearl back. Sharon thought that the insanity her father had suffered may have finally paid him back for the years of anguish he'd been through. All those years ago in his workshop, he'd tried to use a dolly to bring back his lost daughter, and it hadn't worked. When he made Betty for Lucinda, and put all of his love into it, Sharon thought that maybe he'd finally succeeded. Pearl had come back to live inside Lucinda's dolly for a time and to protect Lucinda. Now, Pearl had apparently returned to wherever she'd come from, and Lucinda had Sharon to care for her.

The threat, Deke, had been removed from the equation.

The Texas police never found any trace of Deke. They assured her that no one could have survived such a torrential flood, and that Deke was simply another casualty of Hurricane Gilbert, a grisly statistic more fitting than tragic.

Sharon thought she'd changed, too. She was better able to protect her little girl now than she had been before. She was a different person from who she'd been in Texas. The Sharon who had received the dolly from the UPS guy a lifetime ago was only a victim, someone who allowed things to happen to her.

Now, though, she'd been through the crucible of Deke's hate and abuse and had come out changed. She hoped that, scarred but smarter, she'd never let herself fall into the same situation again.

Though central Georgia never really got frigid, as October came to a close the evenings grew chilly. Sharon watched the leaves of the dogwood in the dooryard turn from green to scarlet, and soon after they began to fall from the tree.

Halloween neared and Lucinda grew excited. Sharon suspected that the prospect of her daughter dressing up and dropping her Lucinda-ness for a couple of hours was intoxicating. Like most of the other children at her school, she lived on a farm, so Trick or Treating presented a bit of difficulty. Some parents thought that an agreeable workaround was to throw a party at the school. While that might have worked, the parents in charge immediately started putting limitations on what costumes the children could wear. First they said "nothing too scary" then a few hyper-religious families got hold of the reins and decided that the children should dress up as their favorite Bible character. Like weeds taking over a poorly kept lawn, soon most of the parents were gushing about what a great, innovative idea it was.

Sharon kept her opinion to herself. To her mind, the other parents completely missed the point of Halloween. She decided that she would take Lucinda into town, where she could go from house to house like the suburbanite kids and get a pillowcase full of candy from strangers.

Lucinda chose to dress up as a witch.

"A nice one, though," she confided to Sharon. Her hair was still short on the side where Doctor Garza had installed the drain tube, but the scar no longer showed, and Lucinda had never exhibited any of the feared symptoms of brain damage. She smiled at Sharon and said, "I don't want to have any nose warts or rotten teeth." Over a few days, Sharon helped her put together an appropriately *witchy* costume, complete with a pointed black hat and orange and black striped stockings, and on October 31, near dusk, she drove her daughter into Caledonia for an evening of trick or treating.

Lucinda seemed to have great fun marveling at other costumes she saw on their walk through a small subdivision at the edge of town. Sharon stayed on the sidewalks while Lucinda approached each door, and by the end of the evening, her cheeks hurt from smiling.

Sharon drove them back out to the farm under an open, starlit sky. With the old pillowcase full of candy on her lap, Lucinda yawned into her fist. The witchy black nail polish was already beginning to chip off of her nails, and in the passing streetlights, Sharon saw Lucinda's excitement fading into contentment.

Outside town, they pulled onto the dirt road and drove back to the farm. Lucinda was anxious to show Aunt Claudia and Uncle Herbert her candy, but when they arrived at the house all the lights were off.

"I guess they already went to bed, Cinda-girl," Sharon said. "That's not a bad idea, either. You've got school tomorrow."

"But Mommy—" Lucinda began.

"No buts, cutie. You can have two pieces of candy before you go to bed, as long as you promise to brush your teeth." Sharon parked the car and turned it off.

"I promise!" she said and opened the passenger door.

They walked up the steps to the front porch, Sharon reached for the doorknob, and a familiar voice growled from the darkness.

"Well, look'a here. I'll be double damned. A witch and a bitch both at the same time."

Lucinda shrieked and dropped her bag of candy, and Sharon turned toward the voice, putting a protective arm in front of her daughter. The voice seemed to be coming from Uncle Herbert's favorite rocking chair.

"Now before you go getting some dumb fuckin' idea, reach in there and turn on the porch light."

"Deke?"

"I didn't fuckin' say stand there and look like a poleaxed mule. Turn on the goddamned light! Now!" He coughed then hawked up a huge wad of phlegm and spat it onto the porch. Sharon opened the door, flicked the switch, and all her fears were made flesh.

41

Lucinda couldn't breathe. She could hear her own heartbeat, thundering in her ears, but she couldn't make her lungs draw air. It was as if Deke didn't even need to touch them, and his very presence could suck the life from them.

He sat in Uncle Herbert's rocking chair, wearing clothes that were the uniformly gray-brown of road dirt and grime. He wore a greasy blue baseball cap snugged down tight on his head, casting his face in shadow. His hair was stringy and matted, and the whiskers on his face were thick enough to truly be called a beard. They, too, looked knotted and filthy.

In one hand, Deke held an old pistol, pointed at Mommy. In the other, he held the detached, deformed head of her Betty dolly. Purple fluff bled out of the bottom of the doll's neck.

The ball cap turned toward her and nodded. He tossed the head a few inches into the air, and caught it. The purple fluff trailed it like a streamer. With a grunt of effort, he stood.

"Yep, I took care of your dolly, you little shit. I don't know how the fuck it did what it did back in Texas, but it won't happen that way this time. You see what that fucking thing did to me?"

He took off the ball cap, then smoothed his greasy hair back from his forehead.

Lucinda screamed again.

Half of Deke's face was pale and sunken, dusted with smears of dirt and angry, open sores on his forehead and around his mouth. The eye on that side of his face was streaked with red veins and its stare had a wet, glaring intensity.

Where the other eye had been was a hole. Not a flat place where the eye had been before, with a slack eyelid hanging down. Deke's eye socket was far from healthy. It looked *eroded*. The eyelid was gone completely, the rim of the hole puffy and bright red with infection, and a lumpy chain of scab ringed the edge of the socket. The hole wept a thick stream of yellow pus.

"Cute, ain't it?" he laughed. The laugh stumbled and turned into a wracking cough, and a big vein pulsed in the center of his forehead. He bent double, the ball cap falling to the wooden planks of the porch.

"Lucinda," Mommy urged. "Run."

Lucinda looked at Deke and her muscles froze. He recovered from his coughing fit with tears standing in his good eye. He blinked a couple of times, hawked and spat again, and pointed the gun at her.

"Fuck yeah. Run. Run so your momma can watch me shoot you down."

Lucinda shook her head, and he turned to Mommy again.

"Don't worry about those old folks. I didn't kill 'em. I got no argument with them. They wouldn't be hurt at all, but the old man had to sass me a little, so I hit him and bounced his head off'n a door. He's laid out on the floor in the parlor, and the old lady is tied into a chair with a hank of clothesline.

"I ain't gonna mess with them no more. I don't have any problem with them. I didn't want them to get in the way of our unfinished business. I got a score to settle with you, and I aim to call it in right now. Y'all done fucked me comin' an' goin'. I didn't get any of my money, I didn't get to Mexico, and I lost both of my partners. That stupid doll of yours took my partner, made me lose my money, made me fall into the goddamned river, and yanked out my eye. My eye, for Christ's sakes! I can't see for shit, and I've got some kind of infection, and I've been barely surviving these last three months." He coughed and spat again, then kept going. "So now you've built up all these debts. You owe me big time, bitch." He held up the doll's head. "It's time to pay up, and this little fuck ain't gonna help you this time." He tossed the head off the porch and it landed somewhere in the tall grass. "I've had nothing but bad dreams about that night, all because of that creepy little doll. I wake up screamin', feelin' those little plastic hands crawling all over me like I'd fallen asleep in an anthill." He considered for a moment, and it almost looked like he was talking to himself. Then his eye squinted and focused on Mommy again.

"I reckon I could shoot you. You'll be dead either way, right? But that wouldn't cover the bill. You don't know what kind of pain I'm in. It feels like my skull's on fire all the goddamned time, and I can hardly eat, and now on top of that, I'm sick. I guess that'll teach me to sleep in the rain and let my goddamned eye socket fill up with rainwater." He stopped, one eyebrow raised as his eye looked up.

"No, I think you need to know what suffering feels like. I'm gonna hurt every day till this kills me, and it's only fair that you hurt, too."

His one eye brightened. "What's out there in the barn?"

"That's only used for storage," Mommy said. "They used to have some livestock, but now they keep their old junk in there. But, Deke, you don't want to do this. Walk away, and we can both forget this ever happened. You made some mistakes. I made some mistakes, and things, well, things happened."

Lucinda heard something in Mommy's voice that she hadn't heard in months. A begging, bargaining wheedle, and Lucinda remembered that tone. It was the tone Mommy had always gotten when Deke got mad. Lucinda knew what would happen next, and knowing made her heart hurt.

"Shut the fuck up telling me what to do, bitch." Another coughing fit rolled over him, and it ended with him gagging. "Bumpin' your gums like you always did. I'm in charge here. The only things you're in charge of are jack and shit. Now go. Lead the way to the barn. And if you try to run, I'm gonna shoot you. Pull the trigger and give you a forty-five caliber ass fuck. Got it? Good. Move it."

Lucinda followed Mommy back down the steps and across the yard to the barn. The big door slid on a track, but that hadn't been opened since before Uncle Herbert built the new shelter for the tractor. A normal-sized door was set inside the larger, and Mommy walked toward it.

Behind her, Lucinda heard Deke's raspy, gurgly voice. He sounded sick, and his face looked like he was already dead and rotting. He snickered.

"You know what they used to do to witches, you little shit?"

Lucinda didn't answer. Even if she'd known, she couldn't make herself speak.

"They burned them. They knew that you can't suffer a witch to live. That's even in scripture. They built big bonfires, tied the witches to a stake in the middle, and lit 'em up."

He snickered again, punctuating it with a phlegmy cough.

42

Just do what he says and avoid the worst of it.

Even as she heard the voice in her head say that, Sharon knew it was a coward's lie. It was the same lie she'd told herself over and over again the last time she'd seen Deke. After all, if she went on what he'd said, he planned to burn up the barn with them inside it. The only way to avoid the worst was to not let it happen.

A chill ran through her. She'd only been in his presence for a minute, and already she was turning into the groveling craven she'd been before. She had to put a stop to this before she lost all her nerve.

She heard him snickering at the idea of burning little witches, and something finally and permanently snapped inside her.

That's my baby girl, you monster!

Suddenly, that righteous feeling of anger came flooding back into her soul, washing away the fears and the doubts. No one was in charge of her life but *her*, dammit. This asshole—that ought to already be dead—should have learned his lesson back at the Mexican border bridge. Rage burned through her veins. If she wanted to survive and save Lucinda, she would have to kill Deke right now.

But how? She needed to stall him while she came up with something. Even though he was sick, and weaker than he ever was before, Sharon worried that he could still overpower her.

She turned and raised a hand.

"Deke wait," she began.

He raised the revolver, put the muzzle on the center of her palm, and said, "Fuck waiting." He pulled the trigger, and the gun erupted with a tremendous roar as her hand snapped backward on her wrist. When it rose back up, she had a hole in her palm. For a split second, it looked almost like an optical illusion, but then the blood started gushing and the bright white pain flared into a supernova. She screamed and fell to her knees, clutching her hand to her chest, and beside her, Lucinda shrieked.

Deke hauled her up with a clawed hand in her hair. He jerked her around then let go. They stood before the barn door. Sharon swung a fist at him, but it went wide.

"Ain't foolin' with you no more. Stop." He let go of her and clamped his free hand onto Lucinda's shoulder, knocking her pointed hat to the ground. Tears flowed down her daughter's face as quickly as the blood flowed onto Sharon's fingertips. "Open up this goddamned door. You try anything stupid and I'll paint the front of this barn with your brat's innards."

Sharon's entire arm felt like it was on fire. She picked up Lucinda's pointed felt hat and crushed it, then wrapped it around her hand. It did nothing for her pain, but hopefully it would keep her from bleeding too much. She ground her teeth as she pulled it tight. The pain was like some living thing at the end of her wrist, and in seconds, the felt was sodden with blood.

"Not so great when you don't have your little voodoo doll to help you, is it?" Deke asked.

He giggled, but it sounded like a noise from a tubercular hog. More snot than snort. He gagged again and hawked out another heavy curd of phlegm.

Sharon opened the door of the barn and stepped in. She flicked the light switch, and the fluorescent tubes overhead came to life. Deke shoved Lucinda in before him, visually checking the dim corners of the barn. Lucinda scrabbled on hands and knees to one of the square support posts, where she sat and looked at the two of them through scared eyes. Along one side were three large pens where Uncle Herbert had once kept a cow and a couple of horses, and along the opposite wall were smaller compartments that had seen various storage uses throughout the years—everything from corn and hay bales, to auto parts and cleaning supplies. There were no windows, and they'd never needed a loft built overhead. The only door into the barn was the one they'd stepped through a moment ago. Bales of hay that had been there for years were stacked in several places across the barn.

In one of the large pens, Sharon saw the stacks of boxes from her father. The old clothes, the notebooks full of heartbreak, and the doll parts on the packed dirt and hay of the floor, the flaps of each box folded shut.

Despite the surreal pain electrifying half of Sharon's body, she began to get a glimmer of an idea. She inhaled, and even the flex of her diaphragm and lungs seemed to make her hand hurt more.

"Deke," she said. "You know my father made that doll you broke. He sent it to Lucinda and we hid it from you until I could make it look like it was from us."

Deke cocked his head to the right so that his one good eye could look at her fully. He bent down and grabbed a handful of old, dry hay from the ground.

"Bullshit."

Sharon struggled to maintain the calm in her voice. "It's true. It came in the mail a few days before Lucinda's birthday."

"That don't matter, bitch."

"It might."

"What do you mean?"

"Come back here and let me show you something. In those boxes back there."

He looked at her suspiciously. Sharon saw the questions flashing across his ruined face, and she could tell he was wondering why she wasn't crying or begging. She thought he was asking himself if he'd missed something important.

Shit yeah, Deke. You missed the fact that I'm not the same woman you dragged across Texas in a tornado of hate. That woman is long gone. I'm the woman that survived that trip through hell. You won't scare me anymore, asshole.

"I told you I'm through foolin' with you."

Sharon turned away from him, toward the stacks of boxes of her father's things. "Whatever, Deke, but this is something you might want to know." She could feel his eyes crawling all over her back and expected at any moment to be knocked forward into the dirt by a bullet. Blood pattered into the dirt from the ends of her fingers. "You're going to kill us. I know that." The thought was one thing, but saying it out loud seemed to make it all the more real. She spoke quickly before the fear could take hold of her heart again. "And you're dying too, right, so maybe it doesn't matter to you. If it were me, though, I think I'd look at it differently. I mean, everybody thinks you're already dead. You can do whatever you want, with no trouble from anyone. If I were you, I'd want to make that last as long as I could."

Deke coughed. "Yeah?"

"Yeah. You won't have to worry about me or Lucinda calling the cops on you, and you destroyed the doll, right?"

"Yeah." He'd followed her to the pen where Dad's boxes were stacked.

"But do you really think that's the *only* doll my father made?"

His stupid, one-eyed expression dimly registered the possibility then his brows lowered again. "Bullshit. You're fuckin' with me. There ain't no other dolls." He put the pistol into the pocket of his baggy, shapeless trousers, exchanging it for a small orange disposable lighter.

"Am I, Deke?" Sharon thrust her hand into one of the open boxes and lifted out a handful of doll arms and legs. "What do you think?" She held them out as proof.

"I think I done wasted too much time with you, bitch." He flicked the wheel of the lighter, then held the twist of dry hay to the flame. She knew he intended to throw it down and run out. Sharon saw that this was her only chance. She turned and picked up a box full of doll body parts, her injured hand screaming, and flung the contents of the box at Deke.

"They're coming to get you *now*, Deke!" A hollow drum roll of the plastic arms, legs, heads, and torsos sounded as the parts cascaded out of the topmost box and all over him. He roared as he stumbled backwards, and the flaming twist of hay fell to the ground. It came apart when it hit, the flaming straws igniting other dry straws scattered about the floor. Those straws ignited still others, and the fire spread.

Deke stepped onto a doll's head, which promptly rolled out from under him. He fell backwards, landing flat on his back. The air was forced from his lungs in a wet whoosh.

On the other side of the barn, Lucinda screamed.

The flame grew, hungrily eating its way across the floor. The scattered hay had probably been replaced last time in the spring to cut the mud of the seasonal rains. It was dry, dusty, and caught fire so quickly it was almost as if it wanted to burn.

Sharon picked up another large box, this one obviously solid, packed with her father's notebooks. It was heavy. She staggered forward then tossed it onto Deke's supine form. She saw a splotchy dark spot at the lower corner of the box, where she'd printed it with her blood. Deke still lay on the floor, his beet red face contorting as he struggled to draw a breath.

The flames were beginning to burn the edges of the boxes, and the stench of scorched plastic began to overpower the cleaner smell of burning hay. The doll parts began to blister and melt, the pink, dimpled features charring to black, then sagging into hollow holes. The acrid smoke stung Sharon's eyes.

"Mommy! Help me!" Lucinda shrieked. Sharon watched as, where the spreading fire approached Lucinda, her daughter kicked the dry straw away.

Lucinda's scream was nearly drowned out by the growing crackle and roar of the fire. It now stretched from wall to wall, and the flames were crawling up the support beams. Thick, black smoke began to fill the barn.

Sharon peered through the gathering smoke, her eyes streaming. "Lucinda!"

At first, she couldn't see anything through the smoke, and the light of the fire cast its own wild shadows. Finally, she saw Lucinda on the floor. The crackle of the flames muted the sounds coming from Lucinda, but Sharon saw that she was screaming. She thought that, somehow, seeing that scream without hearing it was more horrifying than anything else. She dodged past flames that reached out to her like greedy fingers and slid to the ground beside Lucinda.

Sharon picked up Lucinda, and her daughter clung to her in panic. Her entire arm throbbed, and she was sure her hand still bled freely. She stood, turned, and realized that she didn't know where the door was.

The churning smoke and the fire were disorienting to Sharon. Random flares of heat beat against her face like hot wind. Despite the fact that she knew this barn inside and out, she couldn't seem to get her bearings. Where was the goddamned door? For that matter, where was a wall that wasn't completely engulfed in flames? She had to get Lucinda out of here.

She felt more than heard Lucinda coughing and retching against her chest. She stepped forward into a spot that wasn't burning and looked around. She saw nothing familiar, and panic threatened to swallow her thoughts. Sharon forced herself to stop, to compose herself as much as she could in the situation. If she lost her head and panicked, she and Lucinda were as good as dead. She took a thin, shallow breath and tried to calm her galloping heart.

The whole world was hell, an orange and black inferno with no escape. She clutched Lucinda even more tightly and took another step forward. Heat lashed her exposed skin and smoke made her throat lock tight. She looked around again and she finally saw the open door beyond a curtain of flame. She'd been heading in exactly the wrong direction.

She turned toward the doorway, keeping it in her sight. With the black rectangle as a point of reference, she was able to pick out hazy, broken hints of the rest of the barn. The structure itself was burning now, in addition to its contents. The old hay went up as if doused in kerosene, and in the rafters above, individual crumbs of chaff floated and glowed like a million demons' eyes, bullied by the gusting updrafts of heat.

The boxes holding all the notebooks, all of her father's transcribed memories and thoughts, were a bonfire by themselves. On the floor below, the black puddles of melted plastic were also flaming, their acrid smoke indistinguishable from the rest.

The box she'd thrown onto Deke was burning as well. Deke was no longer under it.

She didn't see him anywhere. Panic tried to grab her again in a thorny fist, and she thrust it away. She couldn't allow herself to worry about where Deke was. If he'd made it out of the barn, the door would surely be closed. She adjusted her grip on Lucinda and refocused on the doorway.

Its lines were indistinct, wobbling behind the heat. In the brief glimpses she got of the doorway, it looked more like a distorted funhouse reflection of an opening, warped, wavy lines rippling in the buffeting heat.

She saw no clear path to the door. There were flames everywhere, greedily consuming everything between Sharon and the doorway.

The timbers above her suddenly cracked like a gunshot. If she didn't get out of here quickly, the whole damned place would come down on top of them. She looked around her, but there was no escape other than the door, and that was blocked by walls of fire.

She tried kicking dirt on the first undulating curtain of flame. It worked briefly and knocked down a portion of the flames, but then the loose hay in the dirt caught, and the fire grew again.

When they grew back, they weren't quite as big. Sharon doubled her efforts, and finally the closest flames were low enough for her to step over. She coughed as she kicked more dirt onto the flames before her. The fire was stealing her oxygen, and the smoke made what air she did breathe a mix of hot ash and plastic polymer fumes. She began to grow dizzy. Whether from smoke inhalation or blood loss, Sharon had no idea.

She was able to take another few steps before the fire closed in behind her and Lucinda. It looked like there were only two more areas she'd need to smother before she could get the two of them out of the barn. She shifted Lucinda again, and kicked more dirt ahead of them.

Sharon stumbled forward, kicking dirt onto the last burning area before the threshold of the barn. She felt an errant breeze from outside, and the cool freshness of it was delicious and all too brief. She inhaled, hoping to reap some benefit of the breeze, but instead she sucked the harsh burn of cinders and smoke into her throat. She coughed and stepped forward as the flames began to refresh themselves beneath her feet.

She tripped and fell forward, Lucinda tumbling from her arms and through the doorway before her. A lightning bolt of pain shot from the bullet hole in her hand, up through her arm, and into her neck. Only when she'd landed did she become aware of the wiry strength of the hand that encircled her ankle.

Deke.

He began to haul her backward. Sharon screamed, digging her hands into the dirt and smoldering hay. The sizzling pain of her burning flesh ran a distant second to the gale-force agony of the gunshot wound and the terror of Deke pulling her back into the inferno. She scrabbled forward with all her strength but was pulled inexorably back.

She looked up, and Lucinda was standing before her in the doorway. Her hands were cupped around her eyes as she squinted into the conflagration, her mouth pulled down in a silent scream. Sharon thought for a moment that Lucinda might step back into blaze.

"Run, Lucinda! Go to the house!"

Her blonde head bobbed, and she disappeared into the darkness. Sharon felt Deke adjusting his grip on her ankle, and she kicked furiously at his hand. It closed again around her like a manacle and pulled her away from the doorway.

Ignoring the flames, she rolled onto her back to face Deke. He yanked her toward him then stood, lifting her by the front of her shirt. He pulled her farther into the barn.

His hair was burned away, and his scalp was a domed, smoking black scab. His ears had melted; they sat low on the sides of his head and his earlobes had stretched into thin mozzarella strings whose ends lay on his shoulders. His one good eye focused on her, but the empty socket beside it seemed to glare at her with the same rabid ferocity. His mouth was open in a hideous smile, and blood slicked his chin. His clothes had begun to smoke, and it would be only seconds before he burst fully into flame.

"You killed me months ago, you worthless bitch!" he screamed over the roar of the fire. He coughed then smiled again. "But tonight I'm takin' you to hell with me! Gonna fuck you in the Devil's bed!"

The dragon tongues of fire licking the wood and hay all around Sharon suddenly seemed to slow down. Time stopped and her mind sped backwards. Again she experienced every hurtful thing he'd ever done to her. The physical abuse was bad, but worse was the emotional abuse. He'd torn down every shred of her defenses, and when she was finally reduced to helplessness, he'd consumed her soul. He'd turned her into less than a person, and she'd allowed it. Escape had only been a fantasy seen through a dirty trailer window, a groundless hope with no teeth, no spirit, and no muscle.

He'd taken everything from her and left her a hollow shell. Even that worthless bit of husk was mortgaged to him, and now he was here to foreclose on her.

Deke thought the dolly was their savior, but was it really? Through the dolly, Sharon's father had returned a little of herself to her, and she'd already grown from there, since the harrowing night on the border bridge.

She finally found her way back to herself, to the present. The Sharon who had been knocked from wall to wall in that trailer no longer existed. She'd earned her soul back, and she knew that no one could take that part of her away again.

She balled her hands painfully into fists.

"You already took me to hell, Deke! You're never taking me anywhere again, you asshole!"

She kicked him in the midsection as hard as she could. He stumbled backwards a few steps then launched himself at her.

He jumped then landed heavily on her, driving her back to the ground. She smelled hair burning, and wondered if it was her own. She swung her fists at Deke, but the blows bounced off of him, unheeded and unfelt. She tried to kick as well, but he'd pinned her legs.

He leaned close, and she could smell the rot on his breath.

"Yep, we're gonna die, right here," he whispered in her ear. "Gonna fuck you in the Devil's bed...gonna fuck you so good." A string of saliva pattered onto her cheek. She reached to her side and picked up a doll's arm then swung her hand around hard right as Deke began to lean back.

She plunged the doll's arm into his empty eye socket, and it stuck there. He screamed, blood pulsing out of his wound. He rolled off Sharon as he clapped his hands to his face. Sharon sat up quickly then coughed and stood. She watched him roll back and forth in the flames, his coat and trousers finally catching fire. He looked surreal, his hands clapped over his face and a tiny, blood-smeared hand sticking out between them like Zeus giving birth to Athena.

Get in the Devil's bed if you want to, she thought, *but you're the one getting fucked.*

She staggered through the fire to the doorway. When she finally made it out, she whooped in the cool autumn air and coughed out smoke until she vomited. Lucinda returned with Uncle Herbert, who wore a dark red splash high on his forehead. He threw his old Army blanket around Sharon and smothered out several small flames burning on her clothes. The barn continued to burn, and for a few moments, behind the roar of the flames, Sharon heard a horrible screaming sound that almost made her smile, even though it set her teeth on edge. Deke wouldn't be coming back from the dead this time.

Sharon held Lucinda tight in her arms, coughing and weeping in relief.

"We did it, baby. He's finally gone."

Once again, Sharon and Lucinda had survived. Uncle Herbert went back to the house for a few moments, and when he returned Aunt Claudia was at his side. The four of them sat together on the ground while October turned into November. After a few moments, the barn's roof fell in on itself with a crash, and a cyclone of sparks spun up into the night, their orange glow mixing with the white glow of the fading stars. Sharon and Lucinda held onto each other while the sound of approaching sirens grew.

The county volunteer fire department finally put out the fire, but the old barn was beyond saving. All of John Tibbedeau's notebooks and earthly possessions were also consumed in the blaze. Investigators found the burned remains of a man in the smoking ruin. Eighty percent of his body was covered with the oddly smooth, melted remains of baby doll parts. When Sharon explained to them who it was, the news caused something of a sensation. An abusive monster of a man, believed for months to be dead in a different accident, in an entirely different *state*, suddenly back from the dead and bent on vengeance? The news media would eat that up. The story of a woman, finally overcoming the horror of her life, first by water then by fire, would be huge. It had all the earmarks of a TV movie.

An ambulance came and took Sharon and Lucinda to the hospital back in Caledonia. The doctors there were confident that they'd be able to save her hand, but they suspected it would be a long time before it recovered even fifty percent of its former mobility.

The next day, Lucinda was finally allowed to come into Sharon's room with Uncle Herbert. She held his hand tightly, and there were dark circles under her eyes. She walked in carrying a gym bag at her side.

Sharon's mind was cottony from the pain medication, and sounds echoed in her head. With effort, she focused her eyes and asked, "What have you got there, sweetie?"

Lucinda opened the bag and pulled out her Betty dolly. The doll's hair was disarrayed, and the haunting blue-green painted eyes were cracked.

"Aunt Claudia popped the dent out of her head and sewed it back onto her neck, Mommy. She's still only got one leg, though." She stepped closer and whispered to Sharon, "You saved us from Deke without any help from Betty this time. Now you're hurt, so until you get strong again, maybe she'll be able to protect you. You can cuddle with her while you're here."

Sharon held out her uninjured hand and took the dolly from her daughter with a smile of thanks.

She hugged the damaged dolly close. It smelled clean and radiated warmth in her arms. Because of this strange little doll, she'd found her will to fight and to overcome the beast from which she'd thought there was no escape. She'd never think those words again: *How did I get us into this mess?* That knowledge made her feel good, despite her pain.

As Sharon drifted again into medicated sleep, she imagined she heard, from a strange window that opened on a green hillside in the middle of a beautiful country afternoon, a father joyfully mangling the words to an old Elvis Presley song, singing, "Little sister, don't you cry," and his daughter beside him, laughing.

It was a lovely, happy sound.

ABOUT THE AUTHOR

Dev Jarrett is a writer, a father, a husband, and a career soldier. He spent the first twenty-two years of his life in Georgia, and the most recent twenty-two everywhere else. He's a Chief Warrant Officer 4 in the US Army currently stationed in the heartland at Fort Riley, Kansas.

During the day, he is a 352N and works tirelessly to defeat terrorists. He's deployed numerous times to garden spots like Camp Buehring (in Kuwait), and Kandahar Air Base and Bagram Air Base (both in Afghanistan).

During the night, the *other* kind of monsters come out. Those unkillable kind of monsters that drink your fear and live in the darkest corners of your life. The kind that live on blood and human flesh. The ones you can't protect your children from.

He's had many short stories published, both online and in print, and his newest novels, *Little Sister*, *Casualties* and *Dark Crescent*, are available now from Permuted Press. His first novel, *Loveless*, is available through your favorite online retailer or directly from Blood Bound Books.

You can usually find Dev online on Facebook, Twitter, and (if you want to see all the gory details) here: http://devjarrett.weebly.com/

14

Peter Clines

Padlocked doors.
Strange light fixtures. Mutant
cockroaches.

There are some odd things about
Nate's new apartment. Every
room in this old brownstone has
a mystery. Mysteries that stretch
back over a hundred years.
Some of them are in plain sight.
Some are behind locked doors.
And all together these mysteries
could mean the end of Nate and
his friends.

Or the end of everything…

PERMUTED
PRESS

THE BREADWINNER | Stevie Kopas

The end of the world is not glamorous. In a matter of days the human race was reduced to nothing more than vicious, flesh hungry creatures. There are no heroes here. Only survivors. The trilogy continues with Book Two: *Haven* and Book Three: *All Good Things*.

THE BECOMING | Jessica Meigs

As society rapidly crumbles under the hordes of infected, three people—Ethan Bennett, a Memphis police officer; Cade Alton, his best friend and former IDF sharpshooter; and Brandt Evans, a lieutenant in the US Marines—band together against the oncoming crush of death and terror sweeping across the world. The story continues with Book Two: *Ground Zero*.

THE INFECTION WAR | Craig DiLouie

As the undead awake, a small group of survivors must accept a dangerous mission into the very heart of infection. This edition features two books: *The Infection* and *The Killing Floor*.

OBJECTS OF WRATH | Sean T. Smith

The border between good and evil has always been bloody... Is humanity doomed? After the bombs rain down, the entire world is an open wound; it is in those bleeding years that William Fox becomes a man. After The Fall, nothing is certain. *Objects of Wrath* is the first book in a saga spanning four generations.

PERMUTED
PRESS

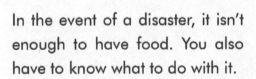

A PREPPER'S COOKBOOK

20 Years of Cooking in the Woods

by Deborah D. Moore

In the event of a disaster, it isn't enough to have food. You also have to know what to do with it.

Deborah D. Moore, author of *The Journal* series and a passionate Prepper for over twenty years, gives you step-by-step instructions on making delicious meals from the emergency pantry.

PERMUTED
PRESS